W9-BJU-406

CIRCUS SEQUINS

Books by Elisabeth Hamilton Friermood

BALLAD OF CALAMITY CREEK

CANDLE IN THE SUN

CIRCUS SEQUINS

DOC DUDLEY'S DAUGHTER

FOCUS THE BRIGHT LAND

GENEVA SUMMER

HEAD HIGH, ELLEN BRODY

HOOSIER HERITAGE

JO ALLEN'S PREDICAMENT

THE LUCK OF DAPHNE TOLLIVER

MOLLY'S DOUBLE RAINBOW

PROMISES IN THE ATTIC

"THAT JONES GIRL"

THE WABASH KNOWS THE SECRET

WHISPERING WILLOWS

THE WILD DONAHUES

ELISABETH HAMILTON FRIERMOOD

CIRCUS
SEQUINS

Doubleday & Company, Inc., Garden City, New York

Lovingly dedicated to the memory of
GROVER R. SEIFERT
Uncle Dodie
a Hoosier circus buff who made circus
day sheer magic for the two Hamilton
children, Tom and Elisabeth.

Library of Congress Catalog Card Number 68–22479
Copyright © 1968 by Elisabeth Hamilton Friermood
All Rights Reserved
Printed in the United States of America

CONTENTS

CHARACTERS

Roxy Clark
Martha Clark, her mother
"Red" Clark, her father
Janet Clark, her sister
Allen Clark, her brother
Douglas Gardner, "the boy next door"

Circus People:
Gracie Riley, superintendent of Wardrobe,
                              Roxy's grandmother
Sadie Modosky, wardrobe assistant
Amy Travers, wardrobe assistant
Jenny Thompson, wardrobe assistant
Mame Anderson, wardrobe assistant
"The Flying Frontenays"—French aerialist troupe
   Marie Frontenay, Roxy's aunt
   Jules Frontenay, Roxy's uncle
   Mimi Frontenay, Roxy's cousin
   Lilly Frontenay, Roxy's cousin
   Henri Frontenay, Roxy's cousin
   Jacques Frontenay, Roxy's cousin
"The Kassel Troupe"—German riders
   Helga and Fritz Kassel

Karl Kassel, their son
Erma, (their daughter) and Bernhard Bremen
Gretchen, (their daughter) and Conrad Hagen
Frieda Jantry, headline rider
Martin Jantry, her husband—circus business manager
Frank Hallock, owner of the Hallock Circus
Louise Hallock, his wife
Miles Wallace, bandmaster
Hap Winters, plays the steam calliope
Rita Donato, headline tiger trainer
Alberto Donato, her husband and headline
elephant trainer
Alice Granville, works elephants in ring three
Midgie Dexter, headline high-wire performer
Angie Heller, ballet girl
Mary Jane Adler, works dogs and ponies
Ted Adler, her husband—walks slant wire
Bogum Bentley, clown
"The Seven Sumokas," Japanese jugglers
"The Eldona Family," Italian tumblers
"The Walton Troupe," highflyers

Side Show People:

Tongo, the dog-faced boy from Borneo
Gertrude, the fat lady
The Marshall Midget Troupe
Mrs. Concello, one of the Marshall midgets
Elva, the tattooed lady
Maximilian, the nine-foot giant
Mary Duncan, the snake charmer
Adolph Duncan, her husband—manager of
the side show
Jim Oldknoe, boss canvasman

8

Jim Daggett, ringmaster
Sam Dowd, bull-whip expert with the wild
West show
Ed Nedosky, boss hostler
Gus, an elephant man
George Tompkins, porter for Wardrobe's car
Henry, porter for Hallocks' private car
Jake Devlin, circus postmaster
Delaware, a groom
Abner Perkins, harness maker
Joe, in charge of hot water
Lem Ames, in charge of cookhouse
Ellen Ames, his wife and assistant

The Children:

Tosho Sumoka
Guido Eldona
Gina Eldona
Juanita Alverez
Johnny Ames
Peter Moon
Susy Duncan

Animals:

Kentucky ("Tucky") Roxy's horse on the farm
Fancy, Grandma's horse
Frieda's horses:
  Sebastian
  Jupiter
  Caesar
  Alexander
The Kassels' horses:
  Bismarck

Otto
Ludwig
Three resinbacks for bareback riding
Five High School horses for dressage
Fritz's twelve liberty horses
Luly, special elephant in Alice Granville's act
Big Bella, hippopotamus
Herman, Bo Bentley's pig
Rajah, one of Rita's tigers
Dogs and ponies in Mary Jane's act

Chapter 1

ADVENTURE AHEAD!

Roxy paused in the doorway and looked back. Miss Merriweather was already looking over the geometry test paper. Roxy took a handkerchief from her shirtwaist pocket and dried the palms of her hands as she walked down the deserted hall to her locker. It had been a difficult hour.

So much depended on that test paper. If she didn't pass geometry on this special examination she wouldn't qualify for graduation, and if she didn't qualify she couldn't leave school now.

Each day during the past week she had stayed after school taking examinations. French and English had been a breeze, but geometry—!

At her locker she took a divided riding skirt from a hook, went into the nearby girls' room, stepped out of her black skirt and into the other garment. Looking in the mirror over the washbasin, she pulled a bit of hair farther down on her forehead and tucked in a hairpin. Well, Roxy Clark, she told herself, the die is cast. If you made it on that test you'll be off next week on the biggest thing in your life, probably the biggest adventure ever offered a senior in Westwood High School.

She took a deep breath to relieve the tension of the past hour's concentration and smiled at herself, studying the reflection of her even white teeth. She was glad her

11

hair was red. No other girl in school had such hair, and she had the spunk and temper to go with it. If she passed that blamed geometry, she'd need the spunk, yes, and probably the temper too to make a success of the job ahead.

Her hat and jacket on, she hurried through the halls and out the front door. Around the corner and three blocks beyond she entered the town livery stable.

"You're late again, Roxy," a grizzled old man said as he got up from his chair. "I've had Tucky saddled up for quite a spell."

"Well, this should be the end of it, Mose. I took the last examination today."

Mose opened the wide front door. "So you're going to join the circus next week, be you? 'Spect your folks'll miss you a lot out there at the farm. You know, I never would've thought Red Clark would let a daughter of his travel with a circus. Red's always been so kind of persnickety in his dealings and I calculate with his family too."

Roxy laughed. "Well, I'm persnickety too *and* persuasive, just like Papa. Yes, he did give me a lot of argument. But he knows that I have circus in my bones because of Mama and that sooner or later I'll have to get it out of my system. Of course he realizes that I have relatives in the circus to keep an eye on me. Grandma Riley is superintendent of Wardrobe and my aunt's family has an aerialist act."

"Yep, I seen 'em last summer when the circus was here. Call themselves the Flying Frontenays as I recollect. You aiming to learn trapeze?"

"No. I'll be helping Grandma in Wardrobe."

Mose chuckled. "Well, I bet my bottom dollar you won't be doing that for long. With your way with horses you could be good in any riding act." He followed her as she led the horse to the street.

"What a flatterer you are, Mose!" Roxy put a foot in a stirrup, got astride the saddle, and smiled down at the old man.

"You got circus in your bones, all right," he said, "and I'd say you got horses in your blood too. I recollect like it was yesterday when Red Clark brought home your mama as a bride, her as had been a rider in the circus. And with him having such a know-how with horseflesh, you was just bound to be a rider. Red used to do quite a bit of racing when he was younger."

"I know." Roxy patted the horse's neck. "He got Tucky for me when he was down in Louisville at a race. That's the reason I named him Kentucky. Well, keep your fingers crossed for me on that geometry test, Mose. If I don't pass it, Papa says I can't leave next week."

As she rode off, a little smile played across her face. Dear, discerning old Mose! He had put into words exactly what she had in mind. Before the summer was over, she *was* going to become a performer in the show! All her life she had heard stories about the days when Mama's family, the Riding Rileys, were headliners in the circus. Gracie and Mike Riley, Roxy's grandma and grandpa, and their two daughters, Mama and Aunt Marie, had played center ring all across the country. Then young French aerialist, Jules Frontenay, joined the show, married Aunt Marie and she gave up riding for the trapeze. Mama had married Red Clark, a young farmer, Grandpa had died, and Grandma had left the Big Top to manage the Wardrobe Department of the Great Hallock Circus.

Tucky's hoofs clattered across the brick pavement of Third Street, then faded out to soft thuds on the dirt of Windam Avenue beyond. At the edge of town, Roxy pulled the horse to a walk and eased back in the saddle.

She supposed she should hurry home and try to baste in those sleeves before supper. If she passed the exam,

13

she would want to wear the new suit she was making. But it was nice to dawdle, to think, to dream.

She would never forget the day right after Christmas that Grandma's letter had arrived. Grandma had written Mama and Papa that she needed another person in Wardrobe for the coming season, someone dependable and handy with a needle. She asked if they would let Roxy come in April.

Roxy looked off across a field; white patches of last week's snowfall still remained in fence corners. Oh, that dear Grandma Riley! A job with the Hallock Circus! How adamant Papa had been. No, not on your tintype would he let Roxy miss the last month of school just when she was about to graduate from Westwood High School!

Mama, however, was sympathetic and had gone to Mr. Lamb, the high school principal. He said that if Roxy could pass all of her examinations by the first week in April, her diploma would be granted with the rest of the class in May even though she was absent.

With such an incentive, how she had studied! Janet and Allen had been wonderful, doing her home chores while she spent every spare moment in her room with her books.

She slapped Tucky's rump lightly and touched his sides with her heels. "Get along, boy. Stretch your legs. You need it after Mose has coddled you all day."

Tucky, only too glad to "get along," broke into a gallop and the wind whistled by Roxy's ears. She gave a yank at her hat to anchor it more securely. More than once it had blown off on this straight stretch of road where she usually gave the horse his head.

Leaning forward, riding swiftly like this, she often imagined herself the heroine of a Broncho Billy moving picture. Whenever she took Janet and Allen into town to the Mecca theater, they always stayed to see the show three times. With two reels of Broncho Billy and a one-reel John Bunny and Flora Finch comedy, the time just flew, even the third time when you knew every move an actor was going to make. Because of the horseback riding, Roxy liked the cowboy picture shows best, although Francis X. Bushman and Beverly Bayne's love scenes in society pictures were thrilling.

Now if things went right this summer, she wouldn't have to pretend she was riding in a show—she would be riding for real in the Big Top of the Hallock Circus. She imagined how her chance would come about. A rider in one of the big acts would become ill or break a leg and someone would say, "There's a pretty little redhead over in Wardrobe who might help us out. I hear she's good with horses. Comes from a riding family; Gracie Riley's her grandmother and you know *her*, Mike Riley's widow." Then they would come for her. She would drop whatever costume she had in hand, slip on a riding habit, and show them what she could do. And then next day, dressed in a sparkling, sequined costume, she would take over at the afternoon performance.

She leaned low over Tucky's neck and cried out, "Ladies and gentlemen, in center ring I now present for your amazement the great Roxy Clark and her performing horse, Kentucky!"

As though he too were thinking of such shared glory, the bay horse sped on faster, his head held high in the wind.

A sharp whistle pierced the air and, ahead, a figure sitting on a fence rail waved both arms.

Roxy pulled up and Tucky responded. Oh, drat it! Why did Doug have to spoil her gallop? She thought she could get by the Gardner farm without stopping. Doug Gardner was going on twenty. Why didn't he get married and settle down, then maybe he'd quit acting like a big brother, always telling her what she should do.

All her life Doug had tried to boss her, without success

15

to be sure, but he was a pest. And now this circus business had made him hopping mad. Well, one thing for sure, he was not going to run her life. Roxy Clark had a big future, and no farm boy was going to stop her! If only she were surer about that geometry, she'd tell him off right now.

Tucky stepped down and up through the muddy ditch and came to a halt by the fence.

"You're late. How'd you do? Miss Merriweather lay it on you, did she?" Doug reached out, took hold of Tucky's bridle, and patted his nose.

"It was hard. I don't know, but I hope I passed. I suppose you hope I didn't."

"Oh, I wouldn't say that. I reckon this circus thing has gone too far to be stopped now. But why your father ever gave his consent I'll never know. You belong on the farm and you know it. You'll be gone all during the summer just when they need you most. You're a self-centered, strong-willed girl, Roxy, and always were."

"And you're a smug, bossy, bullheaded farmer, Doug Gardner! This circus thing, indeed! Who was it that always wanted to play circus after the circus left town? Why, you were the biggest duck in the puddle, trying to walk on the clothesline—nearly broke your neck too—and making a trapeze in the barn." Roxy giggled. "Never will forget how you built a cage for Allen and painted tiger stripes on his overalls and shirt."

Doug grinned. "I remember. How Mom whaled me for that!" He sobered. "But we were kids then. Should have more sense now. We're farmers and we've got to feed the world. The circus is for children."

"Oh, don't be so stuffy! You know as well as I do that when a circus comes to town, the whole community gets excited, not just the children. Thrilling people with dare-devil acts and showing them beautiful performers in glittering costumes are wonderful things. I bet more than

16

one farm woman has pictured herself as a bareback rider in a fluffy dress as she does her chores."

Doug let go of Tucky's bridle and jumped off the fence. He looked up at Roxy. "Well, I guess it's time for us to bury the hatchet. Since you won't have to study now, and you'll probably be leaving next week, would you like to go to the picture show Saturday night? They're starting a continued picture called *The Perils of Pauline.*"

"Now isn't that just like you, when I may be gone next week and can't see how it comes out!" Roxy grinned at him.

"Well, I could write and tell you about it if you give me the circus itinerary."

"You talk as if I were going."

"Oh, I'm sure of it. Miss Merriweather wouldn't dare flunk the great Roxy Clark. And remember, I coached you, and when it comes to math, I'm no slouch. How about Saturday?"

"Oh, sure, I'll go with you, oh great mathematician!" Roxy laughed and glanced over the fence at a roll of wire. "What are you doing out here?"

"We're turning this field into pasture, so I'm stringing barbwire along the inside rails." He looked up at the sky. "And I'd better get back at it if I expect to finish by sundown." He picked up his hammer.

On the road again, Tucky ran swiftly to cover the remaining mile to the Clarks' farm. As she passed the south field, Roxy waved at her father, riding a plow drawn by the team of sturdy, gray Percherons of which he was so proud.

Eager as she was to join the circus, a slight twinge of doubt crossed her mind. She would miss appleblossoms, lilacs, and the first violets by the river, and later on, the ripple of golden wheat in the wind, the smell of blackberry jam simmering on the kitchen stove, the Fourth of July parade, and the Sunday School picnic.

Oh, well, one couldn't have everything. And the farm would always be here. The chance for a circus summer came only once, if ever. But if she became a performer, she might never be home again in summer. What did she mean *if* she became a performer? There was no doubt about it. She would! Hadn't Mama taught her to ride, Mama of the great Riding Rileys?

Tucky clattered across the barn floor; Roxy jumped off, unsaddled the horse, and led him to his stall.

On the back porch, she scraped the mud from her shoes on the metal scraper, then wiped them on the piece of old carpet outside the door. Mama kept up a constant battle with all of them not to track mud into the kitchen; a losing battle, Roxy thought, since the barn lot would be soft all spring.

Mama sat in her rocker by the kitchen window, her mending basket on a stand beside her. She looked up from the stocking she was darning. "Roxy—you're home at last! Do you have any idea of how you did?"

"I'm not sure; nothing stumped me, but with geometry, who knows? Doug seems pretty sure I passed."

"He should be a good judge, helping you with it as he has." Mrs. Clark held a darning needle to the light from the window and threaded it with black darning cotton.

Roxy took off her hat and jacket. "Yes. The way he's crabbed around about me taking the job, you'd think helping me pass geometry would be the last thing he'd do."

"Doug is a good boy. He'll make some girl a very good husband." Mama smoothed the heel of one of Janet's black-ribbed stockings over the darning egg and began weaving back and forth across the hole.

"Well, whoever she turns out to be, she has my sympathy. His wife won't be able to call her soul her own, he's that bossy. He asked me to the picture show Saturday night. Is that all right?"

"Of course."

"I'll go up and change my clothes." Roxy walked toward the door to the dining room.

"Since you don't have to study, how about you getting supper? I'd like to finish the mending. It's stacked up something terrible."

"Sure, Mama." Roxy went up to the room she shared with twelve-year-old Janet.

How could Mama have done it? she thought as she got out of her riding skirt and put on a green gingham dress. How could she have left the excitement of the circus for the dull routine of farm life? You had to hand it to Papa; as bossy as Doug, he had a way of getting what he wanted. Early one spring, long ago, he had seen a pretty little rider in center ring. He had left home immediately, got a job caring for horses in the show, and in the fall he brought Mama back as his wife. And as far as Roxy had observed, Mama had never regretted it.

Back in the kitchen, Roxy put more wood in the cookstove and turned on the electric light hanging on a cord above the table. Mama drew her chair to the table to take advantage of the artificial light.

Roxy filled a pan with potatoes from a basket in the pantry and sat on the other side of the table to peel them. "Mama, don't you ever miss the circus?"

"Too busy to miss it, honey. But sometimes I do like to remember the old days and all the wonderful people."

"What do you suppose I'll have to do on this job? If I go, that is."

"Plenty, since you'll be working for Gracie Riley. Your grandma didn't ask you along just for the trip, you may be sure of that." Mama laughed. "You'll earn your pay and then some. Ever since she took over Wardrobe, the Hallock Circus has been one of the best-costumed circuses on the road. I know Frank Hallock rates your grandma's work as high as that of any of his performers."

At the supper table, Roxy watched her father put a big piece of butter on his mashed potatoes. Working out

19

in all kinds of weather, his face was ruddy and there were squint lines about his blue eyes; his jaw was square, his big mouth firm, and his bright-red hair was thick and wavy. He must have been quite handsome years ago, Roxy thought.

Janet and Allen, also redheads, chattered on about the doings at Round Hill School, a country school two miles from the Clark farm. Janet was in sixth grade and Allen in eighth. Every day next year Allen would ride the four miles into Westwood High School as Roxy had been doing for the past four years.

"And there's going to be this big thing on the last day of school for eighth grade graduation," Allen told them. "You know, speeches and poems and stuff like that just before we get our diplomas. Miss Whitney asked if I'd recite something. What do you think, Mama? Do you know of a poem with two verses that wouldn't be too babyish?" Allen filled his mouth.

"Two verses *would* be babyish for you. You'll have plenty of time to learn something longer, with meat to it," Mrs. Clark replied. "And speaking of meat, cut smaller bites, young man. A boy ready to go to high school should have better table manners."

"There's a wonderful poem about a horse in my English Literature book," Roxy suggested.

"How many verses?" Allen cut a bite of meat in two.

"About fourteen or fifteen, I guess."

"Too long."

Janet passed the bread to her father. "Papa, can I go to the picture show Saturday afternoon?"

"If I finish plowing the north section in time to go to town." Red Clark poured thick cream into his coffee cup, then put in a heaping spoonful of sugar.

At the sharp jangle of the telephone bell, the whole family paused to count the rings—four long, two short.

"That's our ring." Mama rose, walked to the telephone and took down the receiver. "Hello. Yes, this is the Clarks,

Mrs. Clark speaking. Why, yes, I'll call her— For you, Roxy."

"Who is it?"

Mrs. Clark shook her head as she handed over the receiver.

Roxy pulled down the mouthpiece and stood on tiptoe. "Hello. Yes— Oh, hello, Miss Merriweather!— I did? Oh, that's great, simply great! Well, yes, I know that's not a very good grade, but it's passing, isn't it? Uh huh— Yes, I was anxious to know. Now I can get on with my plans— It was so good of you to call to tell me. Thank you so much— Good-by."

Roxy hung up the receiver and grinned at her family. "Ladies and gentlemen! May I present Miss Roxane Clark who has passed geometry and is now an assured graduate of Westwood High! Now, Papa, I can leave for Kingston a week from Friday just as Grandma wanted me to."

Papa pushed his chair back from the table and frowned at her. "Yes, I suppose so. I've given my word. But I must say I didn't think you could manage to jump all the hurdles I put in your way. And I still don't approve. There are so many roughnecks with a circus." He turned to Mama. "You know that's so, Martha."

"Now, Red, we've had this out before. Roxy's done her part, we must do ours. There comes a time when parents have to loosen the rein and give a child his head. I grew up in the circus and I didn't do badly; I got you."

Roxy stood beside her father and stroked his hair. "Now, Papa, simmer down. Just remember Gracie. She'll see that I steer clear of the roughnecks. Although knowing some of them might be very interesting." Roxy laughed. "I may come back with a very colorful vocabulary."

"Roxy Clark!" Papa shouted. "If I ever hear you—!"

"Red, you know she wouldn't. Stop tormenting your father, Roxy, and cut the pie."

That night as Roxy lay awake beside Janet, a chill wind howled outside the bedroom window. Soon she would be hearing the roar of tigers and the trumpeting of elephants. Every day would be circus day filled with beautiful sparkle and stirring band music. And she would be with exciting people like Aunt Marie, Uncle Jules, and her cousins. Uncle Jules was such fun; he had never lost his French accent and to be teased by him was pure delight.

Often Roxy had been told of the January she was born. Aunt Marie and Uncle Jules were there at the time. When Uncle Jules first saw the new-born baby, he was enchanted with her red hair. "Ah!" he had exclaimed. "Such hair I have not seen since I attended a performance of *Cyrano de Bergerac* in Paris! The actress who played Roxane had hair like this. Martha—Red—you should name this child Roxane."

And thus she was called. Roxy liked being named for a character in a French play. In a school full of Marys, Sarahs, and other ordinary names, she enjoyed being different.

She turned on her side and put her hand under her cheek. Tomorrow she would bring Mama's trunk from the attic and start packing. She must finish the navy-blue suit and make two more shirtwaists.

Just think, two weeks from now she would be there, working with Grandma so that the circus could get on the road by May! Oh, the things she would have to tell Doug when she got back. She smiled in the dark. He was an irritating character, but she suspected she was going to miss quarreling with him. During the next months, she should try to keep up that diary Aunt Marie had sent her for Christmas so she wouldn't forget anything. But there would be so much to do, so much to do, she thought as she drifted off.

Chapter 2

CIRCUS CITY

The Clarks' Model T Ford touring car gave a low rumble as Mama pushed the clutch pedal to the floor to climb the hill in low gear.

"Now Mother will probably give you the circus itinerary. You send us a copy so we can write to you," she said to Roxy beside her.

"I'll do that. I'll want your letters. Give the list of towns to Doug too. He said he'd write and tell me what was happening in *The Perils of Pauline*. What a horrible predicament Pauline was left in last Saturday! Any special last-minute orders you want to give me?" Roxy pulled her navy-blue felt hat a little farther down on one side to give it a jaunty angle.

"No. Your father gave you enough instructions for both of us. You'll do all right. Gracie is good at keeping young girls in line. Believe me, I know. There are all kinds of people traveling with a circus, good and bad, as I've told you. It's a complete world on wheels, so there are bound to be the mean, dishonest, and wicked on board. And you won't find them just among the ignorant roustabouts either."

At the baggage window in the depot they checked Roxy's trunk through to Kingston, then stood outside in the bright April sun to wait for the train.

Roxy felt a slight tightening in her throat as she heard

the locomotive roaring down the track. She turned and hugged her mother. "Good-by, Mama."

"Good-by, honey. We'll see you when the show comes to Westwood in July."

"Tell Allen to take good care of Tucky."

"You know he will."

Roxy picked up her suitcase and boarded the train. Finding a seat, she sat next to the window and looked out. Mama was standing beside their Model T near the depot. She spotted Roxy and waved. The train gave a lurch and slowly moved forward. Roxy kept waving as long as she could see Mama. Then, gathering momentum, the train wound its way through the shabbiest part of town.

Roxy took off her spring coat and removed her hat. Looking at the soot-covered window sill, she pulled her jacket sleeves down to cover the cuffs of her white shirt-waist.

She had never taken this train ride in April. In April, Grandma and Aunt Marie's family were much too busy preparing for the coming circus season to have company and, besides, work on the farm in spring was too heavy for anyone to do any visiting.

But what a different April this was! She was leaving the farm and all the work behind. Ahead was the Great Hallock Circus! She settled back onto the faded green-plush seat and looked out at the moist black earth of plowed fields.

She opened her pocketbook and took out a small red book and pencil. She put her feet up on the edge of her suitcase and propped the book on her knees. Now was the time to write something in the diary. Up to now she had written of only three days of 1914.

January 12.   Reading George Eliot's *Mill on the Floss*.

February 14.   Doug sent me a comic valentine about
              an old maid and a horse. But the one I
              sent him was worse.
April 2.   Took geometry exam and Miss Merri-
              weather called while we were eating
              supper to say I passed. Hurray! Now I
              can leave a week from tomorrow.
Roxy turned the pages to Friday, and wrote:
April 10.   Mama brought me to the train and I am
              on my way to Kingston.
"Ticket, please."

She looked up, smiled at the conductor, got the ticket
from her purse, and handed it over.

The conductor tore off a portion, punched it, and returned the remainder. "You have an hour layover in
Indianapolis," he told her.

"Yes, I know. What time does that train get to Kingston?"

The man consulted a timetable. "Three-fifteen."

"Thank you."

She returned the diary to her purse. There was too
much to think about and too much to see outside to write
now. She glanced down at the white face of the little
gold watch on her wrist—a quarter after eight—Allen and
Janet were at Round Hill School by this time, probably
playing in the yard until the principal rang the bell.
Mama would be on her way home, and Papa would have
done a big piece of plowing. Doug, more than likely, was
plowing too. She wondered how that field was working
out as pastureland.

Eyes on the passing landscape, she touched her watch,
enjoying the feel of its small perfection. What a surprise
last night when Papa had handed her the red velvet box
at the supper table. As she had opened it, he had said,
"That's to tick through your circus summer. Every time

you look at it, remember that we're counting the hours till you come back home, Roxy girl."

Her eyes moistened at the thought. What loves they were to give her a *bracelet* watch! Miss Albright, the English teacher, had one and Roxy had admired it. But the teacher's was fastened around her wrist with a black strap, while Roxy's was held in place by a dainty band of gold links. She wished she had had another day at school to show it to the other girls. Not one of them had a *bracelet* watch.

Seeing a man on horseback reminded her of Tucky. She was going to miss that animal. He was probably the best-educated horse in Indiana; every day she had repeated lessons aloud on the ride to school—poems, Shakespeare quotations, even those pesky irregular French verbs. Tucky had heard them all. And when she was mad, she gave vent to her anger by exploding in his ears. She was sure Tucky knew more about her than anyone.

If he were only with the circus too! If he could be there when her chance came, and she could put him through his tricks. What a handsome pair they would make under a spotlight; the color of Tucky's coat complemented her red hair so beautifully. Papa said he had thought of her the minute he laid eyes on the horse.

With so much to watch along the tracks and such delightful daydreams to fill her head, the morning passed quickly. In the Indianapolis station, she ate the sandwich and apple Mama had put in her suitcase.

The train north was on time. Roxy got on, arranged her things in a seat, and settled back to observe the other passengers still boarding.

Across the aisle a group of people spoke to one another in a foreign language as they stowed away their bags and seated themselves. It sounded like German to Roxy. She wished she knew who they were and what they were saying.

The beautiful, older woman and the distinguished, gray-haired man sat directly across from Roxy. She decided they must be husband and wife. And were the younger ones their children? The two young women resembled the older couple and so did the handsome, blond fellow sitting directly behind them. Perhaps the two dark-haired men were the daughters' husbands since they had paired off in the seats ahead.

As the train started, the blond boy caught Roxy watching him. Quickly she looked out the window and did not look back until the conductor collected tickets.

He took hers first, then those across the aisle. Roxy watched the older man hand over a sheaf of tickets and make an inclusive gesture toward the others. The conductor nodded, punched and pocketed the tickets, and gave the group a friendly look.

"Going to Kingston are you? I bet you're circus folks."

Roxy sat up straighter and cocked her ears.

The older man nodded. "Yah, Hallock Circus."

"Thought so." The conductor grinned broadly. "I've been on this run a good many years and, come early spring, I can usually spot you performers on your way to Winter Quarters. What's your act?"

Puzzled, the older man turned to the young man in the seat behind.

"My father doesn't understand English very well," he told the conductor. "We are the Kassels from Germany. Our horses are well-known in Europe. For the first time we will ride in America."

"You don't say!" The conductor put his ticket punch in his coat pocket. "Well, I'll have to plan to lay off when the circus comes to Indianapolis and take my kids to see you. They love the circus and so do I."

"Doesn't everyone?" The young man laughed, glanced across the aisle, and winked at Roxy.

Quickly she looked away and felt her cheeks burn.

27

Why, the nerve of him! She should have kept her hat on. Mama had cautioned her that red-haired girls had to be extra careful about mashers. But really, that wink hadn't seemed fresh, just friendly. After all he was with the circus and so was she, he was a rider and so was she. That wink might be the beginning of a very interesting friendship. Here she was, just a few hours away from the farm and already—!

Cautiously she glanced back. He was looking up at the conductor.

"Do you know how far the Wayne Hotel in Kingston is from the station?" he asked.

The conductor set his cap on the side of his head and thought briefly. "Well, now, I can't just rightly remember." He turned across to Roxy. "You're going to Kingston, Miss. Do you happen to know the location of the Wayne?"

"Why, yes. It's around the corner from the station and about three blocks down Main Street." Roxy was aware that the eyes of those across the aisle were upon her.

The older woman smiled and nodded, plumes swaying gracefully over the edge of her big black hat. "Thank you. You will show us?"

"Of course." Roxy smiled back.

The conductor moved on and Roxy again faced the window. A slight commotion caused her to turn. Mrs. Kassel was standing in the aisle. She looked down at Roxy, pointed to the place occupied by Roxy's hat and purse and asked, "May I sit here, please?"

Roxy quickly removed her things. "Oh, please do."

"My English is not good," the woman said as she settled in the seat beside Roxy. "I would like to practice."

"You speak very well. I wish I knew some German, but I don't. I heard that you are going to be with the Hallock Circus this season. I am too, in the Wardrobe Department."

Never had the ride from Indianapolis to Kingston slipped by so fast. Roxy learned all about the Kassels and Mrs. Kassel about the Clarks, Mama's circus background, Grandma, and Aunt Marie's family.

She had been right, the two young ladies were the Kassels' daughters; Erma married to Bernhard Bremen and Gretchen married to Conrad Hagen. Their son Karl, Mrs. Kassel told her, was unmarried. Roxy smiled inwardly at this bit of information.

Mrs. Kassel leaned across the aisle and spoke to Mr. Kassel in German. Roxy caught the name of Riley. She must be telling him about Grandma and Grandpa's riding act. Karl, she noted, was listening too.

Mr. Kassel replied to his wife and smiled at Roxy.

"Fritz says he has heard of Mike Riley, your grandfather," Mrs. Kassel said. "Do you like horses? Do you ride?"

"Oh, yes." Roxy described Tucky and the tricks he could do.

"You miss your horse already, do you not?"

"I do indeed," Roxy answered. "Tell me about your horses. You must use a great many in your acts."

"Oh yes. Five High School horses, three resinbacks for bareback performance, and Fritz has twelve matched black beauties for his liberty number. They are all like family. Like Kassel children. You know?"

"I know. I know." Roxy gave a little shiver of delight. All those horses! And she would be there to see them perform every day until late fall! That is she would if Grandma didn't keep her busy all the time in a tent someplace in the circus back yard. She had to remember that she wasn't being hired to watch the show like a paying customer; she was a behind-the-scenes *part* of the show.

What luck to meet the Kassels before anyone else in the circus. Of course Mr. Hallock had met them last year when the contract was signed in Berlin. But to Roxy, Mr.

Hallock was only a shadowy figure, someone whose big, pillared mansion was the showplace in Kingston and whose name appeared on the circus posters that blossomed every spring on billboards, barns, and sheds across the country. Grandma and the Frontenays often talked about Frank Hallock and his beautiful wife, Louise, but Roxy had never seen them.

As the train passed through Watsonville, Roxy put her hand on Mrs. Kassel's arm. "The next station is Kingston. Perhaps we should get our things together."

Mrs. Kassel nodded and rose. "So nice to talk," she said as she stepped into the aisle.

Roxy watched the stately, beautiful woman as she directed one of her sons-in-law in the removal of a bag from overhead. Dressed in a black-tailored suit, a white blouse, with a stock collar fitting high about her throat, black kid gloves, and the big, black-plumed hat, she was as theatrical a figure as Roxy had ever seen. What a fine appearance she must make in center ring.

Roxy put on her own hat, coat, and gloves and sat down to wait for the next stop.

"May I carry your suitcase to the front of the car?" It was Karl smiling down at her.

"Why, yes, thank you." She returned his smile. What deep blue eyes he had, and his hair gleamed as gold as corn tassels in the sun. If his riding ability matched his looks, he was a big star for sure, she thought as he picked up her suitcase.

The conductor called out, "Kingston!" He assisted the lady passengers off the steps. As the Kassels gathered up their bags and moved toward the depot, he waved, and yelled after them, "I'll be looking for your act in Indianapolis."

Roxy took up her suitcase and walked beside Mrs. Kassel. Karl and his father had gone ahead to check on their trunks and to make arrangements to have them sent to the Wayne Hotel. Roxy knew that Uncle Jules would drive down and get hers later. At the corner of the depot she pointed out for Mrs. Kassel the way to the hotel and said good-by. "I go in the other direction," she told her new acquaintance.

"We shall see you at rehearsal, shall we not?" the older woman asked.

"That's hard to say. I don't know exactly what my job will be in Wardrobe. As I told you, Grandma's boss and I've heard she's a regular Simon Legree in her department. But surely I'll be seeing the show sometime."

"Your grandmother has a big job, a big responsibility. But of course I shall see you. We have the whole nineteen-fourteen season to get better acquainted. Thank you for listening to my bad English."

Roxy crossed the street and walked down Fourth, then turned on Wheeler Avenue and continued the five blocks to the house where the Frontenays and Grandma lived each year from late October to the first of May.

It was a large brown house trimmed in white. Sometimes during the winter months, Grandma lived here alone, for the Frontenays often went on vaudeville tour. But Grandma never had time to be lonely; she was too busy designing and making next season's costumes. All winter, the women of Kingston plied their needles on garments of satin, velvet, and sequins.

On the porch Roxy put down her suitcase, lifted the doormat, picked up the key, and unlocked the front door. Inside, she looked around the familiar sitting room furnished with rocking chairs, center table, and worn sofa. One corner was taken up by a big heating stove standing on a large square of linoleum to protect the carpet. It was a typical living room, Roxy knew, but what made it so special were the photographs that covered the walls, photographs of the famous performers Grandma had

31

known. And they were all autographed—most of them saying, "To Gracie, with love."

Roxy went upstairs to Grandma's room, unpacked, and hung her things in the closet. She took off her suit and put on a housedress.

Downstairs again, the house seemed chilly. She put on the work gloves lying on top of the coal bucket in the living room, opened the stove door, stirred up the red coals with the poker, and tossed in some big lumps of coal.

In the kitchen she built up the fire in the cookstove and glanced up at the clock. Twenty after four. She wondered what they were planning to have for supper. Knowing Grandma and Aunt Marie, she doubted if they had planned anything. Mama said Grandma was the worst cook in Indiana and Aunt Marie a close runner-up for the title. Because they ate the well-cooked, nourishing food put out in the circus cook tent for six months of the year, Grandma always said they just had to teach their stomachs to coast for the other six months.

Roxy took an apron from a hook on the back of the pantry door and tied it on. She would surprise them and have supper ready. She had time to make gingerbread.

By a quarter to six the house was filled with the odor of clove, ginger, and cinnamon, and the smell of frying meat began to permeate the kitchen. The lighted chandelier over the dining-room table shone down on settings for eight. Roxy took the napkins in their initialed silver rings off the sideboard and put them at the proper places, and got a clean one for herself.

Returning to the kitchen, she pulled the boiling coffeepot to the back of the stove then stuck a fork in the potatoes. They were ready to mash as soon as the family arrived.

The back door flew open. Mimi burst in and threw her arms about her cousin. "I just knew you would be here!

32

That's the reason I came on ahead with Grandma." She gave a deep sniff and glanced at the stove. "Roxy, you darling! You've cooked supper! I'm starved. What is that heavenly smell?"

"Gingerbread. Mimi, you look wonderful. Take off your hat and let me see how you're doing your hair now."

Mimi pulled off the hat. "It's just pinned up tight. We've been rehearsing all day."

Roxy looked at her cousin fondly. Mimi was so pretty, dark-haired and vivacious, with eyes that sparkled as she talked. And oh, how magnificent she was in performing tights and leotard! Flying through the air to catch Uncle Jules' waiting hands, Roxy thought Mimi the most beautiful thing alive. She was like some dainty bird soaring confidently from perch to bar to the hands of her father.

"Where's Grandma?"

"Unhitching. I should have helped her, but I just had to see you. How are Aunt Martha and Uncle Red and Janet and Allen?"

"Fine."

"How's Doug?"

"As bossy as ever. Oh, Mimi, I must tell you. On the train today—"

At that moment Gracie Riley opened the door and clasped Roxy in her strong arms. "Welcome, Roxy girl. Glad you arrived. Hmmm. So you got supper. Smells good. How are the folks?"

"Very well." Roxy smiled at her grandmother. "And how well you look, Grandma. Did you make that coat? It's lovely on you. Pretty hat too."

"No. I bought this coat last spring in Chicago. I just don't have time to do any sewing for myself." She turned to Mimi and gave her a good-natured smack on the seat. "I'm too busy seeing that the likes of this gets dressed in satin and sequins."

"Should I mash the potatoes yet?" Roxy asked.

"Better wait, honey. Jules was having an argument with Jeff Anderson about some new equipment when I left. Come on, Mimi, let's get our things off and give Roxy a hand. How wonderful it is to have supper ready."

At the table, compliments about Roxy's cooking came from all sides. Roxy grinned. She knew she had better gather these bouquets now, for once she saw the Frontenays act again she would feel like a clod tied to earth.

With the training they had had since childhood, her cousins—Mimi, sixteen; Henri, seventeen; Jacques, eighteen; Lilly, fourteen;—would probably become the world's greatest aerialists. Uncle Jules was not only a marvelous performer, he was also a thorough teacher.

Roxy passed the butter to Lilly. "On the train, I got acquainted with some circus people, the Kassels from Germany."

Aunt Marie put down her fork. "The Kassels! So—they have arrived. Louise Hallock says they're magnificent riders. She was with Frank last year when he signed them up in Europe. What are they like?"

Roxy described the family and related her visit with Mrs. Kassel.

"That would be Helga Kassel," Grandma said. "From what I hear, she may be doing Frieda Jantry out of headline billing. Old Frieda isn't going to like that. Frank is so sentimental about Frieda. I still can sit a horse with the best of them, but who wants to see a wrinkled, white-haired old woman when there are talented young ones around? Sometimes I wonder if Frieda ever looks in a mirror."

"You could still look great and pull off a spectacular act, Mother." Aunt Marie smiled. "But I think you enjoy being boss of Wardrobe and having your oar in everyone else's act. Frank says you're the backbone of the show. Without all the shine and glitter of costumes who would pay to see us?"

"Will there be other new acts this year?" Roxy asked, helping herself to the gravy.

Grandma nodded. "Yes. Frank rounded up quite a few on that European jaunt of his. He told me he thinks things are brewing over there. That's the reason he went scouting for talent before something happens."

"Like what?" Roxy watched Grandma stir her coffee slowly.

"I don't know. But Louise Hallock said she never saw so much parading of soldiers in her life as she saw in Germany. So—I suppose anything can happen. Right, Jules?"

Uncle Jules frowned, narrowed his eyes, and nodded. "Kaiser Wilhelm has not raised that army just to parade the streets of Berlin. I distrust the Kaiser. So much France has suffered from Germany."

Roxy gave an involuntary shiver. She liked the Kassels. How would Uncle Jules react to the German family in the season ahead? From his tone, some fur might be flying.

Jacques put his hand on his father's arm. "What happens in Europe shouldn't concern you, Papa. You are an American now."

"Even Americans must be on the *qui vive* where the Kaiser's concerned."

Mimi and Lilly did the dishes, refusing Roxy's help since she had cooked supper. She sat by the table and listened to circus talk.

"Oh, Mimi, I started to tell you that the Kassels' son Karl is the handsomest fellow I've ever set eyes on." Roxy described Karl in detail, how he had winked at her, and carried her suitcase.

Mimi sighed and her hands remained motionless in the soapsuds. "How nice to have someone new on the lot. He sounds dreamy."

"When Mimi looks like that, Roxy, it means Karl

Kassel is a goner. And she's got beaus galore already." There was a tinge of envy in Lilly's laugh.

Watching Mimi's large dark eyes, Roxy felt a surge of irritation. "Well, look out, Mimi Frontenay, I saw him first. I aim to give you competition on that one."

Mimi gave a slow smile, washed a plate, and said teasingly, "All right, if you can. But you'll be working with Grandma and, if I know her, you won't be out from under her thumb very often. And I'll see your handsome rider every day in the back yard. Of course he *is* a German," she added more thoughtfully, "and Papa has such a bad opinion of them."

"Since when has Papa's opinion about your fellows mattered?" Lilly dropped silverware into a drawer as she dried it. "My sister has grown into an awful flirt this past year, Roxy. Beware of her. Whenever our act is on, all the fellows who can, gather in the side entrance to watch. And believe me they aren't there to watch the rest of us."

Roxy examined Mimi anew. She *had* changed since they had last been together. There was an aura about her, something more than beauty. She loved Mimi and she was not going to be jealous of her. And yet, with Mimi fast becoming a star, what chance would a red-haired cousin in Wardrobe have? Roxy jumped up and began putting dishes in the cupboard.

That night, lying on a cot in a corner of Grandma's room, Roxy was wide-eyed, her mind on tomorrow. Early in the morning she and Grandma would drive out to Winter Quarters where her new duties would begin.

What a magic place this city of Kingston was! Since everything in town revolved around the big show, it really should be called Circus City. If only she were a performer instead of just— But if she hadn't got in by means of her needle, she probably wouldn't be here at all. Now if Mama had married a performer instead of a farmer, she might be in an act too and could give Mimi a run for her money.

But before next fall, she just might be able to work her way into an act some way or other, an act in which she could wear a gorgeous costume, one of green, or lavender, or yellow to go with her red hair. Red-heads were supposed to have lots of fire, get-up-and-go, and temper, and she had enough of all of them to get what she wanted! Look out Mimi Frontenay!—You up there in your silk tights! Here comes Roxy Clark!

Chapter 3

WINTER QUARTERS

Next morning at a quarter past seven, Roxy and Grandma drove along Main Street.

"I want to stop at Jenny Studer's. She had to make over Luly's spec blanket. It just didn't fit." Grandma held the reins in one hand.

"Luly? She's one of the elephants, isn't she? But what's to fit on an elephant's blanket?" Roxy enjoyed watching Grandma drive. She did it with such style, as though she were taking part in the opening grand entry around the hippodrome track.

"You'd be surprised the trouble those big galoots give us. Like women, they come in all shapes. Some are enormous across the rear and then slope toward the shoulders, some are narrow in the middle, while others are huge. Old Luly girl leads the elephants in the new Arabian Nights opening spec. Her rose velveteen blanket has to fit properly over that big behind of hers."

They stopped briefly at a house. Roxy held the reins while Grandma went in. Coming back out she dropped Luly's blanket, a large roll of gold-sequined, rose-colored velveteen, into Roxy's lap. "Pretty color, isn't it?"

"Gorgeous." Roxy examined the sequins.

"Take a good look at the way those are sewed on. One of your jobs will be to replace them from time to time during the season. Wardrobe has to have constant care. Costumes must look as fine in August as they do in May."

"It was good of you, Grandma, to give me this job. I didn't think I'd ever get to travel with the circus."

"Well, you were not hired because you are my granddaughter, young lady, but because you are as handy at sewing as anyone I've ever known. You're neat, methodical, and, as much as I've seen of you, level-headed—all attributes that will be useful in handling temperamental performers. Also you've got enough spunk to prevent them from bamboozling you."

Roxy laughed. "I know. Mama has told me many a tale about jealousies and fights over billing and center ring."

Grandma chuckled. "Well, things haven't changed a bit from Martha's day." She reached in her pocket and pulled out a piece of paper. "Here, I thought you'd like to have this. It's our official tour sheet for the season. Now you'll know where you are going."

Roxy's scalp prickled at the roots of her hair as she ran a finger down the list of towns and states—South Bend, Indiana, Chicago, Illinois, Indianapolis, Indiana, Terre Haute, Indiana, Rockford, Illinois. Her finger moved faster down the long list—Minnesota, South Dakota, Iowa, Nebraska, Missouri, Kansas—and on and on.

"Heavens, Grandma, by the time I get back I bet I'll be the most-traveled girl in Westwood."

"Shouldn't wonder. But you won't see much of the country except railroad yards and circus grounds. We travel at night and by day you'll be on the lot, either in my wardrobe wagon or in the back yard dressing tents keeping costumes in order. Some of the girls make fast changes. We have to be on hand to grab what they take off."

"I've never been to Chicago."

"Yes, I know. And now that's a horse of a different color. We play there for a whole week in Grant Park. I

39

think I'll have time to show you around a bit. If I don't, perhaps Mimi or Marie can. It's a great city."

"What's the new spec like? I'll never forget the year Cinderella was the theme." Roxy rubbed her hand over the rose velvet.

"Well, this year there are a lot of oriental dancing girls in each ring. There's a stage where the Sultan lolls around on a cushioned throne while Scheherazade introduces him to Aladdin, Ali Baba and the Forty Thieves, Sinbad, and all the other characters from the Arabian Nights. Did Mimi tell you that she is doing Scheherazade?"

"No. Oh, she'll be lovely! What's she wearing?"

"Pink satin and pale-green chiffon with gold sequins. It's one of the loveliest getups we've ever made. The whole number is *splendiferous.*"

Roxy closed her eyes momentarily. Mimi in another act in which she probably would look more gorgeous than ever!

Now they had left the town and were nearing the Hallock farms. Roxy could see the long rows of red and yellow circus barns, buildings, and sheds coming into view. Winter Quarters covered acres and acres.

This, Roxy knew, was the pulse of Kingston, in fact of the whole county. For miles around, the farmers raised timothy hay and oats to feed the circus animals during the winter months, and circus work occupied a large portion of the town's population. The Adler Carriage and Wagon Company furnished all the fancy vehicles for the show. No fairy-tale coach, chariot, or fancy cart was ever too much for Tom Adler and his workmen to tackle. And besides making the new, they repaired the old—the band wagons, cages, ticket wagons, floats, and calliopes. Some years, the Carriage Company had to put on an extra shift from November through April.

If anyone in Kingston wanted his house or barn

painted, he had to wait until the circus left town, for all painters were occupied at the Quarters, brightening up the rolling stock. And as for a carpenter—Roxy had heard Grandma say that in winter you couldn't get a carpenter for love or money.

Grandma drove in the main gate above which a huge red and gold sign proclaimed: *The Great Hallock Circus.*

Roxy had visited Winter Quarters before, but never at this final stage of preparation. "What's going on now, Grandma? What will be happening today?"

"Well, all the practice rings and training barns will be in use. Some of the performers are still coming in, like the Kassels you met yesterday. Their acts will have to be timed, then probably cut, and retimed. Next week full rehearsals will get underway. Putting a show together is some job. There must be no waits. No performer may have more than his allotted time. But Frank Hallock is a genius at this big business. Turns out one of the smoothest-running shows in the country."

Grandma pulled on a rein and the high-stepping horse turned down a side road between rows of buildings and sheds. Freshly painted red wagons, their wood carvings gleaming with gold paint, stood under the sheds, ready for the miles and miles of parade routes to be covered along the main streets of the land.

The gaudy wagons gave Roxy a thrill. She could almost hear the brass bands and the clack of horses' hoofs. There was nothing like a circus parade! Absolutely nothing!

"Well, here we are at Wardrobe." Grandma pulled up at a two-story building. A man came running from behind it.

"Been watching for you, Mrs. Gracie," he said. His grin showed several teeth missing, and his face was bristly with unshaved whiskers.

"Good for you, Del. You remember Roxy, don't you? She's going with us this season."

41

Roxy smiled at the old man. "Hello, there, Delaware. How've you been?" she asked as she stepped over the wheel.

"First rate. My, how you've growed, Miss Roxy. So you're following in your mama's footsteps, be you? What a rider she was! I never thought she'd stick to farm life. What kind of a act you got? Did you bring your own horses?"

Roxy laughed. "Didn't bring a one, Delaware. I'll be doing all my performances with needle and thread, working in Wardrobe."

The old man frowned and grumbled. "'Taint right, 'taint right at all with no Rileys in the ring."

"Aunt Marie's there."

"But not on a horse like she ought to be." He shook his head as he climbed into the seat Grandma had vacated. "Mrs. Gracie, you got no business giving up your act. Anybody can take care of Wardrobe; Gracie Riley belongs in center ring."

"Oh, go along with you, you flattering old coot. See that you give Fancy a good currying today and not too many oats."

"Mrs. Gracie, they's no need to remind me after all the years I been tending your horses." He looked down at Roxy and grinned. "If working in Wardrobe ever sours on you, Miss Roxy, come 'round to the barns and I'll put you on a horse. Martha Riley's daughter's bound to be handy with a bridle. And, being Gracie and Mike's granddaughter won't hurt you either."

"Don't put ideas in her head, Del. She's here to tend costumes. Come on, Roxy. I've got a million things to do." Grandma opened the door as the carriage rolled away.

Inside, the whole first floor was one huge room, filled with open wardrobe crates, bright-hued, glittering garments hanging on the long rods running down the middle of each.

42

"What colors!" Roxy exclaimed, touching a piece of red satin near her.

"Those are the parade outfits. We're still working on those for the spec. And we have to finish the machine work on the ones for latecomers as soon as they get out here for fittings."

"You mean you'll be seeing the Kassels?"

"Yes. They ride together in the parade. They sent their measurements, but we've just basted the clothes until they try them on. They carry their own costumes for their acts; we just made their parade duds."

"What color?"

"Bright green."

"Oh, how stunning! Mrs. Kassel and the daughters are blondes. Sequins on them?"

Grandma laughed. "Naturally. The ladies ride sidesaddle in the parade, and believe me those full skirts are some job. Come on upstairs."

"Is Sadie still with you?"

"Oh, sure. Couldn't run Wardrobe without Sadie Modosky."

Roxy followed her grandmother up a flight of stairs and into a loft-like room above. Two long tables ran down the middle of the room. Some women were already seated at the tables working on satin, velvet, and chiffon.

"Sadie, where is everybody?" Grandma opened the watch pinned at her shoulder, then clicked it shut. "It's four minutes to eight."

A wiry, little old lady hopped up from the end of a table and walked to a window. "Keep your shirt on, Gracie, there they come now. The interurban was probably late." She smiled at Roxy over her gold-rimmed spectacles. "Hello there, Roxy. So—you've come to give us a hand."

"Hello, Sadie."

There was the sound of feet on the stairs and a group

of women entered, hung up their coats, and hastened to the tables.

Grandma looked at her watch again. "Well, girls, you just barely made it. I insist upon punctuality. And we begin work here at eight o'clock as I've told you again and again."

Girls, indeed! Roxy looked at the seamstresses. Practically all of them had either gray or white hair and wore glasses. What had she let herself in for? Oh, well, only a few of these would be going on the road, and there were lots of young people among the performers, she thought. Karl's face flashed across her mind.

"The interurban was ten minutes late this morning, Mrs. Gracie," one lady explained.

Grandma removed a fancy comb from the back of her wavy white hair, smoothed up a loose strand, and returned the comb to its place. Roxy watched her, remembering the photographs they had at home of a younger Gracie Riley seated firmly on the back of a rearing horse and waving to an admiring audience. Now she managed Wardrobe with as firm a hand as she had controlled the horse, and her figure was as striking as ever.

All morning Roxy sat at one of the several sewing machines along the windows and hemmed bright-red velveteen camel blankets. Grandma and Sadie darted about the room, assigning work, inspecting finished garments, folding them, and lining them up in neat, labeled stacks for packing in the crates on the first floor.

By half past ten Roxy felt as though she had been born guiding red velveteen under the machine needle. How come so many camels? How come the ladies in town hadn't made these along with those for the elephants? She asked Sadie as the latter came for those that Roxy had finished.

"Mr. Hallock got a bargain in camels two weeks ago when the Wagstaff show went into bankruptcy. So we had to order more velveteen to cover the creatures. When you get these hemmed, I'll show you how to sew on the gold braid."

Roxy straightened up and sat back in her chair to ease the ache through her shoulders. She liked to sew, to make a dress or a suit for herself or clothes for her family, but this was ridiculous! All this beautiful material to cover dirty, old haughty-looking camels!

At home when she got tired of sitting at the sewing machine, she could run out to the barn and give Tucky a vigorous rub down to work out the kinks in her shoulders. Then, astride the horse, she would go for a gallop down the lane and back again, returning refreshed to the machine.

She glanced across the room and saw Grandma watching her. Guiltily, she spun the wheel with her right hand and pedaled below with her feet, the whir of her machine adding its noise to that of the others in the line along the windows. Coming to the end of the hem, she cut the threads and tied them, then stood up to fold the material and put it in a box on the floor beside her.

As she picked up another piece of unhemmed material from a table nearer the window, she looked out. A long line of black horses was passing by toward the big circular building Grandma had called the practice ring. How beautiful they were! Their black coats shone sleekly in the sunlight, and they walked with delicate precision as though conscious that they were indeed thoroughbreds of the ring. Roxy longed to run after them and watch their workout.

"Well, Roxy."

She jumped at Grandma's voice behind her.

"Just getting another blanket to do." She quickly returned to her machine.

Grandma looked out the window. "Hmmm. Nice bunch. Must be Fritz Kassel's liberty horses. I heard they

45

had arrived. Wish Mrs. Kassel and her daughters would get over here to be fitted." She looked down at Roxy. "Suppose you leave that for the moment and take that box of jackets downstairs. Sadie's down there and will show you where to hang them. I expect you're feeling a little restless by now. You need a stretch. After a while you'll get used to it, but I don't want to make you miserable the first day. You work downstairs with Sadie the rest of the morning. She'll show you the dining room."

"I know where it is."

Roxy picked up the box Grandma had indicated, a box of short, sleeveless jackets, covered entirely in gold and red sequins. What a glitter they would make when the oriental dancing girls wore them in the Big Top!

Below, Sadie pointed out where they belonged; one to be hung over each of the satin, baggy-trousered costumes of the harem girls. Every costume was marked with a girl's name, having been made to her measurements. How on earth could all these be kept in their right places during the long season of one-day stands across the country? This was going to be part of her job, Roxy supposed. Her dream of performing might be just that! A dream! She'd just be sewing camel blankets and putting away costumes the whole summer, while Mimi—! Oh well, she was here on the lot where the excitement started and for now that had to be enough.

"Come over here, Roxy," Sadie called from a front window. "That's Mr. Hallock driving up in his seven-passenger automobile. Wonder who all those people are with him?"

Roxy looked. "They're the Kassels. I met them on the train yesterday." She watched the open touring car draw up before the door and stop. Would Karl remember her? Sure he would; who could forget her red hair? Thinking of his wink, she grinned. This wasn't a bad job at that. Sooner or later, everyone had to deal with Wardrobe.

The big man got down from behind the steering wheel and opened the back door of the car. So, that was Frank Hallock! Tall and broad-shouldered, and, she judged, about Grandma's age. With a courtly air, he removed his hat and bowed as the two Kassel daughters descended from the automobile. Mrs. Kassel gave him a big smile as she stepped onto the running board. The circus owner extended a helping hand and his mouth broadened under his gray mustache. Roxy had heard Mama say that one of the reasons for the success of the Great Hallock Circus was Frank Hallock's ability to handle his headliners, the stars who drew the crowds to the Big Top.

She saw Mr. Kassel speak to Mr. Hallock, then to Karl and his sons-in-law. Mr. Hallock pointed to the practice building and the men walked off toward it. Roxy was disappointed. Karl wasn't coming in.

She watched him stride along beside his father. How jaunty he was, dressed in riding breeches, polished riding boots, a black slip-on sweater high about his neck, and a black cap on his blond head.

Sadie left the window and returned to her work, as the door opened and Mr. Hallock and the three ladies entered.

"Sadie, please call Gracie downstairs."

"Yes, Mr. Hallock." Sadie ran upstairs.

A sequined jacket in her hand, Roxy came from behind a crate and nodded to Mrs. Kassel. "Good morning."

"Ah, Miss Clark! And it *is* a good morning!" Mrs. Kassel stepped forward and took Roxy's hand. "A good morning when I see a friendly face."

Erma and Gretchen smiled and nodded as their mother turned to Mr. Hallock. "We met yesterday on the train."

"So?" The circus owner looked Roxy over from head to foot. "Just who are you?"

"Roxy Clark, Gracie Riley's granddaughter."

Mr. Hallock put his hat in his other hand. "Well, well! You must be Martha's girl. So you're working in Wardrobe, are you? Welcome to our circus family. You know I've always had it in for your father taking your mother away from show business." He turned to Mrs. Kassel. "About twenty years ago this girl's mother was one of our prettiest and most-accomplished riders."

At this moment Grandma came downstairs, introductions were made, and she led the three German ladies up the steps.

Mr. Hallock took hold of the doorknob and looked back at Roxy who, by this time, was again hanging sequined jackets over oriental costumes.

"Has your mother taught you to ride, Roxy?"

Roxy's heart skipped a beat. "Yes, since I was five and had my first pony." Was her chance coming this soon? Was he going to suggest—

"You couldn't have had a better teacher unless it was Gracie. It was a crying shame when the Riley act broke up." He opened the door. "Well, good luck in Wardrobe, Roxy. A mighty important job, here. Circus couldn't roll without Wardrobe. Glad Gracie has you with her this season." He closed the door behind him.

Roxy sighed and her vision of a red-haired rider in the grand entry vanished. He had only been making conversation. He wasn't really interested in her riding. But then why should he be? He had the best riding acts in the country already, not to mention those from Europe. And now he had the Kassels.

Presently Grandma escorted Mrs. Kassel and her daughters to the front door. They waved at Roxy from the other side of the room as they went out.

"Nice people," Grandma said to Sadie. "Didn't find any fault at all with their parade clothes." She turned to Roxy. "Often the big ones are hard to please. How are you getting on?"

48

"All right."

"Well, you've nearly three weeks to learn the layout. We open here in Kingston on Friday, May first, next day we'll be in South Bend, then we have over Sunday to get to Chicago and set up for a week in Grant Park. Keep your wits about you and you may be worth your salt by that time."

All the jackets distributed, Roxy counted the oriental costumes. There were sixty! That meant there would be twenty dancing girls in each ring for this one number. No wonder it was called the *Great* Hallock Circus. Everything was scaled to match the herd of elephants advertised on Hallock posters: The Ponderous Prodigious Pachyderms.

Roxy moved from crate to crate, reading labels, and examining contents. There were white costumes for Living Statues; long, rainbow-colored, diaphanous chiffon dresses for the Iron Jaw Ballet; red velvet uniforms for band wagon number one; blue velvet for band wagon number two; and for three and four, green and purple.

As she looked in box after box at the brilliant costumes, her admiration for Grandma grew. What an organizer and manager! Her skill with this behind-the-scenes job was as great as her former performances in the ring.

At noon, with two other ladies, Roxy and Sadie walked along the road to the dining room. Grandma was waiting for Rita Donato, expected for a fitting, Sadie said.

"What does Rita Donato do?" Roxy asked.

"Animal trainer. She works five Bengal tigers. We made her a lovely white satin uniform with red braid. Her husband Alberto works the elephants. Such a fine couple, the Donatos."

"Oh, I remember their acts!" Roxy exclaimed. "The way she can make those tigers perform! It's amazing!"

As they neared the dining-room building, the noise

49

from the animal barns became louder; trumpeting elephants, roaring cats, and a screeching that Roxy couldn't identify.

Taking a skipping step to catch up with Sadie, Roxy took a deep breath. The Great Hallock Circus! Elephants, horses, spangles, tigers, and sequins! And she was a part of it! A small part right now to be sure— But being on the lot every day, anything could happen, and she was bound to see Karl Kassel, and who knew what might come of that? Oh, great day! Great, splendid, colossal day!

For the moment she forgot Mimi.

Chapter 4

REHEARSAL

During the following days, Roxy stitched what seemed like miles of hems and seams on the machine, and sewed on so many sequins that she doubted if she'd ever see their glitter again without distaste.

It grew warmer and, with the windows open at Wardrobe, brassy music floated in as acts rehearsed with the band. Roxy tried to imagine what was going on out there in the practice rings.

So far she hadn't been able to see any one rehearse, not even the Frontenays. In the evenings at home she listened to their remarks about their work and about other performers. During noon meals in the Quarters' dining room, Grandma told her the names and specialties of those sitting around them. Slowly people's names and their parts in the show became familiar.

There were the seven Sumokas, Japanese jugglers; the Eldona family of tumblers; the Walton troupe of high-flyers who worked rings one and three at the same time the Frontenays performed in center. There was a tiny young woman named Midgie Dexter who, Grandma said, was one of the greatest on the high wire. And there was Alice Granville who helped Alberto Donato work the elephants.

One day in the dining room, Grandma took Roxy's elbow and guided her between tables to the far end where a man and woman sat at a special table. Roxy knew it was special, for, whereas all the others were covered with red-checked tablecloths, this one had one of white linen.

"Frieda and Martin, this is my granddaughter, Roxy Clark. Roxy, this is the great Frieda Jantry. Martin Jantry is a behind-the-scenes great; he heads up our office and bookkeeping department." Grandma let go of Roxy's arm and smiled down at the couple.

Martin Jantry rose and bowed to Roxy. He was bald and had a pointed gray beard. Roxy thought his wife, Frieda, for all of her bleached-blond hair, looked the older. The wrinkles creasing her sharp features did not match the hair at all. Roxy cast a side glance at Grandma. How much more attractive she was with white hair that softened the lines in her face. Seeing Frieda this close, it was unbelievable that she could ride so well, for Roxy had seen her perform in Westwood.

"So this is Martha's girl." Frieda looked Roxy over critically. "Do you ride?" There was a glint in her eyes as though on guard against a competitor.

"Not professionally. I'm with Wardrobe," Roxy answered.

"Good!" Frieda exclaimed. "I'm sure Gracie can use you." She turned to Grandma. "You're going to have to do my spec costume over, Gracie. I don't like the long sleeves and the neckline is too high."

"Now, Frieda, are you going to get notiony again? You said you liked it." Grandma frowned and her eyes narrowed as she looked down at Frieda.

"What if I did?" the elderly performer asked petulantly. "I've changed my mind. You fix it, Gracie! Do you hear me? Fix it!" Frieda's voice rose angrily to a high pitch.

Grandma's eyes flashed. "Don't you scream at me, Frieda Jantry! I'll change the costume without you cutting any of your temperamental didoes. I'll take out the sleeves entirely and cut the neckline down to your navel if you say so. But don't you scream at Gracie Riley!"

Roxy suppressed a giggle and wanted to shout, "Bravo, Grandma!" What tartars these two old ones were!

"Now, Gracie, I didn't mean to raise my voice," the circus star placated in a lower tone. "But you know me, anything I consider not in tune with the spirit of my performance upsets me dreadfully. And that costume is definitely not me. I must think of my public image."

Martin Jantry put his hand on the back of his wife's chair and looked into Grandma's face. "We'll bring the costume over at four o'clock this afternoon, Gracie. All right?"

"Fine, Martin, fine. Come on, Roxy." Grandma walked away.

Roxy glanced into the man's face. He smiled, looked after Grandma's retreating figure, down at his wife, and then back at Roxy. His smile turned into a grin as he shrugged his shoulders. Roxy knew she was going to like the business manager of the circus. Heavens, what he must have to put up with!

Outside she caught up with Grandma. "Whew! Do all stars yell at you like that?"

"No one yells at me and gets away with it, least of all Frieda. I know very well what's eating her. She has heard what Helga Kassel is wearing in the spec. News travels fast on the circus grapevine. While you were running that errand for me this morning, Mrs. Kassel brought her costumes in for me to check and list in my master files. Her spec costume is perfectly magnificent. She'll be the most stunning woman on horseback."

"Oh, tell me, Grandma."

"She will ride sidesaddle on a white horse. The costume is a white satin, sleeveless evening dress embroidered in red sequins. With it she wears a big white hat with red plumes. So you see why Frieda wants a lower

53

neckline and no sleeves. When I made hers with a high neck and long sleeves I was trying to do the old girl a favor, trying to cover her wrinkles. I suppose she chooses to ignore the fact that Helga Kassel is twenty years younger."

"Mrs. Kassel *is* beautiful for her age," Roxy said.

"I happen to know she is forty-two, right in her prime. In her perfect physical trim, she could pass for thirty. How old is her son Karl I heard you and Mimi talking about?"

"I don't know. About nineteen or twenty, I expect." Roxy's lower lip protruded in a slight pout. She still hadn't spoken to him since that first day. Mimi had not only talked with him but also had watched him rehearse. Mimi's excessive rhapsodizing over his riding skill and handsome appearance was getting on Roxy's nerves. Stuck in Wardrobe under Grandma's sharp eyes, while Mimi, she was sure, was doing her best to add Karl to her string of beaus—it just wasn't fair. Somehow she had to slip over to rehearsal and remind Karl she existed.

On Monday, April 20, hundreds of men began to swarm onto Winter Quarters' grounds. Huge, burly fellows they were for the most part, with bulging muscles. From a window at Wardrobe, Roxy watched fascinated as the gangs set to work in the open space beyond the buildings.

Coming up behind her, Grandma said, "That sight is as exciting as the performance itself."

Roxy gave a guilty start. "Oh, Grandma, I just had to look. I'm almost finished with the tassels."

"Go ahead and watch. The way the boys get up the Big Top is quite a spectacle. Jim Oldnoe has been boss canvasman for about twenty-five years. He's the fellow wearing a big white hat. He's more important to this circus, I expect, than our greatest star. See? He's already laid out the lot there, measured it off with a tape measure, and marked the exact spots where the boys will raise the poles."

"When will Big Top rehearsals start?" Roxy asked, idly fingering the fringe of the gold tassel in her hand.

"A complete run-through for timing is called for tomorrow afternoon. The first full-dress rehearsal will be on Saturday. That's when Wardrobe will have to be cracking. But we're ready. Just a few odds and ends to clear up." Grandma turned away. Roxy followed reluctantly. "Oh, you go on and watch the set up, honey. You may not have the chance once we get on the road. I think I'll drop over to rehearsal tomorrow and take you along. I want to see if those Kassels are as good as their advance notices."

Roxy gave a happy shrug. "Oh, fun, Grandma, I'll like that!" At last she would see Karl ride!

Back at the open window she watched an eight-horse hitch draw the pole wagon to various spots, where the men rolled off the poles in proper positions. The great center poles were as tall as the masts on huge sailing vessels. Once Mama had told her that each pole weighed about a ton. Now several elephants in harness padded across the space and strained at the chains, adding their strength to the gangs of men to raise the center poles. Smaller poles began to rise around what would be the walls of the Big Top's perimeter. A wagon drove around the edge, dropping off stakes for the guy ropes.

Roxy put the gold tassel on a table and pulled a chair to the window sill. What a show *this* was! And to think that all of this putting up and then tearing down went on every day the circus was on the road. She wished she were closer. She'd like to hear the clang of the sledge hammers on the iron stakes. She grinned. She might hear some of that colorful language too that Papa was afraid she would repeat. Sweet old Papa! He couldn't protect her forever. Maybe as the summer progressed and

Grandma saw how mature and reliable she was, Grandma would let her get to know all the people who made up this world on wheels.

She wondered what those roustabouts were like. Where did they live during the winter months? Did they have families?

It was amazing the way those sledge gangs worked. Gathering around a stake, they moved with the precision of a machine, one sledge stroke following the next by a fraction of a second, and not one hammer was hit by its successor. A forest of stakes had quickly sprung up over the whole space.

Roxy watched huge bales of canvas unloaded from wagons, saw the canvas sections laid on the ground, unrolled, and laced together into one enormous piece.

When Grandma returned the whole gigantic tent was up, flags fluttering from the center poles. "Well, think you could do it now?" Grandma chuckled.

"It's a miracle! A real miracle. And they do it so fast."

"A miracle it is, and no mistake. Well, young lady, you've dawdled long enough. I want those tassels finished by noon. They have to be sewed on the red parade blankets for the band-wagon horses. Get a move on."

Early next afternoon, Roxy and Grandma sat in the Big Top opposite center ring. Here and there a few other employees also perched on the tiered seats to watch the performance. But without the thousands of upturned faces of a thrill-seeking audience, Roxy thought the huge tent as bare as a cornfield in November; the vacant seats were sightless eyes, offering no encouragement to performers at all.

Miles Wallace, the bandmaster, raised his baton and the band blared into the grand entry number. Grandma tapped her foot in time. Just below them Roxy saw Mr. Hallock talking with Jim Daggett, the ringmaster.

56

The first horse-drawn, glittering wagon rolled through the entrance and started around the hippodrome track, followed by horseback riders, elephants, camels, and men and women on foot. The faces of the performers were expressionless until they reached Roxy and Grandma and smiled up at them.

"You know, Grandma, it just isn't circus without the costumes, is it? And the people look so—so uninterested."

"Right. Wardrobe is important, that's for sure. And it takes a big audience to turn on the smiles and charm. There come the Kassels. Nice-appearing family."

Roxy waved as the group on horseback neared. All returned her greeting. Karl smiled recognition, took off his cap, and bowed.

"That's Karl, Grandma, Karl Kassel, the son, the one I told you about." Roxy spoke excitedly. He had doffed his cap to her! Her eyes followed him around the track until the family disappeared at the exit.

"Yes, I know." Grandma gave Roxy a fleeting glance.

Fascinated, Roxy watched the spec. Mimi as Scheherazade wore a dark cape over her black practice tights. But she was beautiful even in these. What a vision she would be in the oriental costume Roxy had hung in its proper place only yesterday.

The ballet girls went through their routine in the three rings while the Arabian Nights pantomime took place on the side stage. Without costumes and spotlights, Roxy thought it rather silly. But she knew that once the circus got on the road, the magic would be there, enough magic to transport thousands of people to the mystical land of Arabia.

Jim Daggett, watch in hand, signaled the change of acts by sharp blasts on his piercing whistle. Frequently, in a voice that penetrated to the farthest canvas walls, he would call attention to a headline act: "Ladies and gentlemen! In center ring I call your attention to the great—!"

Now Roxy took more interest. The band music stirred her blood; she leaned forward, elbows on knees, chin in hands. Beside her, Grandma remarked on performers and changes in their acts.

"Now that was a new bit for Rita's cats. Don't know as I ever saw cats stand on their hind legs all at the same time. Rita's been mighty busy teaching it to those tigers."

"Oh, Grandma, she's wonderful! Look there! She made him jump through *two* paper hoops!"

Frank Hallock climbed up and sat beside Grandma. "Rita's new routines are good, don't you think, Gracie?"

"First-rate. But then we expect that of Rita Donato."

"Wardrobe all in shape?"

"Of course, Frank, or I wouldn't be here."

The circus owner looked across at Roxy. "Beginning to feel at home with us, Roxy?"

"Well, not really," Roxy answered. "It's all too exciting. I don't suppose I'll ever be able to take circus life for granted."

"Wouldn't want you to. It's the excitement and challenge of thrilling the people that keeps us at it. Isn't that so, Gracie?"

"I suppose so. Although I've lived through days when I've wondered why I ever took up with canvas and sawdust."

Mr. Hallock grinned. "Oh, sure. But then what job doesn't have its bleak side on occasion? Ah, there's the whistle for your kinfolk, Roxy."

The nets up under the maze of wires and trapezes, aerialists ran into all three rings and climbed rope ladders to their high perches.

Roxy watched above center ring where Uncle Jules, Aunt Marie, the boys, Lilly, and Mimi went into their act. Uncle Jules, as catcher, hung by his knees from a swinging bar on one side and caught and returned each member of his family as they swung out in turn from the opposite side. Then came the specialties. There was a quick exchange, Jacques from his father's hands to the bar which Mimi had just left to be grabbed by Uncle Jules. Roxy caught her breath as Mimi swung back to the perch. Henri, attempting a double somersault, fell into the net. Roxy gave a muffled scream.

Mr. Hallock laughed. "That little devil is a born performer, Roxy. He missed this trick last season, then got such a big hand when he made it that he's kept the miss in the routine ever since. It's good showmanship to make a stunt look difficult. The audience then appreciates the perfect execution all the more. Applause is meat and drink to a performer and he'll do anything to get it."

Roxy relaxed. She knew that claims on circus posters often were exaggerated, but everything said about the Flying Frontenays was true. They were marvelous.

"See out there at the entrance." Grandma pointed. "The Kassels are next."

Roxy looked across at the entrance passageway. Mounted on a handsome white horse, Karl, his head tilted back, had his eyes fixed on the Frontenays. Roxy felt a lump slide into her throat. At every performance in the coming season, he would be in this exact spot at this time watching her beautiful, talented, cousin Mimi, dressed in tights and a sequined satin leotard that enhanced her perfect figure. And as if that weren't enough, she was an expert flyer too. What chance did she, Roxy, have even if she did have pretty red hair?

She looked speculatively across at Mr. Hallock. If only she could somehow become a performer, a performer dressed in a striking costume, she might have some chance of attracting Karl. But as it was, the cards were all stacked in Mimi's favor.

At Jim Daggett's whistle, the aerialists came down and

ran out as the Kassels rode around the track. Erma and Gretchen and their husbands worked rings one and three, while Mr. and Mrs. Kassel and Karl performed in center.

"Now there's some riding, Gracie," Frank Hallock said, pushing his hat to the back of his head. "Good, heh?"

"Very good, Frank." Grandma nodded approvingly.

Fritz Kassel, long whip in hand, stood in the middle of center ring, guiding the broad-backed white horse around the edge, while Helga, standing on its bare back, jumped through the paper hoops Karl held for her. Then Karl leaped up behind his mother and the two performed a routine of jumps on and off ending with Karl climbing up and standing on Helga's shoulders, as she stood on the circling horse.

Roxy clutched Grandma's arm. "Oh, aren't they wonderful? And I thought I could ride!"

Grandma laughed. "They've been practicing that bit ever since Karl was a little boy, no doubt. Now it's fairly easy. What else do they do, Frank?"

"Well, their High School horses are a joy to watch. Fritz got his training at the Spanish Riding School in Vienna, so he knows what's what when it comes to dressage." Mr. Hallock turned to Roxy and explained. "Dressage is putting a High School horse through a variety of maneuvers without the use of the whip, bridle, or any noticeable movement of the rider's heels or knees. Dressage is the highest art of horsemanship. The rider and horse are as one, so well-balanced that the slightest movement from the rider brings a quick response from the horse." The circus owner slapped his knee and laughed. "Great day! Why am I explaining dressage to you, daughter and granddaughter of Rileys!"

Roxy smiled. "Well, yes, I do know about it. I've always thought the 'dancing horses' the best things in the circus."

"You'll see the greatest in the Kassels' next act," Mr.

Hallock replied. "And then later on Fritz has a great liberty horse number."

Roxy rubbed her moist palms on her skirt. Horses, horses, horses! Such beautiful creatures! And Karl, so handsome and lithe out there, leaping on and off that moving resinback as though he had wings.

As the Kassels disappeared through the connection tent, the band swung into "There'll Be a Hot Time in the Old Town Tonight," and the hippodrome track became thick with clowns, each going through some crazy antic. But, without grease paint, wigs, or costumes, Roxy thought they seemed absurd.

During the clowns' routines, crews set up the rigging for the living statues. Huge black circular coverings were lowered into the three rings from above so that the "statues" could arrange themselves underneath. Then, the coverings were raised again, revealing the artistic tableaus. Roxy had seen living statues at circuses in Westwood. Today only the horses and dogs were white. But in a real performance, the men and women would not only be dressed in white, but their faces and all exposed skin would be covered in white grease paint.

One of the covers stuck at the top of the tent; the work crew pulled and jerked frantically at the ropes. After several minutes delay, Frank Hallock uttered some strong language and leaped down the bleachers. The crew boss, letting out an oath that Roxy could hear above the band, climbed a rope ladder and, at the top of the tent, set the thing free.

"Whew! How come such a fuss?" Roxy asked.

"Mustn't be any delays when we open," Grandma answered. "The only acts that can run overtime are the animal acts. Each animal must be made to go through his routine every time. So, if one gets contrary we have to wait until the trainer makes him do it. If he gets away with disobedience once, he might refuse to do the act next time."

Roxy was at the front door when old Del brought Grandma's carriage around to Wardrobe late in the afternoon. Mimi was in the back seat.

"Some company to ride home with you." The old man grinned down at Roxy.

"Sit back here with me, Roxy," Mimi invited. "I saw you there at rehearsal."

Roxy climbed in beside her cousin as Grandma came out and took the reins from Del.

"How did you think rehearsal went, Grandma?" Mimi asked as the carriage rolled down the road.

"Oh, about as usual. I like that new bit you and Lilly do on the bar in unison. Very effective. How that child has grown! Tall as you are. Shouldn't wonder but what she'll outstrip you in another year." Grandma gently slapped the reins and the horse increased his speed.

"She's getting prettier too," Mimi said. "With a pretty red-haired cousin and an attractive sister on the lot, what chance will poor little Mimi Frontenay have this season?" Mimi laughed and gave Roxy a playful hug.

"Oh, Mimi, you're just perfect," Roxy said sincerely. "I've never seen anything as lovely as the way you fly up there so near the top of the canvas. It's, well, it's—oh, I can't tell you how it makes me feel."

"Hush, Roxy," Grandma expostulated. "Don't you know the minx is just fishing for compliments? Why shouldn't she fly well? She's had the world's best teacher. And Mimi, my girl, don't forget that conceit can soon make you an ugly person, your pretty face notwithstanding."

"All right, Grandma, all right! With you always fussing at me I'm not likely to think well of myself at all." Mimi made a little face at the back of Grandma's head.

Roxy watched the western sky grow rosier as they

approached the outskirts of town. Filled with the sights of the afternoon, her thoughts were jumbled. There were the iron-jaw girls whirling about high in the tent, hanging with their teeth locked around fitted mouthpieces, their arms free to hold out the varicolored chiffon costumes they would wear at the real performance. There were the elephants walking around the hippodrome on their hind legs, front legs resting on the elephant in front, and beautiful Alice Granville, the girl who helped Alberto Donato work the "Ponderous Pachyderms."

There were those two cute children in the Eldona tumbling troupe and the Japanese jugglers had a darling little girl. And how exquisite tiny Midgie Dexter was on the high wire! And the chariot race and the wild West show at the end!

But best of all were the horses! The one Karl rode in the dressage number reminded Roxy of Tucky. She closed her eyes and wished for a moment that she were feeding that dear creature a lump of sugar, and then she could ride at a gallop down the lane to the Gardners to see what bossy Doug had been up to. She kind of missed the old crab.

Mimi leaned against Roxy's shoulder and whispered, "Karl looked me up after rehearsal and told me he liked our act."

Roxy opened her eyes. "That was nice."

"Nice! Oh, Roxy, it was beautiful. He said the most complimentary things, about the act of course. He's too polite to get personal on so short an acquaintance. And isn't he a magnificent rider?"

Roxy swallowed her resentment. "Yes. He rides well. Almost as well as his father and mother."

"Oh, but he's young and handsome. That makes up for any difference in skill."

"He'll get better as he grows older, I expect," Roxy

said. "He waved at me when he passed in the grand entry. So you see he remembers our train ride together," Roxy said, putting in her one claim to the young man's attention.

Mimi hugged her again. "Oh, nobody would ever forget you, darling Roxy. Even Karl Kassel must have been impressed by your beautiful hair."

Perhaps, Roxy thought, but even Karl Kassel would forget her if he never saw her again. And certainly he wasn't likely to, hidden as she would be behind hundreds and hundreds of costumes!

Chapter 5

PARADE

Trying to return discarded garments to their proper racks in the utter confusion of the women's dressing tent at Saturday's dress rehearsal, Roxy fought growing panic. With only a few minutes to remove the spec oriental costumes until they were on again as the "World's Largest Aerial Ballet," the ballet girls tossed the baggy satin pants and sequined jackets onto a rising heap, then ran off to the Big Top in the tights they wore underneath.

Roxy's hands trembled and a hastily hung jacket fell from its hanger. Watch it, she told herself, keep calm; do it right the first time. All these must be in place for the next performance.

Almost every pair of harem pants had been pulled off wrong side out. Roxy frowned in irritation. Now there was no sense in this! At next rehearsal she was going to lay down the law to the girls beforehand. If she didn't, she'd be dealing with this kind of mess the whole season. The flash of anger restored her confidence; her hands became steady, and the mountain of pants and jackets turned into neat rows of hanging costumes.

Around the edge of the large tent, canvas walls partitioned off private dressing rooms. From within came frequent calls for someone from Wardrobe to help fasten the new outfits. Roxy caught her breath as she watched performers step out in brilliant, glittering dresses, riding

65

habits, or leotards and run off toward the Big Top where the band played their cues.

"Will you please hook me up?" A pretty girl stood beside Roxy.

"Sure. Turn around." Roxy hooked the knee-length blue satin, sequined dress. "You're Alice Granville, the marvelous girl with the elephants, aren't you?"

"Yes, I'm Alice. And you're Roxy. Mimi told me about you." Alice looked over her shoulder at Roxy. "You're much too good-looking to stay behind the scenes. I'm going to tell Frank he should work you into an act."

"You do that. Need any help with the elephants?" Roxy laughed as she fastened the last hook. "There, you're fastened up. Here, let me fix your hat. Oh, you do look lovely. I hope those big brutes appreciate having you as a trainer."

"Scoot along, Alice," Grandma said, coming out of a dressing room. "The Sumokas' music is starting and you follow them."

"On my way, Gracie," Alice said. "Thanks, Roxy."

The Kassel ladies ran in wearing their short, white, fluffy, bareback riding dresses and disappeared into their dressing room.

"Would you like some help?" Grandma called into them.

"If you would be so kind," Helga Kassel replied.

"Come on, Roxy, they have a quick change."

Roxy gasped in delight at the riding habits the Kassels were putting on for the dressage number. Long, full, divided skirts they were, the dresses entirely covered in sequins. Gretchen's was royal blue, Erma's red, and Mrs. Kassel's deep purple. Each wore a large hat to match.

Roxy smoothed the back of Gretchen's skirt and hooked the belt. "A beautiful dress," she murmured.

"Thank you." Gretchen smiled at Roxy briefly then

looked in the mirror, pulled her hat to the proper angle, and stuck a long hatpin through the crown.

"Ready, girls?" Helga asked, pulling on long purple gloves.

"Ready, Mama."

Roxy stepped outside the small enclosure and watched the three women hurry out of the tent. She picked up a riding habit from a chair and hung it away. What, she wondered, was Karl wearing for dressage? With all there was to do out here in the back yard, she'd probably never know.

Mimi, her two appearances over, brushed past Roxy, calling over her shoulder, "See you later, Rox. I want to catch the Kassels' dressage number."

Roxy dug her nails into her palms and frowned at her disappearing cousin. In the empty Big Top, Karl was bound to see Mimi sitting in the grandstand admiring his skill with a dancing horse. But my time will come, Mimi Frontenay, Roxy thought. You're only a flyer; I'm a rider like Karl. The thought bolstered her spirit, but only for a moment. How ordinary her ability would appear to the great Karl Kassel.

In the racket and hubbub of the dressing tent, the wardrobe women went about calmly hooking up, picking up, hanging up. Roxy sighed and put a hat in a box. Such confusion out here, but even so—co-ordinated confusion.

That night, sitting on her cot, Roxy unbuttoned her shoes slowly. She was more tired than she had ever been after a strenuous day of farm work, even the days she had helped Papa in the fields. Perhaps in time, she would grow accustomed to the rush and noise. She could still hear the band blasting away at her eardrums with clashing cymbals and blaring horns. No matter how good the selections, two and a half hours of band music were just too much. Only when one was in the Big Top, watching daring performances, could brassy music continue to thrill.

There was a brief knock and Mimi came in. "Roxy, I have to show you. This magazine came in today's mail. See here, all these pictures of Mr. and Mrs. Vernon Castle showing how to do the Castle Fox Trot. Let's put a record on the victrola in the morning and see if we can do it." She sat beside Roxy and opened the magazine on their laps.

"Oh, how lovely she is!" Roxy exclaimed. "You can see there, under her hat, that her hair is cut short. Did you read all that to-do in the papers when she cut it?"

"I sure did. I wanted to cut mine, but Mama said no, circus audiences wouldn't like it. Short hair might be all right in big cities but not in the smaller towns. Aren't they the most marvelous couple? I'm going to ask Mama if I can buy a pair of white-topped button shoes like these." Mimi pointed to Irene Castle's dancing feet below her ankle-length, accordion-pleated dress. "Look at the nice curve in the high heels. And doesn't he look handsome in his white flannel suit?"

"What did Karl wear for dressage this afternoon?" Roxy asked, then could have bitten her tongue for asking; Mimi waxed so eloquent it was sickening.

"Roxy, he was absolutely devastating in a white satin uniform with gold braid! And at the end of every number he removed his hat and and had his horse kneel right in front of me! Isn't he the handsomest, most exciting man you have ever seen?" Mimi closed the magazine, hugged it to her, got up, and danced around the room.

"What's going on in here?" Grandma asked as she entered. "Get along to bed, Mimi. Can't you see Roxy is dead-tired? It's no picnic being under fire in that dressing tent for the first time." She turned to Roxy. "But you'll get used to it, honey, in time. You did fine today."

Later, in bed, with Grandma's breathing the only

sound, it came to Roxy. She would not only be in that dressing tent two and a half hours in the afternoons and during the hours of the evening performances, but, also, every morning to help care for parade costumes. What kind of a summer had she let herself in for? And all the time Mimi would be seeing Karl in the Big Top! Oh, my! A white satin uniform with gold braid! And—on a black horse!

Rehearsals continued the following week; acts were timed, added to, or cut, then timed again. Certain costumes were adjusted, taken in, or let out to the wearer's liking. Roxy began to know the women performers by name and at just what point each needed help with a quick change. And, by Friday, after several outbursts from the redhead in Wardrobe, the ballet girls removed their harem pants right side out.

The ten o'clock circus parade through the streets of a town was to advertise the show, to make the crowds so excited by the glamor and glitter that they would hurry to the circus grounds and buy tickets to see more. There was really no need for the Great Hallock Circus to advertise in Kingston. In the home town they paraded for love. For the most part those along the sidewalks would be friends or relatives, who themselves had worked in some way for the circus.

Friday, May 1, was a clear, beautiful day. A good omen for the season, Aunt Marie said at breakfast, and fine for the parade.

Uncle Jules drank the last of his coffee and said, "Well, we've slept our last night in beds. From now on it's sleeping cars for all of us. How will you like that, Roxy?"

"I've never slept on a train. But I expect it will be exciting." Roxy rose to help clear the table.

Mimi laughed as she stacked plates. "The word for our sleeping cars is *crowded* not *exciting*."

All along the railroad tracks near Winter Quarters, red, yellow, and silver railroad cars were lined up to move the show to South Bend after the night performance. Roxy and Grandma drove by the tracks and put suitcases in their car in the second section. There was only time for Roxy to cast a hurried look down the aisle of the car. With as many curtained double-decker berths on either side as possible, the word, just as Mimi had said, was *crowded*. Grandma laughed when Roxy mentioned it.

"You think this crowded! You should see the roustabouts' cars. Their berths are triple deckers, some even quadruple. With nearly a thousand of them, we have to pack 'em in. Just leave your suitcase there in the aisle. It has your name on it. George will put it in your upper berth. You'll be above me."

"George?"

"Our porter, George Tompkins. He's been with Wardrobe's car for years. He takes care of the beds, keeps things clean, and looks after us in fine style."

"Where will Aunt Marie's family be?"

"They'll be in the third section; the boys in an all-men's car, and Mimi and Lilly in a family car with Jules and Marie. All performers are in that last section. That way they get more sleep than the rest of us. Usually by the time the third section arrives, things are pretty well set up. Performers get on the lot just in time to eat breakfast and dress for the parade."

Stepping off the car after Grandma, Roxy looked across at the Big Top in the field beyond. Flags rippled in the breeze and its canvas sidewalls billowed in and out. What a beautiful circus day!

"Now I expect that this morning will be about the only chance I can give you to see the parade," Grandma said. "So, as soon as the girls are dressed for the procession, you skip off down to the gate and give it a critical eye.

It'd be a good idea to take pencil and paper and jot down any duds you think need alteration."

Later, pencil and tablet in hand, Roxy made her way across the fields toward the gate. In the vast open spaces, wagons rolled into place, riders mounted, elephants lined up trunk to tail, and on the band wagons, musicians tooted a few test notes to get ready for the blasts to come.

Roxy's heart beat fast with excitement. This was her circus, her parade! She had helped add the glitter and grandeur! She was part of it even if she wasn't riding in it.

Beyond the gate and down the road a way, she climbed onto the top of a rail fence and tucked her feet onto a lower rail. Several small boys, unable to wait for the parade in town, rode up on bicycles, dismounted, and sat on the fence near Roxy.

With a twenty-four horse hitch, band wagon number one drew near the gate. The musicians on top raised their instruments to their lips, and a Sousa march rent the air. A man on horseback galloped through the forming parade inside the grounds and out in front of the band wagon. He signaled to the driver above and then rode through the gate.

It was Mr. Hallock himself, wearing a natty red flannel riding habit and a tall black silk hat. His bay horse was so like Tucky that a lump rose in Roxy's throat. She wondered if the circus owner always headed the parade or if only for today, because it was the home town.

He lifted his hand to Roxy as he rode past, and she returned the gesture. The band drowned out the rattle of the huge crimson and gold wagon as it rolled by. Roxy looked up at the driver, his hands were so full of leather lines it was a miracle how he managed those twenty-four horses. With tall red plumes bobbing up and down on their heads, the handsome matched white Percherons, six rows, four abreast, stepped along proudly. Oh, how grand they were!

As the procession went by, Roxy forgot the list she was supposed to be making. Twelve ballet girls in flashing pink, riding sidesaddle, waved and called her name. The Sumoka family, wearing brilliant kimonos, rode on top of a silver and white wagon. The Frontenays followed, riding matched palominos. Lilly saw Roxy first and called out, "Hey, Roxy! Get a horse and join us."

Roxy waved and smiled.

"How are we doing, Rox?" Jacques yelled.

"You're beautiful, simply beautiful," Roxy yelled back. The Frontenays were as spectacular in red-sequined riding habits as in tights and leotards.

Mimi, sitting very straight in her saddle, made only a brief movement of her hand to Roxy. The reason for the small acknowledgment was soon apparent; the Kassels followed. Karl saw Roxy, spoke to his mother, and then all of the Kassels waved at her.

In green and on black horses, what a magnificent parade troupe they made! Gretchen and Erma rode beside their husbands while Helga followed between Fritz and Karl.

Roxy watched them move on down the road. Every day from now on Mimi would ride up there in front of the Kassels where Karl would see her. Mimi, as beautiful as a princess, in red satin and brilliant sequins, whose dark eyes other young men in the circus had already found irresistible.

"Hi-yah, down there, Red!"

Roxy looked up. A figure on top of a clown wagon was looking down at her and wiggling huge ears back and forth on the sides of his head in a ludicrous fashion. Roxy laughed and waved. This was the first time anyone had ever called her Red. She wondered what that fellow looked like under the various colors covering his face.

Orange-and-black-striped tigers, vivid in the sun, paced back and forth in their cage wagons. Roxy shivered as she looked through the glass of the snake wagon. Pretty Mary Duncan, the snake charmer, sat unperturbed in one end, a spotted snake across her shouders; others slithered around her feet.

Frieda Jantry was the sole rider in a white open coach drawn by four white horses; the driver of the splendid vehicle wore a white uniform. Frieda was regal in a gold-brocaded dress and a flowing cape of purple chiffon. Eyes straight ahead, the old performer's expression was grim. She was saving her charm and smiles for the crowd in town, Roxy surmised.

Now came band wagon number two followed by more ballet girls on horseback. The seven Eldonas, the tumbling troupe, were sure to make a hit with the children in town. Their eight-year-old girl and nine-year-old boy, mounted on small ponies, waved at Roxy and at the boys near her. They reminded her of Janet and Allen when they were younger.

Cages of monkeys, panthers, and lions passed by. Ten horses drew the huge hippopotamus wagon. In its sunken pool, Big Bella lolled and drowsed in tropical luxury and occasionally winked an eye at the spectators staring at her monstrous corpulence. Roxy laughed; Big Bella seemed so bored with the whole thing.

Roxy felt especially drawn to the camels padding along with their heads held haughtily in the air; their blankets had caused her such trouble that first day.

Wagon after wagon passed, each lavishly decorated in wood carvings covered with gold leaf. Before the season was over she hoped she would have time to examine each wagon carefully, for no two were alike, and they were so beautiful. There were even wood-carved panels fitted between the wheel spokes. Colorfully painted, the effect was gorgeous as the wheels turned. She knew that as soon as the parade was over each wagon would be covered by a "hushcloth", a specially-lined canvas cover to protect the gilded carvings.

Several tableaux wagons carried ballet girls in a variety of costumes. One portrayed the fairy queen and her attendants, another Mother Goose and nursery rhyme characters, and still another a Spanish theme, the girls wearing high combs and lace mantillas.

Then came the wild West troupe, cowboys in fur chaps, and cowgirls in divided-leather skirts mounted on fractious horses. Indians in feathered headpieces rode without saddles; several Indian women had papooses on their backs. Anna Lowry, a cowgirl Roxy had met one day at lunch, waved at her. The boys on the fence eyed Roxy with envy. It was clear to them that the red-haired young lady perched near them was part of the circus; she knew so many in the parade.

Alberto Donato on a black horse led his herd of twenty-seven elephants. Seeing Roxy he pulled his horse up on its hind legs as he waved at her. Roxy clapped her hands. Two other men rode by on horseback. In town they would warn those on the sidelines, "Hold your horses, the elephants are coming." There was something about the smell of elephants that was likely to set town horses crazy.

At the head of the procession of elephants was the dependable Luly. High on her back in a colorful howdah rode Alice Granville wearing a red and blue oriental costume.

"Hello up there, Alice," Roxy called.

Alice let loose of one side of the swaying howdah to wave. "Hello Roxy! Lovely day!"

The elephants following Luly held trunks to tails. This not only kept them in a straight line but also kept their inquisitive trunks out of trouble when they got in town.

And last of all, drawn by eight horses, came the steam calliope! The steam piano, Roxy had heard her mother call it. Black smoke already rolled out of the smokestack as the fireman tended the coal-burning boiler to generate the steam. The operator, seated at the keyboard in the rear, saw Roxy and the boys on the fence. He lifted his red cap to this first audience, then dropped his hands, and the shrill notes of "On the Banks of the Wabash" sailed out on the wind. Holding her hands over her ears, Roxy was sure people could hear the tune two miles away.

The boys jumped from the fence, mounted their bicycles, and rode down a side road, hurrying over a short-cut to see the parade again in town.

Roxy picked up the tablet and pencil from her lap. Not a single notation! Well, she hadn't noticed anything wrong. It was all just beautifully, gaudily gorgeous!

She climbed down, removed her jacket, and put it over her arm. The sun had dispelled the early-morning chill. She looked at her starched, white shirtwaist. Soon there would be the problem of washing and ironing clothes on tour. She would have to work out a schedule. Her main job was to keep the performers looking grand, but she still had to keep up her own appearance. And just when and where would she take a bath?

Noting the dust on her high-button shoes, she stepped in the tall grass to dust them off. Sometimes there would be mud on the lot, she thought. Keeping neat was not going to be easy.

But, oh, that glorious parade! She wished she could watch it again in town. She hurried past the side-show tent and around the Big Top to the back yard. Grandma had said Wardrobe ate lunch early in order to be finished by the time the parade returned. They must be on hand to pack away the parade clothes for South Bend to-morrow.

Roxy took a deep breath, held up her ankle-length skirt and ran across the open space to the dressing tent.

Chapter 6

THE CIRCUS ROLLS

The train lurched, the wheels whined, and Roxy turned over in the narrow upper berth. Would she ever get to sleep? She was so tired! It seemed years since she had watched the parade this morning. Afternoon and evening band music from the Big Top still throbbed in her ears.

They had had a big audience at both performances. The county's whole population must have been there to twice fill their twelve thousand seating capacity.

And what an operation the teardown! The loading order had to be exact so that first things would be first for the setup in the morning. By the time Roxy had the last costume shut away in its crate, the menagerie and side-show tents had been struck and loaded, the seats were torn down, and the Big Top itself lay as flat as a pricked balloon, the canvas ready to be rolled into bundles and hauled to the train.

With the others from Wardrobe, Roxy had walked across the fields to the tracks. Here, amid shouts, curses, the rumbling of wagon wheels, the roars of animals, trumpeting of elephants, and neighs of horses, hundreds and hundreds of workmen loaded wagons, tableau floats, and other rolling equipment onto flatcars. It was a clear, starlit night, and Roxy had wanted to stay outside to watch. But Grandma had herded her staff of sixteen into their car—as though they were horses, Roxy remembered resentfully.

"Daylight will be here all too soon," Grandma had said as she sat on the edge of the berth below Roxy's. "We must be up and at 'em by six in the morning."

Roxy turned over again. It was so hard to get comfortable in this blamed thing. It would be six before she ever got to sleep at this rate.

There might be a letter from Mama in South Bend or maybe one from Doug. Her life had been so full the last three weeks she had seldom thought of home. But it would be good to see the folks when the circus showed in Westwood late in July. She wondered if she would get a chance to go out to the farm. Probably not. But maybe Allen could bring Tucky to the circus lot. How she missed that horse! She closed her eyelids firmly and imagined herself on him, galloping down the lane to Lazy Creek where he would pause to drink. Then they would fly on down a rolling hill; her hairpins would fall out and the wind would blow her hair back like a tawny mane. Roxy was asleep.

It was as though she had just closed her eyes when she felt her shoulder shaken. "Up with you, Roxy! Get yourself dressed. We'll be off to the cookhouse in a bit."

It had been difficult enough to undress in an upper berth but dressing was even worse. Roxy bumped her head, knocked her elbows and knees, and wished she dared use some strong language. Climbing down the ladder at last, she finished hooking her skirt placket, and buttoning her waist. She looked for her buttonhook. It was not in her bag of toilet articles, not in the bedclothes, nor in her purse. Darn it! Buttoning shoes with a hairpin took so long.

Mame Anderson stood just beyond, brushing her long gray hair. Roxy glanced down at the woman's feet. "Mrs.

Anderson, you're wearing button shoes. May I borrow your buttonhook. I've lost mine."

"Sure. It's right there on top of my suitcase. How'd you sleep?"

"All right once I got there," Roxy answered, sitting on the edge of Grandma's berth to button her shoes.

"Well, it takes all of us a few days to get used to sleeping on the move. This is going to be a good season for us. I knew it the minute I saw your red hair. It brings good luck, you know, to have a redhead on board. And it's like a fresh drink of water to have a *young* lady like yourself here in the 'old ladies' retreat.'"

Roxy slipped the hook through the top buttonhole, pulled the button through, then stood up and returned the instrument. If red hair was so lucky how come she was working in the "old ladies' retreat" instead of riding in the Big Top? She pulled on her kimono to keep loose hairs off her skirt, unbraided her hair, and brushed it. She was tucking the last hairpins into the knot on the back of her head, when Grandma returned from the washroom.

"See here, Roxy," she said as she pointed inside her berth. "This little rope George has hung across the end of each berth is for your washcloth and towel. You better get along to the washroom. It isn't too full right now. Several of the girls have gone on to breakfast."

The cookhouse tent had been the first erected on the lot. It had come in on the first section, with the menagerie cages, the parade wagons, horses, animal men, hostlers, grooms, blacksmiths, and roustabouts—or razorbacks—as the husky workmen were often called.

By the time Wardrobe staff came for their breakfasts, the hundreds of crewmen had been fed and were already hard at work.

Roxy paused and looked up and down the rows of red-checked covered tables, where circus personnel were eating generous portions of ham, eggs, fried potatoes, bread and butter, and cups of strong coffee laced with thick cream. The cookhouse tent could seat one thousand at a sitting, Grandma said, and before the day was over would serve about five thousand meals. Roxy wondered if the section carrying performers ever got in soon enough for them to eat this early.

It was cold in South Bend. Roxy wore her jacket all day and wished she had brought her coat from the car. Her fingers were numb as she hooked and fastened costumes. When the performers left on cues, their bare arms were covered with goose bumps, but activity in the ring warmed them and they returned in a glow.

Saturday night, her second on the circus train, Roxy slept better. George had put an extra blanket in each berth to keep out the chill of the early May cold snap. Thoroughly warm at last, the movement of the train rocked her to sleep almost at once.

Next morning they were in Chicago. Looking outside at the puddles and mud in the railroad yard, Roxy went to the end of the car and got her rubbers from her trunk. With umbrella and raincoat in one hand, her suitcase in the other, she followed the wardrobe ladies across the tracks to the street where they boarded a streetcar to the Loop. During the week in Chicago they would have rooms at the Auditorium Hotel on Michigan Boulevard.

From the streetcar window Roxy gazed in amazement at the great city. Even this early, horse-drawn wagons and carriages and automobiles crowded the streets. The motorman's foot kept up a constant clang on the bell to keep the track clear. And what tall buildings!

They got off at Wabash and Congress and walked east to Michigan Boulevard. Roxy repressed an exclamation at the size of the hotel, not wanting to reveal that she was a green, Indiana country girl.

She found that she was assigned to a room with three

of the ladies. It was nice to be independent of Grandma for once. Maybe she could see some of the sights on her own.

Mrs. Anderson took the cot next to hers. "Now today we can do as we please, Roxy. Circus folks anticipate Sunday as children do Christmas. We do our laundry, wash our hair, visit, write letters, or sleep. Of course, in Chicago we usually take streetcar rides, or a trip on the elevated, or just walk around and look in shop windows. As soon as you unpack, we'll walk across to Grant Park where the show's setup, and have breakfast."

Roxy put her blouses, petticoats, and underwear in the dresser and went into the large bathroom. She looked at the broad, six-feet-long bathtub, standing high on ornamental legs. Back in the room she found the others putting on their hats.

"Would you all mind if I didn't go to breakfast now? If this day is ours then I'd like to start mine by taking a bath in that marvelous tub." Roxy picked up her jacket from the bed and hung it in the closet.

"Why, of course, you do that, honey, if you want to," Jenny Thompson said. "Come here to the window and I'll tell you how to get to the park."

Alone in the big room, Roxy reveled in the privacy—privacy she would seldom have on this tour, she was certain. She undressed, pinned her hair high, and soaked for fifteen minutes in the porcelain tub. What luxury! She felt like a princess. At home there was no bathroom, family ablutions being performed in a big zinc washtub in front of the kitchen range.

Imagine, Roxy Clark staying in this grand hotel! She wondered if the Kassels were staying here too. And Mimi? Since she would be getting over to the cookhouse later, might not the third section have arrived and the performers be there for breakfast too?

She took her time dressing, combed and put her hair

up with care. After all if she did see *him,* she wanted to look her best.

She looked in the mirror and was not displeased. Her plain, navy-blue, tailored suit had good lines. Her blue-and white-striped shirtwaist had a high, white, starched collar. A navy-blue windsor tie made a soft flowing bow under her chin. She brushed her shoes to a glow, then pinned her hat on at a rakish angle.

She looked out the window. No sign of rain now and the sun was out. She put her key in her purse, left the room, and pushed the button for the elevator as she pulled on her kid gloves.

Downstairs, she walked across the lobby with her head high. In spite of seeming to take all this grandeur for granted, she observed details—the leather chairs and settees, the many shining, brass cuspidors, and the thick red carpet.

On the sidewalk she held her hat, not trusting the hatpin against the brisk wind that blew in from Lake Michigan. So this was windy Chicago! She probably should have worn her coat, but it was two-years-old and not nearly as stylish as her suit.

At the corner, she waited with others until the policeman in the street blew two sharp blasts on a whistle and stopped horses and cars while the people crossed. Two elephants and a circus wagon crossed at the same time. So—they were still unloading.

On the other side of Michigan Boulevard, Roxy discovered that the people with whom she had crossed were also going her way, probably those who couldn't wait until tomorrow for a glimpse of the circus.

Just before she headed into the park she heard a sharp whistle. She turned her head. It wasn't the policeman this time. She smiled, stepped to one side of the pedestrians, and waited. Karl Kassel hurried toward her.

"I saw you cross the street just as I came out of the hotel," he said. "Going to breakfast?"

Roxy nodded. "What do you think of Chicago?"

"What I've seen is good. Very different from Berlin, but then one cannot compare a mature adult with a growing child, can one?"

"I suppose not. It seems grand to me, though, but then I've not traveled as you have."

Exhilarated by the sharp wind and fascinated by the handsome young German, Roxy's feet scarcely touched the ground as she and Karl approached the tents extending across Grant Park.

"Mimi is taking me for a ride on the elevated railroad this morning. Out to a university, I believe. Would you be able to come with us?"

Roxy's heart gave a bounce. "I'd love to. What time?"

"Around nine-thirty. Mimi said she would be over for breakfast by nine and will meet me at the cookhouse."

Roxy glanced at her watch—a little before eight. She had almost an hour before Mimi arrived. She better make the most of it. Mimi wasn't going to like having her along on the elevated ride. But she would have to realize that her cousin also knew a thing or two about men. How lucky it was that she had waited until now to come to breakfast. She hoped Grandma was off someplace and wouldn't come horning in.

Seated across from Karl in the cookhouse, Roxy slowly pulled off her gloves as she had seen Clara Kimball Young do in a film in which she was trying to vamp Conway Tearle.

The eggs could have been paper and Roxy would not have known the difference. She ate leisurely but her thoughts darted about as rapidly as her feet did in the dressing tent during a performance. She must make the most of this opportunity. No telling when she would be alone with him again. How blue his eyes were! And, oh those wonderfully strong hands! She was sure they could manage any horse in the world.

"Do you notice any differences in audience response to your acts in this country?" she asked and was quite pleased with the sound of such an intelligent question.

"Not really, so far. Of course I can hardly say for sure with only four performances. And the enthusiasm in Kingston is not likely to be found in any other city." Karl broke a piece of bread.

"Well, back in Wardrobe I could hear your applause and it seemed tremendous." Roxy put sugar in her coffee.

Karl laughed. "Oh, that probably was for Mother. As you say here, Helga always brings down the house."

"She *is* wonderful."

"Your mother was a circus rider too, Mimi told me. Why did she leave the circus?"

Roxy laughed. "Love! What else?" She wiped her mouth with her napkin and dropped it back in her lap. Encouraged by the interest in Karl's face, she launched into the tale of the farmer and the circus rider. Then she found herself telling about the farm, Allen and Janet, Tucky, and even Doug.

Karl laughed at the right places and kept prodding her with questions when she paused. She had never felt so appreciated. He *did* like her!

"Well, well, what are you two gabbing about?" Mimi stood behind Karl.

He rose, stepped over the bench, and pulled it out so Mimi could be seated more easily. "Roxy has been telling me about her family and their farm. And I must say she is a fascinating storyteller. I could almost smell the lilacs and hear the birds in the orchards. It must be beautiful."

"When we show in Westwood, I'll take you out there if you like." Roxy glowed at his praise.

Karl left to get Mimi's breakfast plate and coffee.

83

"Did he tell you about his grandfather's place where he grew up?" Mimi asked.

"No. I guess I didn't give him a chance."

"Well, Karl spent a lot of his childhood on his grandfather's estate along the Rhine. Lived in a castle too. He was so modest in speaking of it; he said it was quite a small castle."

Roxy felt herself shrink to the size of one of the Marshall midgets. Bragging about the Clark farmhouse and *he* had lived in a castle on the Rhine!

"There you are, Mimi," Karl said, putting a plate of food in front of her.

Mimi looked into his face as he climbed over the bench and sat beside her. "Thank you, Karl."

Roxy felt pain. Mimi might be a flirt, but right now she wore her heart on her sleeve, as Mama would say. And the way Karl returned the look! How had this thing between them progressed to such a point in so short a time? If she were going to be able to make Karl notice *her,* she'd have to work fast.

"Karl has asked me to go along on the elevated ride this morning," she told Mimi.

"That's good. You've never been on the el either, have you?" There was no displeasure in Mimi's voice.

She must be awfully sure of him if she raised no objection to three on the expedition, Roxy thought resentfully. "Of course not. I've never even been to Chicago. Remember?"

"Oh, that's right. I forgot."

"Well, what are you young ones going to do with this beautiful day?" Grandma stood behind Roxy.

"I'm acting as a guide on an elevated ride to Jackson Park," Mimi answered.

"Good. No, Karl, stay seated. I've had my breakfast," Grandma said. "Be sure to show them the few remaining buildings of the Columbian Exposition out there in

Jackson Park. We were here in ninety-three while that World's Fair was going on and I've never seen anything so grand in my life. With all the crowds out there it was a wonder we had any circus business at all. But we packed them in twice a day." She turned to Roxy. "I was just at the post office tent. If I'd known you'd be here I would have brought your mail. There were two letters for you. Better get over there. Jake Devlin likes to close up early on Sundays."

"I'll be through here in a minute, Roxy," Mimi said. "Suppose Karl and I meet you in the front yard and then we'll go over to the Loop to get the train."

Roxy walked out of the cookhouse tent, and around the horse tent to the small canvas top that housed the circus post office.

"My grandmother said you had some mail for me," she told the bent old man seated behind the counter.

He squinted at her a moment. "Well, Roxy Clark, our little redhead! Yep." He took two letters from one of the pigeonholes at the back. "These must be the letters you were asking me for back in South Bend."

Roxy noted the envelopes, one from Mama, the other from Doug.

"You got here just in time. I was about to close up. What are you aiming to do today? Out on some kind of a gay time, I reckon."

"I'm going on the elevated out to Jackson Park. This is my first visit to Chicago."

"Out to Jackson Park? What a sight that place was in ninety-three when we showed here."

"Oh, were you with the circus then?"

"Sure was. I was a clown. Had a good bag o' tricks too, if I do say so. Sometimes when your grandma stops by here, we chew the fat about the good old days." The old man took off his glasses and cleaned them with a red-bandanna handkerchief. "You know, Roxy, there's never been a female rider since as could hold a candle to her. My, but Gracie Riley was a handsome figure on horseback. She never saw a horse she couldn't manage."

Roxy gave a short laugh. "And she's never seen a person she couldn't manage either."

The postmaster joined in the laughter. "You're right there, young lady. But here I'm keeping you from reading your mail."

"I'll read it later. I've got to meet Mimi and Karl in the front yard."

"Say, that cousin of yours sure has a way with the boys this season. Seems only yesterday she was a skinny little girl just learning to fly. And now I hear that new rider, Karl Kassel, is her latest beau. Well, you have a good time. And listen, when you get out there on the Midway of the old World's Fair, say a big thank you for Little Egypt from Jake Devlin. My, but she was a cute little trick of a dancer. I'll never forget her, no sir, never!"

Roxy smiled. She had heard of all the marvelous buildings, the educational and scientific exhibits at the Fair. But what was it this old man remembered? An oriental dancer named Little Egypt! "I'll do that, Mr. Devlin."

"Oh, call me Jake, Roxy honey. You belong to the family now."

"Good-by, Jake."

That was a nice way to put it, she thought, as she made her way to the front yard. She *did* belong to the family now, the circus family, and with her real family so closely related to the Big Top her ties were even stronger.

She walked past the side-show tent to one of the ticket wagons. She'd wait here where they'd be sure to see her. She watched the Big Top canvas rise like a mammoth umbrella being opened to cover a giant. No matter how often she saw this happen, she knew she would still be thrilled at how swiftly it was done.

She turned as Mimi and Karl approached. A wave of loneliness engulfed her and she tried to ignore what she saw—two people entirely engrossed in one another. She felt as helpless in her secret and growing emotion toward Karl as a swimmer caught in an ocean's undercurrent.

"Did you get your letters? How are Aunt Martha and Uncle Red?" Mimi asked when they reached her.

"I haven't read the letters yet."

"Well, go ahead and read them. We'll wait. I bet you got one from Doug. Did she tell you about him, Karl? He's her farmer beau. Lives on the next farm and he's always been crazy about her. Hasn't he, Rox?"

Roxy's face flamed. "Douglas Gardner is not my beau, Mimi, and you know it! Why we fight like cats and dogs! Always have!" With effort she fought down her anger and said to Karl. "I've never been interested in any fellow." She wanted to add—*until now.*

"Well, maybe not. But plenty have been interested in her," Mimi said, winking at Karl.

"I'm sure of it," Karl said.

With Karl walking between the girls, the three made their way out of the park, crossed Michigan Boulevard and walked toward the Loop to an elevated station. Mimi chattered all the way, talking about Chicago.

"It's a wonderful city," she said enthusiastically. "There's so much I want you to see. Down on Michigan Boulevard is the Art Institute. We must spend at least one morning there. After the parade tomorrow, all the rest of our mornings will be free for sight-seeing."

Roxy wondered if Mimi meant that "we" to include her, too. Just how often could she tag along without annoying Karl? She mustn't make him sick of her. Perhaps this infatuation with Mimi would pass and then he would turn to her. He probably had gone with lots of girls and, since he was unmarried, he was still looking for a wife. Well, she was going to stay in the picture, Mimi or no Mimi!

They climbed the stairs leading from the sidewalk to the elevated; Karl purchased tickets and they walked out onto the long platform along the tracks above the street. A train roared in and the three boarded.

Seats stretched along either side of the car. Although Karl sat between them, his head was turned toward Mimi most of the time. The train's roar made conversation difficult. Karl bent his head so Mimi could speak in his ear, but kept it erect when Roxy tried to address him. When he couldn't hear her, he just smiled, and shrugged his shoulders. Roxy gave up, looked out the window, and watched Chicago flash by.

Jackson Park was fresh in spring green. The beauty of trees and flowers acted as balm to Roxy's low spirits, and the walk through the site of the Columbian Exposition further revived her. It had taken place four years before she was born, but Mama had a book of pictures of the great Fair and had told Roxy many tales about the week the circus had played in Chicago in ninety-three. Mimi pointed out the Midway. Roxy smiled and told them about old Jake Devlin's remembrance of the Fair—a dancer called Little Egypt.

Karl was impressed by the Gothic buildings on the University of Chicago campus. Roxy admired the way he spoke of architecture. He spoke of it with as much assurance as Doug did of harrows and plows. She wondered what Doug had written her. Had he been over to check on how Allen was caring for Tucky?

On the ride back to the Loop she might just as well not have been there, so infrequently did the other two speak to her. It was nearly one when they walked along Congress to Michigan Boulevard. At the corner they paused to wait for the policeman's whistle.

"I think I'll let you two go on to the cookhouse without me," Roxy surprised herself by saying. "I'm going up to the room and read my letters before I eat."

"I wondered how long you were going to wait to read what Doug has to say." Mimi smiled.

"Now, Mimi, I told you—" Oh, what was the use? "There's the traffic whistle. I'll be over in a little while."

She turned and walked toward the hotel. At the door she looked back and watched the couple step up the curb on the opposite side of the boulevard and continue toward Grant Park.

Oh, Karl, why couldn't you have preferred a redhead? Why did Mimi have to be so attractive? And why did she, herself, feel so mean toward a cousin she loved?

Chapter 7

CHICAGO

On Monday morning the wardrobe staff reported for duty at eight-thirty to prepare for the parade. Since they would parade only one day during the week's run in Chicago, Grandma had told Roxy the night before, this procession must be perfect.

Roxy's eyes burned. Last night she had cried quietly as she lay on her cot at the hotel. She wasn't sure whether she had cried because of Karl's polite indifference toward her or because the letters had made her a little homesick. Mama had described what Papa and Jeff Murray, their hired man, were doing in the fields; Allen was memorizing his poem for the last day at school; Janet was baking a cake without any help; Mr. Lamb had asked Papa and her to be present at high school commencement to receive Roxy's diploma—Roxy had to admit the letter had moved her deeply. Strange too, considering the exciting circus world in which she was now living. But perhaps not so strange either, since she was a half-and-half girl—half-farm, half-circus.

Then there was Doug's letter, full of advice and warnings to stay out of trouble. "I worry about you, Rox. You are such a rash, madcap of a daredevil; no telling what you'll get into without me there to look out for you— I took Agnes Johnson to see the *Perils of Pauline* last Saturday. Agnes is a nice girl, agrees with everything I say.

What a contrast to you! Oh, yes, we left Pauline in a railroad wreck. Next week I suppose she'll get out of it and then into another hair-raising predicament— Stay away from the wild animal cages, Rox, and watch out for the elephants. You may be an impudent girl but I wouldn't want you squashed by one of those big critters— Yesterday I saw Allen riding Tucky into town to the blacksmith shop. Tucky looks good. Allen's pretty pleased to be looking after him. But I'm sure old Tuck misses you— Write and tell us farmers about circus life— Your apple tree is in bloom."

The last statement had added to Roxy's nostalgia. "Her" apple tree was a huge one in the Gardners' front yard. It had the pinkest blossoms and the reddest, juiciest apples of any tree in all the Clark or Gardner orchards. Best of all, it had a rope swing in which Roxy, in her younger days, had felt she was reaching the sky when her toes touched the top branches.

That Doug knew how to stick the homesick knife into a person's heart and turn it. Darn him!

In the midst of parade preparations in the dressing tent, Aunt Marie came to Roxy. Dressed in glittering red, she was very beautiful, Roxy thought. She tried to imagine her own mother in such regalia. Even though they had pictures at home of Mama in fancy riding costumes, it was gingham and calico that most often came to Roxy's mind when thinking of her.

"Listen Roxy, how would you like to visit Marshall Field's department store with Mimi and Lilly and me in the morning?" Aunt Marie asked.

"But I thought Mimi and Karl were going to the Art Institute tomorrow morning. In fact they asked me to go along."

Aunt Marie frowned. "Yes, I know. That's the reason —well, I might just as well tell you. Your Uncle Jules is having a fit about Mimi and Karl. Says I have to break it up at once. Jules laid down the law to Mimi last night after he saw them in the afternoon walking along the lake, holding hands. You'll have to help me Roxy."

Roxy felt a surge of hope. With Mimi forbidden to see Karl, perhaps—!

"Don't tell Mimi I told you. She's quite upset. I've promised she could buy those white-topped button shoes she's been wanting." Aunt Marie laughed. "You know, the ones like Irene Castle's she's been raving about. But even white-topped shoes didn't seem to interest her last night."

"But why, Aunt Marie? Uncle Jules hasn't objected to Mimi's other beaus, has he?"

"Well, no. You see, it's because Karl is German."

"What does that have to do with it?"

"The fact that Jules is French has to do with it. Oh, it's too much to explain right now! I've got to go. Want to tell Del to change my bridle."

Roxy watched her aunt make her way out of the crowded, noisy tent, then picked up empty hangers and hung them on a rod. Now she remembered Uncle Jules' bitter tone when he had spoken of Kaiser Wilhelm of Germany. Well, maybe she was to have a clear field with Karl after all.

Roxy's exhilaration was short-lived. Across the tent she saw Mimi emerge from a dressing room. Even at this distance one could notice that she had swollen eyes. Roxy melted. Oh, poor Mimi! Unrequited love was awful but how much worse to be thwarted in a love that was returned. For, as much as she hated to admit it, Roxy was sure Karl cared for Mimi. Yesterday's trip to Jackson Park had shown that, although she had not acknowledged it completely to herself until now.

But if Karl couldn't see Mimi, might he not turn to her? If only Mimi weren't her cousin, if Mimi could just be a stranger for whom Roxy had no feeling. But, that poor girl! With eyes that swollen she must have cried all night. Roxy's own few tears seemed insignificant in comparison.

"Hey, Roxy," Lilly called out as she followed after her sister. "Are you going to Field's with us tomorrow?"

"Yes."

"Good. Mama says I can have a new dress." Lilly paused and said in a confidential tone, "Oh, boy, you should have heard the family row last night! Papa's mad as hops about Mimi going around with Karl Kassel. And you know, I think she's really gone on Karl too. I've never seen her act this way about a fellow before. She kept me awake crying last night. Of course maybe it's just because Papa is saying no, but I don't think so. What do you think, Rox?"

"I think you better skidaddle." Roxy looked at her bracelet watch. "It's ten minutes to ten and you know what Mr. Hallock said about being ready to mount at ten."

With a flash of sequins Lilly ran out, and Roxy returned to her tasks. Grandma bustled across and gave her granddaughter a slap on the back.

"Good girl! I see you have this side under control. Why don't you skip along and see the parade on Michigan Boulevard. I know you're dying to. I'll finish up here."

"Oh, thank you, Grandma." Roxy buttoned her jacket, got her hat and purse from the top of a crate and ran out, pinning on her hat as she went.

Outside she darted and dodged around tableau wagons, mounted groups, cages, and the elephants Albert Donato was lining up trunk to tail. When she reached the boulevard she gasped. Sidewalks on both sides of the street were packed to the curb. This might be the big city all right, but when it came to the circus, the people were as eager and as childlike as the most unsophisticated small-town population.

Not able to see over the crowd, Roxy, staying on the

east side of Michigan, wriggled her way through, going north, hoping to find a place where she could get closer to the curb. If only she were taller! Spotting the Art Institute building ahead, she made for it and found a place to stand on a high step.

From her vantage point Roxy could see policemen in the street keeping the crowd up on the curbs. But no sooner had the uniformed men passed on, than the children in front slipped out into the street again to see if the parade was coming. Glancing at the buildings across the street, Roxy noted the windows on every floor were filled with people looking down. What a grand place from which to see the parade!

She could feel tension and excitement all around. Behind her a man held a small boy on his shoulders. Balloon men pushed in and out, their enormous inflated wares held above their heads like clusters of rainbow bubbles. The crafty circus vendors centered attention on the children, knowing that the cry of "Buy me a balloon, Papa," often ended with Papa reaching into his pocket.

Roxy held her pocketbook close to her. With her circus background, she knew well that shady characters followed the show to pick pockets in the crowds. Mr. Hallock ran a "clean" show, but it was inevitable that there would be some undesirables among the circus employees. The crooks would be sure to have a field day here in the Chicago crowds.

"It's coming! It's coming!"

Roxy felt that no matter how old she got, or how many parades she saw, the sight of tall bobbing plumes on horses' heads, the rumble of wooden wheels, the vision of brilliant wagons and horseback riders, and the sound of brassy bands would always make the blood pound in her temples and her throat ache with the gaudy beauty of it.

Mr. Hallock led the parade down the middle of Michigan Boulevard. He held his tall black silk hat aloft as he bowed first to the left and then to the right. His beautiful horse stepped high, occasionally rearing on hind legs to thrill the crowd. Watching from here was much better than last Friday on the rail fence. Even the horses were playing up to the crowd.

Seeing her friends ride by in such magnificence, Roxy wanted to tell those around her, "That's Charlie Carter driving that twenty-four horse hitch and managing that many horses is nothing at all for Charlie. He used to drive a forty-horse hitch for Barnum and Bailey.

"That snake charmer is Mary Duncan. She's married to Adolph Duncan, manager of the side show and they have a dear little girl Susy who is learning to ride bareback.

"That woman riding in the barred-off section inside the tiger cage is Rita Donato. She works those cats fearlessly, but is afraid to ride horseback.

"And that's my cousin Mimi who—" No she wouldn't want to tell them about Mimi's trouble. There was no droop to Mimi's shoulders; she sat erect on her horse, her head high, and she smiled at the crowd along the curbs. Mimi was too good a showman to let her personal life affect her performance. At this distance Roxy couldn't see the swollen eyes.

The Kassel troupe followed. Did Karl know yet about Uncle Jules' ultimatum? Roxy wondered. Probably not. Would Mimi have a chance to tell him? From now on, Uncle Jules would be keeping close watch on his older daughter.

When Roxy heard the calliope at the end of the parade, she started working her way south along Michigan Boulevard. She must be back on the grounds before the first of the procession returned.

For the Chicago run all extra seats had been installed in the Big Top. Coming out of the cookhouse at twelve-thirty, Roxy was sure every seat would be taken, for the front yard was already swarming with people.

The crowd packed in front of the side show listened open-mouthed to the nasal tones of the barker, bold and self-assured in his shirt sleeves and straw hat.

"Right this way, ladies and gentlemen! See Tongo, the dog-faced boy straight from the wilds of Borneo! See Baby Gertrude, 617 pounds of feminine pulchritude! See the world's tiniest entertainers, the Marshall Midgets, the perfect *Little People!* See Elva, the tattooed lady who dances and sings and entrances the eye! See Maximilian the nine-foot giant! And don't forget our beautiful Mary who charms hundreds of the world's largest snakes and pythons, wears them around her neck, on her arms, and about her waist!" On and on he yelled his singsong spiel. "All this, ladies and gentlemen, for ten cents, one tenth of a dollar, one thin dime! Step right up and get your tickets!"

Roxy glanced up at the huge posters mounted along the side-show tent. She knew very well the barker exaggerated. She doubted that Gertrude really weighed 617 pounds or that Mary Duncan had that many snakes.

The refreshment stands were doing a good business in hamburgers, pink lemonade, cotton candy, peanuts, popcorn, and crackerjack. Long lines stood at the ticket wagons, and already there was a crowd at the entrance waiting for the one o'clock opening. The main performance didn't begin until two, but everyone wanted time to look at the animals in the menagerie tent before finding his seat in the Big Top.

Roxy made her way around to the back yard. She had just reached the main dressing tent when Mimi caught up with her.

"Lilly said she told you about Papa and me." Mimi's eyes were normal again, but her usual vivacity was missing.

"Yes and I'm sorry." Roxy pulled up her skirts a trifle and dusted her shoes in the grass.

"He'll be watching me like a hawk from now on. Could you tell Karl that I can't meet him in the morning?"

Roxy looked up. "Why, I guess so. If I don't see him on the grounds, I could telephone him from our room at the hotel in the morning. But I may see him in the cook-house."

"Oh, Roxy! What am I going to do?"

"Mind Uncle Jules, I expect."

"But Karl is so—he's so different from the others."

"Yes, I know." Roxy wished that she didn't know.

"And from now on the only time I can see him is when he's in the ring. And if Papa catches me hanging around the connection to watch him after our act, he'll probably put a stop to that. I'll be seventeen next month. Surely I'm old enough to choose my own friends."

"Oh, don't kid me, Mimi. You're not thinking of Karl as just a friend."

"No, I guess not." Mimi sighed and turned away. "Oh, there comes Grandma. Don't say anything to her. She wouldn't understand."

"Roxy," Grandma said. "This afternoon I want you to help Rita Donato get dressed. She was rehearsing Rajah this morning in that new routine and the old devil gave her a nasty clawing. Before you go, see that your racks are in order and Amy will take over your station for the ballet girls."

"Was Mrs. Donato hurt badly?"

"Well, she had to go to Doc Markley's tent and get sewed up and bandaged. It happened right after the parade. Anybody but Rita would have gone to bed. But she wouldn't miss putting those cats through their paces even if she was at death's door. Why the long face, Mimi? Anything the matter?"

"No, Grandma, nothing at all." Mimi forced a smile and gave Roxy a glance.

Roxy nodded briefly and went in to check the girls' spec costumes. That done, she proceeded along the outside of the main dressing tent to three special small ones at the back belonging to the three stars, Frieda Jantry, Midgie Dexter, and Rita Donato.

"Mrs. Donato," she called, pausing at the opening flap.

"Yes, come in, Roxy."

Inside the small enclosure, Roxy paused. Lying on a cot with a coverlet spread over her, Mrs. Donato, the tamer of wild beasts, appeared tiny and helpless to Roxy.

"Mrs. Donato, I'm so sorry you were hurt. Can you really go on this afternoon?"

"Of course. Don't let this in-bed business fool you. Alberto was just here and I promised him I would lie down for twenty minutes. What time is it?"

"Twenty-three minutes until two."

Rita threw back the cover and sat up. "Nice of Gracie to let you come over to help me. I really could dress myself, I expect, but Gracie likes to pamper me. Between her and Alberto—" She laughed. "If I can't dress myself I wonder how they think I can manage my kittens in the ring. Oh, well, since you're here, we'll let you help. My trousers are hanging behind you."

Roxy got the white satin breeches and knelt down to slip them over Rita's feet. Standing, the woman pulled them up under her kimono and fastened the belt, then removed the kimono.

Roxy gasped. One arm was bandaged from the wrist to across the shoulder. It was not the bandage, however, that caused the exclamation but the deep scars on the bare portion of Rita's chest, her other arm, and back.

Mrs. Donato laughed. "You see before you, honey, the beat-up old body of an animal trainer. Alberto wanted to work my cats this afternoon. But I have to get in there and show Rajah who's boss. Hand me my coat, please."

Roxy took the spangled white satin jacket from its hanger and gently worked one sleeve up over the bandaged arm. Then she brought the high, white leather boots from the trunk and, kneeling on the grass, put them on the performer.

At the small dressing table, Roxy watched Rita apply dry rouge to her cheeks and powder to her face; then, dipping her little finger into a jar of creamy lip rouge, Rita spread it evenly over her pretty mouth.

"No use doing anything to my hair. That tall hat Gracie made me is pure destruction to any hairdo. It's there behind the trunk." Taking the tall red-braided hat from Roxy, Rita put it on and fastened the matching strap under her chin. "I told Gracie that in this getup, I look as if I'm ready to lead the band. When Miles Wallace first saw me in the outfit he said, I could stand in for him any day. I used to wear an evening dress for the act. But that was before I had several run-ins with obstreperous cats. Now the main thing is to cover up." She took a long white whip from the corner. "Thanks, Roxy."

"Oh, it was a pleasure, Mrs. Donato. And I think you're wonderful."

"Call me Rita, honey. Now I must get out there and mount that blamed horse to ride in the grand entry. I'd rather be riding Rajah around the track."

"Aren't you ever afraid of your tigers, Rita?" Roxy asked.

"No. But I never trust them entirely. Even the friendliest and seemingly tame cat will have a bad day and take it out on a trainer if he has the chance. From my scars you can see that even I have guessed wrong in my time."

The first blasts from the band filled the small tent. Roxy followed Rita outside where performers were lining up for the opening procession around the hippodrome track.

99

At the front of her private dressing tent stood Frieda Jantry. "Roxy Clark, come here," the old performer called out. Roxy approached. "What were you doing in Rita's tent?"

"Helping her dress."

"So—now they're furnishing her with a private maid, are they? Well, we'll see about that. I'll speak to Frank and ask him what the hell he thinks he can pull off around here. Why I was doing center ring before she was born!" Frieda grasped her riding crop tightly and hit her thigh with it.

"But Mrs. Jantry, Rita was hurt this morning. Rajah chewed her up some. And Grandma thought—"

"Oh, so it's Gracie again, is it? Concerned for Rita's scratches is she? And what about me? I've had rheumatism for years and she's never sent anyone to help me with my quick changes. I'll give Gracie Riley a piece of my mind, you can bet on that! Well, don't just stand there! Get along to your work!"

Roxy got along quickly, only too glad to escape Frieda's tongue. What an old devil she was! With so many other excellent riders why did Mr. Hallock keep her?

At eleven that night, tired but contented at the huge, appreciative audiences at both performances, Roxy walked back to the hotel with Amy Travers. As they crossed the lobby toward the elevators, Karl rose from a chair nearby and approached them.

"Roxy," he said. "May I speak with you for a moment?"

"Why, of course." At the sight of him, Roxy fought down the inner tumult that caused her heart to beat faster. She had to lick this thing; she just had to or she would be miserable for the rest of the season. "Excuse me, Amy."

Hat in hand, Karl bowed to Amy as she went to the

elevator. "Will you sit over here?" He led Roxy to a leather settee.

"I was hoping I'd see you," Roxy said. "Mimi asked me to give you a message."

Karl brightened. "She did? Good. You see I thought I might have offended her in some way. She hasn't spoken to me all day. Every time I saw her and tried to get to her, she was gone. I keep wondering what I've said that displeased her."

"Oh, it's not you at all," Roxy hastened to say. "It's, it's—" Should she come right out with it and tell him? Sure, why not? Truth was best even if it did have a sting to it. "It's her father, Uncle Jules. He's forbidden her to see you, to go places with you, or to be—to be, well, friendly."

"Mr. Frontenay? But why? What have I done? I have treated Mimi with the highest respect. My behavior has been above reproach. Why?"

"Because you're German." There, she had let him have it. Seeing the pain in his deep-blue eyes, she wished she had softened the statement in some way.

"Because I am—! I see. But I thought Mr. Frontenay was an American."

"A naturalized American. He came here from Paris in eighteen-ninety and even after all these years he's never forgotten he's a Frenchman. Haven't you noticed his accent?"

"Everyone's speech here seems strange to me. I had not noticed his particularly. I wonder why Mimi didn't tell me. She must have known how her father feels about Germans."

"I expect she was hoping for the best. She wanted me to tell you that she will not be able to go with you to the Art Institute in the morning."

"I suppose not. But somehow, Roxy, I will have to see her. We cannot travel all season with the same circus and not have an occasional meeting. Perhaps I can get better acquainted with Mr. Frontenay so that he may learn that I am not a monster."

"I wouldn't count on it. Uncle Jules is very stubborn. He—"

"I must try anyway. Mimi is—is—well, so very special, I—"

"Yes, she is."

"Well, it's late and I expect you want some rest." Karl rose. "Perhaps *you* would like to show me the Art Institute in the morning since Mimi cannot go."

Roxy stood up and again had to fight her fast-beating heart. To have him all to herself in the morning! Roaming that big place full of paintings and statues, might he not forget Mimi? No, of course he wouldn't. And then too, there was Mimi herself. It wouldn't be fair to try to horn in. Mimi was just too pitiful right now to have a calculating cousin take advantage of her plight.

"No. I think not. But thank you. I'm going to Marshall Field's department store in the morning with Aunt Marie, Mimi, and Lilly."

Karl's eyes widened with interest. "Marshall Field's? Do you have any idea in what part of the store you will be?"

"Why all over, I suppose. Although Mimi will be looking at shoes and Lilly at dresses."

"Good night, Roxy. I think I shall take a walk before I go up," Karl said as they neared the elevator.

Roxy pressed the button and heard him murmur, "shoes and dresses," as he left her.

Chapter 8

LADY'S MAID TO A TIGER

Whenever she thought about the week's run in Chicago, it was the Mimi-Karl affair that came to Roxy's mind more often than the sights of the great city. The astonishment on Aunt Marie's, Mimi's, and Lilly's faces at seeing Karl sitting in the ladies shoe department at Marshall Field's when they walked in, had been something Roxy would never forget. Nor would she forget Mimi's animation as she tried on the white-topped shoes with Karl looking on.

The right size found, the clerk had buttoned both shoes to the top with a pearl-handled buttonhook. Mimi had walked across the floor to see how they felt, then twirled on one toe so that her dress swirled around her.

And how Mimi had smiled when Aunt Marie had accepted Karl's invitation to take them all to lunch in one of the store's very fancy dining rooms. Roxy wondered at Aunt Marie's acceptance. Perhaps long ago, Grandpa Riley had been upset at having a French aerialist persuade his daughter to leave the "Riding Rileys." Roxy knew that Grandpa certainly had objected to *Papa* from the minute he got a job with the circus the summer he courted Mama. Yes, Aunt Marie probably was sympathetic to difficult young love.

They had lingered too long over the linen-covered table and almost ran back to the grounds. Roxy was glad she was still assigned to help Rita so Grandma didn't see that she just barely had time to get the trainer ready for the grand entry.

Each evening that week, Karl had managed to speak to Roxy after supper, and very casually she would drop the information about the next morning's expedition upon which she and the Frontenay ladies would be embarking. And each morning Karl showed up in the right place.

Several times during the Chicago week, Roxy visited the tent that protected the performing horses and had thrilled at the sleek beauty of them. Including those for heavy work, the Hallock Circus carried more than a thousand horses.

Each horse was brushed and cared for every day. The performing horses were not only groomed by the hostlers, but their riders often came to give them special attention. Roxy began to learn the riders by name as she questioned them about their horses.

Wandering up and down the tent's roped-off stalls, inhaling the strong, pungently mingled odor of hay and manure, Roxy reveled in the sight of so much magnificent horseflesh. Here, with horses, the farm girl and the circus girl became one. The longing to ride, that for a time had been overshadowed by the excitement of her new life, had returned in full force. If only someone would give her a chance to straddle one of these beauties for just a small run!

After Chicago the circus went to Milwaukee, then to Rockford, Illinois. Now Rita did not need special help and Roxy returned to the main dressing tent and the ballet girls.

"We sure missed you, honey," Angie Heller told her. "Amy forgot to remind us to get rid of our chewing gum before the parade yesterday, and Frank gave us the devil afterward. Be sure to keep at us."

"Sure, Angie. Here, give me your jacket. There's a split seam under the arm. I'll fix it."

Grandma had been right about her not seeing the country on this tour. Every railroad yard in which she wakened was like the one of the day before, and the set up on the circus lot was always the same. Roxy seldom saw any other part of the city or town in which they were showing.

While the parade was in progress downtown she often had to work in Grandma's enclosed wardrobe wagon mending costumes. The wagon, wired for electricity provided by the circus generating system, carried two sewing machines and all kinds of hooks and eyes, buttons, braid, sequins, beads, and other material needed for repairs. Nearby stood the laundry and dry-cleaning tent.

On sunny days circus life was wonderful; when it rained it was wretched. Mama had known what was what when she insisted on buying Roxy a long raincoat, new rubbers, and a big umbrella before she left. Sloshing about on a muddy lot was depressing. And of course the worst of it was what it did to business. Many bad days and the circus could not meet its huge payroll.

Seeing the crowd of employees lined up at the paymaster's wagon on payday, Roxy began to realize the importance of a full Big Top at every performance. And there was all that food to be bought, food for people, food for animals. In every town the commissary crew preceded the show and made arrangements for supplies to be delivered.

They made good time from Cedar Rapids to Malden City, Iowa and Roxy finished breakfast early. Getting a bucket from the wardrobe wagon she went to the back of the cookhouse tent for hot water.

"Good morning, Joe," she said to the boy who doled out the bathwater.

"Morning, Roxy. You're early."

"Thought I'd come before you get so stingy with the hot water."

"You're the first, so I'll give you a full bucket this time." He filled her bucket from the huge cans on the stove. "There, how's that?"

"Good. Thanks."

Back at the wardrobe wagon she set the bucket on the floor just below a high window in a curtained-off corner, then bolted the wagon door. Taking a bath in this transitory city of canvas was not easy. There were times when she wished she could have a good soak in the washtub at home.

She had just gotten her clothes back on and put the soap in its box, when there was a knock.

"Roxy, are you in there?"

"Yes, Grandma. I'll be right out. Just finished taking a bath."

She hung up her towel, fastened the belt of her lavender gingham dress, and opened the door. At the bottom of the steps Mr. Hallock stood beside glowering Grandma.

The man smiled as he looked up at Roxy, framed in the doorway. "I say, Gracie, there's a picture for you. As fresh and pretty as this May morning."

Roxy returned the smile. "Why, thank you, Mr. Hallock. It *is* a fine morning, isn't it?" She descended the steps.

"You won't think it so fine in a minute," Grandma growled. "Go on and tell her, Frank."

"Well, Roxy, it's this way." The circus owner set his Panama hat on the back of his head. "Ever since you spent that week with Rita Donato, Frieda hasn't given me a minute's peace. Says she has to have someone to help her and she insists on having you."

Roxy stuck a hand in her dress pocket and clenched her fist. "But, Mr. Hallock, why me? I'm new," she expostulated. "Somebody else in Wardrobe would be a lot more useful to her. Why, I scarcely know the ropes around here. Grandma—" She turned to Gracie pleadingly.

"Don't look at me, honey. I've said all that. Honest-to-John, Frank, the way that she-devil wraps you around her little finger! It's a crying shame! It's a good thing there's only one Frieda Jantry with this show."

"Now, Gracie, you know I'd do anything for *you* that you asked me to."

"Yes, everything but tell Frieda off in no uncertain terms." Grandma sniffed in disapproval.

Frank Hallock took a handkerchief from his pocket, removed his hat, wiped the inner band, then dried his forehead. "You will report to Frieda's tent right now, Roxy, and help her get dressed for the parade. From now on you will be working for her."

"And just when Roxy is getting to be a good hand in Wardrobe too," Grandma grumbled.

Mr. Hallock shrugged, smiled at Roxy, and walked away. Roxy looked at Grandma. The latter clicked her tongue, shook her head and said, "Well, that's that. She's got her way again. I'm sorry for you, Roxy. But I tell you one thing, it will be a real test of your character. If you can get along with Frieda, you can do anything. As for me, I'd just as soon be a lady's maid to one of Rita's tigers." Grandma stalked away.

Slowly Roxy stepped up into the wagon again, brought out the bucket of water and emptied it underneath. Hanging the bucket inside, she took a look in the mirror. If she had to do this, well—she had to. She smoothed her hair into place and tucked the pins tighter before leaving.

A test of character, Grandma had said. Well, she should be a match for Frieda Jantry any day, she thought as she approached Frieda's tent.

She paused at the opening. "Mrs. Jantry, may I come in? It's Roxy Clark." The canvas flap was pushed aside and Martin Jantry came out. "Oh, good morning, Mr. Jantry. Mr. Hallock said I was to help your wife."

"That's fine, Roxy. I'm just leaving. Frieda's resting but you go on in." He leaned down and whispered in Roxy's ear. "I'm glad you're here to give her a hand. Take good care of her for me. She is a rare and wonderful woman."

"I'll do my best, Mr. Jantry." Rare, indeed! She watched him walk across the lot to his "office" wagon. How could such a gentle man be in love with cantankerous Frieda all these years?

"Good morning, Mrs. Jantry," Roxy said to the woman lying on the cot inside.

Head propped high with pillows, Frieda looked her over critically. "So—Frank sent you, did he? And, in spite of Gracie too, I'll wager." She gave a pleased chuckle at her victory. "Turn around slowly."

Roxy gritted her teeth at the peremptory command, but complied. "Well, will I do?" she snapped as she faced Frieda.

"Watch your tone, girl. I'll not put up with impertinence. Yes, you'll do. In fact you're very attractive, but don't get uppity because I tell you so. Did you make that dress?"

"Yes." Roxy was astonished at the compliment.

"Lavender is a good color for you." Frieda lifted her arms with difficulty and put her hands back of her head. "Now, to business. Sit down there." Roxy hoisted herself onto the star's battered trunk. "I shall want you to keep my costumes in good order, take my wash to the laundry every day, and call for it when it's finished. Be here at nine each morning to get me ready to parade. Then, when you see my coach come back on the lot, I shall want you to bring two buckets of hot water for my bath. I'm sick and tired of having my tent smelling to high heaven after one of those roustabouts brings water in here. Whew! How those guys stink!" The old performer curled her nose.

Roxy laughed. "After all these years, I'd think you'd be used to it. What with all the animal smells, a circus certainly is no scented flower garden."

"Oh, animals! Their smells I can take, but dirty people—!"

"I know what you mean." Sitting on the trunk, Roxy's feet did not quite reach the ground. She drew one leg up a bit and clasped the knee with both hands. "I always liked the smell of horses in our barn at home. Here I run over to the horse tent frequently just to get a whiff and to see the horses."

Frieda gave her a penetrating glance. "So—you like horses, do you?"

"Love 'em!"

"Being kin to Gracie, I suppose you would. Well, to get back to what I shall require. I have four changes at each performance. With my stiff elbows, I have trouble with back hooks." Slowly she withdrew her hands from the back of her head and held them out in front of her. "Thank heavens there's no rheumatism in my fingers. They're still as strong as iron on the reins. There's not a horse on the lot I can't manage."

"I'm sure of it, Mrs. Jantry."

"Don't call me that! I'm Frieda Jantry, equestrienne, queen of the ring!" She laughed dryly, sat up, threw back a silk coverlet, and put her feet on the ground. "That's the way they used to bill me in my heyday. Now it's the Kassels this and the Kassels that. Why, when I was Helga Kassel's age I—" She broke off and her shoulders sagged a bit. Then she stood up and flung off her blue silk kimono.

"All right, don't just sit there! Get me ready for the parade. Frank won't let me ride horseback in the parade anymore, but my coach and I are admired more than anything else in the whole damned shebang!"

"You do make a grand appearance, Frieda. I saw the parade in Chicago and the people around me applauded like everything when you went by." She might just as well humor the old girl, Roxy thought. She took the gold parade dress from the hanger and slipped it over Frieda's head.

During that first week in June, Roxy's whole routine changed. Each morning after breakfast in the cookhouse, she hurried to Frieda's tent to have all in order before the old tartar arrived on the lot. She arranged the folding cot with spread and pillows, unpacked the trunk, and hung the costumes. Frequently she took them over to the wardrobe wagon and pressed them. How, she wondered, had they cared for costumes in the old days, before the circus carried its own generating system? The electric iron was a marvelous modern convenience.

During the parade one morning, Martin Jantry came in and said, "Roxy, at every performance I want you to be in the Big Top connection entrance as Frieda comes off after her last appearance. If it's raining, put her raincape on her and have an umbrella. If it's chilly, bring a wrap. In other words make her as comfortable as you can. In her last number she gives that dressage all she has. Often she is exhausted at the end, though she won't admit it. I'd like her to give up the ring, but she won't." He stroked his beard and smiled wistfully. "Says she wants to die in the saddle."

So—afternoons and evenings, as soon as she had dressed Frieda in white riding breeches, red coat, black boots, and tall black silk hat, Roxy followed her to the Big Top where Frieda mounted Sebastian, one of the most beautiful horses in the circus. Roxy admired the way her employer handled the nervous, fractious Sebastian. Oaths and curses she flung at those around her, but there were only soft, gentle words for the black horse.

While Frieda waited outside for her cue, Roxy stood inside at the edge of the performers' entrance and caught the last of the Kassels' dressage numbers. The applause for their dancing horses was always deafening. Whenever Mimi could elude Uncle Jules' watchfulness, she slipped in beside Roxy to watch Karl.

To all outward appearances these two were avoiding each other, but seeing the look on Mimi's face there in the connection each day, Roxy wondered. As for herself, there was only a dull ache in her chest now as she watched the young man in the white satin uniform.

What had happened to the Roxy Clark who had joined the circus determined to become a performer and who had set out to win the attention of the handsome Karl? Had she lost her spunk? No, she didn't think so, but living in this ever-changing yet never-changing circus world, she was looking on the whole operation with different eyes. The performers were extraordinarily talented people; dressed magnificently, all applause was directed at them. What the audience didn't know was that the clapping acclaimed not only the performers, but also every dirty roustabout, every cook, every ticket seller, every wardrobe lady like herself, every blacksmith, groom, and animal man. All of them had to do their job or there would be no show.

And as for Karl—well, one had to know when to put the brakes on when there was nothing but dangerous heartbreak ahead. Was Mimi going to be able to put on the brakes? Was she even trying?

After her first week with Frieda, Roxy had written to Doug and humorously described her new job as *"lady's maid to a tiger."* Doug answered, "Do you good to toe the mark for once. Maybe that Frieda will take some of the contrariness out of you— Hallock's advance man was in town yesterday arranging for supplies for your outfit when it gets here on July 28. Dad and I signed contracts with him for some hay. I'll put in an extra bale for you."

Roxy wrinkled her nose. That devil! Always razzing her! She'd tell him off next month. Home and Westwood seemed like part of a different world. Her world now was a rolling bed by night and a canvas city by day and the circus people, her people.

Occasionally Roxy would pick up a newspaper that Mr. Jantry had left in Frieda's tent, but she found that reading about what President Wilson was doing in Washington was rather dull compared to the excitement Luly was causing on the lot.

Always the most reliable of Alberto's elephants, Luly was acting up these days and causing no end of trouble. Alice Granville told Roxy she had stopped trying to teach Luly the new routine. In fact Luly had become so bad-tempered that another elephant was wearing her rose-colored blanket and performing in the spec.

On Sunday morning, June 14, they were set up in Omaha, Nebraska. It was comfortably warm, but very dusty on the lot. Frieda had come over from the train at eight and, right after breakfast, had asked for her bath-water. A bucket in either hand, Roxy made her accustomed trip to the back of the cookhouse tent.

There was a line for hot water and Roxy took her place at the end. Her two buckets filled, she walked slowly around ropes and stakes. During her first days she had tried to hurry on this two-bucket journey and had soaked her dress and shoes. Now she took her time.

"How about me helping you, Red?" A young man seated on a stool near a wagon rose, pushed back a shock of wavy black hair, and came forward.

Roxy set down the buckets to ease the pinch on her

fingers and looked him over. There was something familiar about the voice but the face didn't ring any bells. "Thanks, but I can manage. My name is Roxy," she said.

He grinned. "Sure, I know. Roxy Clark, Gracie's granddaughter and Mimi's cousin. But you've been Red to me ever since the first time I saw you sitting on the fence back at Winter Quarters. The sun made that top of yours as red as all get out."

Roxy smiled. "Well, of course! I remember you! The clown with the big wiggly ears!"

He bowed. "Bogum Bentley at your service, ma'am. And my friends call me Bo. Here, I'll carry these over to Frieda's for you." He picked up the buckets.

"How did you know the water was for Frieda?"

"Oh, word got around that the old girl had a pretty redhead fetching for her. Whatever that old spitfire does around here is news." He walked beside Roxy. "You know, I've seen you around for some time. This morning I decided we should get acquainted. Any objections?"

"Why no. Before the season's over I expect to know everyone on the lot."

"That's a tall order. But for now you just concentrate on me. All right?"

"Sure, if you say so, Bo." Roxy laughed. It might not be too hard to concentrate on him either, she thought. He had nice eyes, and must be about Karl's age.

At Frieda's tent she said, "Just set them right there. And thank you very much."

"Roxy!" Frieda yelled. "Who's out there with you?"

"It's me, Frieda," Bo yelled back before Roxy could answer. "Bo Bentley."

"Well, come on in here."

Bo picked up the buckets and stepped inside as Roxy held back the tent flap.

Setting down the water, Bo put his hands on his hips

and looked down at Frieda leaning back in her cushions on the cot. "How ya doing, Frieda?"

"As usual." Frieda's sharp eyes darted from one to the other. "Since when did you get so interested in *my* well-being, Bogum?"

Bo grinned. "Why, ever since Red started working for you, of course. I know better than to try to kid *you*. I just happened to see her carrying your bathwater this morning and thought I'd give her a hand with it."

"Just *happened* to— Oh, go on with you! You saw her go over and waylaid her on the way back." Frieda sat up. "Now, go along. I want to take my bath before the water gets cold."

"See you later, Red." Bo smiled and disappeared quickly.

Roxy pulled the curtain across the corner and set the water in the enclosure. Towels on her arm, Frieda went behind the curtain.

Roxy smoothed the spread on the cot, straightened the pillows, and sat down to wait until it was time to go in and wash Frieda's back. "What kind of a fellow is Bo Bentley?" she called out.

"Well, he's young yet, but I'd say he has the makings of an excellent clown; comes from circus people. His father and mother were killed in a railroad wreck when he was twelve. There were no close relatives, so Frank sort of looked out for him till he was grown."

For several minutes there was only the sound of sloshing water behind the curtain.

"Come do my back, Roxy."

Roxy left the cot and went behind the curtain. She soaped, rinsed, and dried Frieda's back, admiring the firm muscular arms and shoulders of the accomplished rider.

"There you are. Now what would you like to put on today?"

"Get out the pink voile."

"All right. You know, Frieda, I think I'll wash out your petticoats myself after this. The laundry isn't very careful of them, and the lace is so lovely." With the petticoats Frieda had just removed in hand, Roxy turned to go.

"Good. It's about time someone around here appreciated that Belgian lace. There's a clothesline in the trunk."

"After I wash these out, will you want me for anything else today?"

"I guess not. As soon as I'm dressed I'm going over to see that the blacksmith shop shod Sebastian to suit me. Want to go along?"

"Frieda, I'd love to."

"Very well. We'll stop at the cookhouse and get some sugar. Sebastian will be expecting it."

Roxy ran to the cookhouse for more hot water in which to wash the petticoats. Outside the tents, all across the back yard, wet garments flapping from clotheslines proclaimed Sunday as circus washday.

Shortly thereafter, Roxy walked beside Frieda toward the horse tent. Working for this old circus rider was not all bad. In fact, if it was going to bring her into closer contact with the horses, it was very good indeed!

Chapter 9

COLOSSAL TOOTHACHE

By the time they reached Wichita, Kansas, Roxy knew Frieda's dressage routine perfectly; she had watched it so often from the connection. Eight women performed around the hippodrome track before her number, three on each side and one at either end. Then Frieda and Sebastian came to the best spot, the one in center ring. Dressed in the white breeches and red coat, Frieda stood out from the other black-clad riders like a cardinal in the midst of a flock of ravens.

Roxy admired her employer's skill. Sebastian seemed to respond to Frieda's thoughts rather than to any pull of rein or pressure of knees. At each change of music and tempo, the sleek black horse changed his gait and step. It was a beautiful sight and Roxy thrilled as the audience applauded. And how exciting at the end, when Frieda pulled Sebastian onto his hind legs to acknowledge the thunderous applause with a dramatic wave of her hand and then galloped out with a yell of "Hike, you! Sebastian!" No wonder Frieda didn't want to quit the ring. While she was there, who knew she was old?

One morning, watching the returning parade in Salina, Missouri, Roxy waved at Bo Bentley as he climbed down from number three clown wagon.

"How ya doing, Red?"

"Fine. What's new with you?"

"Got some new business in my act. Take a look this afternoon and see what you think."

"I'll try, but Frieda keeps me on the go most of the time."

"Oh, tell the old hellcat to take a jump for herself!" Bo took the tiny hat from the top of his stringy wig, then pulled off the red bulbous nose covering his own.

Roxy bristled. "Don't call her that! Sure she's strong-minded and wants her own way, but with all that talent she deserves it."

"Oh, come off it, Red! She's no more talented than hundreds of others around here and you don't catch them trying to rule the roost. You haven't lived through as many seasons with her as I have. When I was a kid she was always telling Frank how I ought to be punished when I pulled something on the lot."

"Well, since yesterday she's ace-high with me. She let me ride one of her horses in the practice ring. And next Sunday, she says I can have a once around on Sebastian to get the feel of him. Lately I've been feeding him sugar while Frieda waits for her cue. I think the old boy likes me."

"Well, catch my act when you can. I bought a little pig a way back and have been training it. It's kind of a cute little thing. I call him Herman."

"I'll try to."

"Good."

Roxy watched Bo enter the cookhouse. In spite of his hard-boiled attitude, she thought, there was something appealing about him. Poor guy! With no parents, he had been fighting his own battles for a long time. How his voice had softened when he spoke of Herman.

Seeing Frieda's white coach appear, she went for the buckets to bring the bathwater.

The following Sunday they were set up for a three-day

run in St. Louis. In the morning, Roxy slipped into the pair of brown riding breeches Frieda had loaned her. She stuffed some paper into the toes of a pair of riding boots. Frieda's feet were a little longer.

Thus attired, Roxy sat at the dressing table and took a look in the mirror. She unbuttoned the top button of her high-collared, yellow shirtwaist, then reached up to stick in two loose hairpins. If she did get to ride Sebastian and he got rambunctious, *all* the pins might fall out. Decisively she removed them entirely. The mass of auburn hair fell about her shoulders and reached below her belt. Gathering it together in the back she plaited it into one thick braid, fastening it near the end with a piece of ribbon from Frieda's sewing box.

Today, along with the usual shouts, growls, roars, and neighs on the lot, a new sound was added—one long continuous trumpeting from Luly. On the way to the outside practice ring, Roxy walked toward the sound.

Surrounded by elephant men, Alberto, Alice, and several others, the elephant swung her head from side to side and bellowed piteously. Seeing Roxy, Alice walked to her.

"Haven't you found out what's the matter with her yet?" Roxy asked.

"No. The poor old thing seems in agony. It breaks my heart to see her suffer and nobody seems to be able to do a thing." Alice noticed Roxy's clothes. "Riding again with Frieda? Say, she's going to make a performer out of you yet. When Luly gets better I'll give you a ride on *her.*"

Roxy stuck a hand in her breeches pocket feeling extremely jaunty and free without skirts. "Good. I've never been on an elephant. So far Frieda has let me ride only Jupiter, but today I'm to have a go at Sebastian. Can you imagine that?"

Alice raised her eyebrows. "Well, well! What kind of a spell have you cast on Frieda? You know, sometimes I wonder if she doesn't think more of Sebastian than she does of Martin."

"Oh, no! It isn't like that at all! You don't understand Frieda." Roxy shook her head and frowned.

"And you think you do? Well, I'm glad it's you instead of me working for her. Say, how are things going with Mimi and Karl?"

"Things aren't going at all, as far as I can see."

Alice gave a short laugh. "You've been cooped up with Frieda too long, Roxy. You're way behind the times. Jules may be under the impression that he has stopped young love, but everybody else on the lot knows differently, except you, evidently."

Roxy watched Alice return to the crowd around the sick elephant, then made her way around a ticket wagon toward the practice ring. So—Mimi and Karl's romance was progressing in spite of Uncle Jules. What an explosion there would be if he found out. Glancing at her watch, she walked faster. She and Frieda had the practice ring from ten to eleven. She didn't want to waste a minute of it.

Gretchen and Conrad Hagen were working out a new bareback routine in the practice ring. Helga and Fritz Kassel watched their daughter and son-in-law and occasionally called out suggestions in German. Frieda was not in sight. Roxy waved at the Kassels and went on to the horse tent.

Stepping inside, she heard Frieda before she saw her. Her employer's complete repertoire of oaths cracked the air like a bull whip, as four grooms worked furiously on Frieda's horses. Roxy waited until the storm was over.

The horses curried to her liking, Frieda turned and saw Roxy. "I caught these birds red-handed," she said as Roxy approached. "I've told them again and again that my ring stock doesn't know Sunday from any other day. But these lazy good-for-nothings pay no attention to anything I say." She glanced back at the busy grooms. "And don't think Frank Hallock isn't going to hear about this, you ignoramuses!"

At this point Ed Nedosky, the boss hostler, came in. "What's eating you today, Frieda?"

The air got bluer as she told him. Roxy was filled with admiration for Ed as she heard him soothe Frieda. While he talked to her, he fed carrots and sugar to Sebastian, Jupiter, and Caesar. This gesture to her ring stock had a more calming effect on Frieda than his words, Roxy surmised.

When Sebastian and Jupiter were saddled outside the tent, Frieda and Roxy mounted and rode the short distance to the practice ring. Roxy patted Jupiter's graceful neck while they waited for the Hagens to finish.

Not as high-strung as Sebastian, Jupiter, Roxy had found, was quite easy to handle. Early in the circus program, Frieda drove Jupiter around the track, hitched to a dainty two-wheeled cart all intertwined with roses. Frieda wore a flowered full-skirted dress and a big picture hat covered in flowers. Putting Jupiter through a series of gaits and fancy steps, Frieda ended the number by having the horse rear up on his hind legs again and again before the exit. Special harness was required for this number so that the cart did not overturn as Jupiter rose.

During the hour, Frieda instructed Roxy in the fine points of dressage, demonstrating the dancing steps on Sebastian. Every time she failed in her efforts to make Jupiter do likewise, Roxy expected to be "cussed" at. But her teacher was strangely patient.

"Now practice the hind legs bit you've been doing," Frieda said.

"All right. Jupiter, let's show her. Up, up, boy!" Roxy gave the special pull on the reins and pressed hard with her knees. Jupiter responded, his front feet high in the air.

"Good. Do it again, and this time grab the pommel with your right hand and lean back as far as you can."

Again Jupiter reared on command and Roxy, holding onto the pommel, leaned back, feeling her long braid fly out.

"Good, good! Unbraid your hair!" Frieda yelled.

Puzzled, Roxy sat up and did as she was told, wondering if Frieda wasn't a little batty this morning.

"Up again, Roxy, and lean way back." Roxy and Jupiter complied. "Ah, beautiful! Beautiful!" Frieda cried. "Your hair is magnificent against Jupe's whiteness!"

Standing outside the ring, Mary and Adolph Duncan and their five-year-old Susy applauded vigorously. Roxy flushed excitedly. Could it be that she was doing something spectacular enough for the Big Top?

"Now," Frieda said, "ride around the ring and do that bit on every count of ten. Here put a glove on." She removed a leather glove and handed it to Roxy.

Again and again Roxy and Jupiter circled the ring; the horse reared on command, and, holding on with the gloved hand, his rider leaned back displaying her tawny hair above his snowy hide.

Dismounting when their time was up, Frieda and Roxy led the horses from the ring. Adolph Duncan, holding the bridle of a resinback, said, "Nice going, Roxy. You've got a good pupil there, Frieda."

Frieda smiled briefly, then turned grim. "She should be. She was born to the saddle. And Gracie thought she could keep her in Wardrobe! Well, I'll show her, the bossy old know-it-all!"

So—Frieda was teaching her just to spite Grandma, Roxy thought, as she led Jupiter and followed Frieda and Sebastian. At the horse tent she remembered. "Oh, Frieda, you forgot. I was to ride Sebastian this morning."

Frieda stroked the black horse's neck. "Well, so I did. Guess we got carried away with the red hair bit, didn't we? Here, Elmer, take Jupiter," she called to a groom near the entrance. She turned to Roxy. "Come on, mount and take a turn around the tent here. Hold still, boy." She held Sebastian's bridle while Roxy got in the saddle. "Be a good fellow," Frieda added as she released her hold.

Sebastian quivered slightly as Roxy took the reins, but complied with Frieda's command and trotted obediently around the tent. After the exciting performance she and Jupiter had just put on, the ride on Sebastian seemed tame.

Later, in her tent, Frieda said, "You know, Roxy, I think that stunt you and Jupe were doing would look better with a sidesaddle. Of course it would be more difficult, but there's nothing as grand as the sweeping skirt of a sidesaddle riding habit." She bent her head as Roxy rubbed the back of her neck. "And it should be lavender. Yes, with that hair, it should definitely be lavender. I'll talk to our harness maker, Ab Perkins, about making adjustments on one of our sidesaddles so that it will have a handle to hang onto. Then you will learn to let loose of the rein so you can wave with the other hand." She chuckled dryly. "Guess that would show old Gracie Riley. She never had any routine like that."

As she took a bath in the wardrobe wagon, Roxy wondered if Frieda really had it in mind for her to have an act. Were all those hopes of riding before an audience in the Big Top going to come true? A lavender riding dress of satin and, of course, covered in sequins!

Every Sunday afternoon Midgie Dexter conducted "school" outside her private dressing tent. At the beginning of each season, the circus children missed school during the month of May and, at season's end, the months of September and October. Midgie drilled them weekly in reading, spelling, and arithmetic. Soft-spoken, but a firm disciplinarian, the tiny high-wire performer was adored by the children. In spite of all the excitement of the other days, it was Sunday afternoon school that was the highlight of their week.

Wherever the circus moved, a special trunk went with Midgie's baggage. It contained readers, primers, spelling books, arithmetics, a small blackboard, pencils, and tablets. In good weather the children sat on the ground outside the small tent and inside if it rained.

This afternoon, while Frieda took a nap, Roxy sat on an overturned bucket near the tent. She wanted to dream about a rearing white horse and a rider with flowing, bright hair. The back yard was always noisy, but she had learned to ignore the sounds. Today, however, ignoring Luly's uproar was difficult.

Roxy watched the children gather at Midgie's. There were seven of them, a varied group in this outdoor schoolroom—Japanese Tosho Sumoka, Italian Guido and Gina Eldona, Spanish Juanita Alverez, American Johnny Ames, Peter Moon, and Susy Duncan.

Suddenly Angie Heller came running. "Midgie, come on and bring the kids. They're going to pull Luly's tooth. They think she's putting up all that fuss on account of a toothache."

Dropping books and pencils, the children followed the teacher. Roxy joined them. A toothache, she thought; that poor old elephant. No wonder she yelled.

From every corner of the lot, circus folk came running. Too short to see, Roxy spotted the wardrobe wagon, squirmed through, and climbed up the wheel. Standing on top, she looked across the crowd of heads to the strange scene beyond. Mr. Hallock, Alberto, all the elephant men, and other animal trainers were present at the mammoth extraction about to take place.

From just below the wardrobe wagon Lilly's voice called out, "Oh, look where Roxy is! Let's get up there so we can see." She and Mimi scrambled up and stood beside Roxy.

"Say, this is like being in the reserved seat section," Mimi said. She turned to Roxy. "I heard that you put on a good show this morning in the practice ring."

Roxy gave a pleased smile. "Who told you?"

"Karl. He saw you from the blacksmith shop. Said you sat Jupiter very well."

For a moment Roxy's infatuation burst into flame again. With effort she extinguished it. No use stirring that fire up again.

"Everybody wonders how you've bewitched Frieda into letting you ride her horses," Lilly said.

Roxy laughed. "I think she's just doing it to spite Grandma, to get me out of Wardrobe. You know the running feud between those two."

"Well, I'd say you're out of Wardrobe now. We seldom see you any more," Mimi said. "Oh, look!"

They watched as Luly was chained down and her trunk securely tied up over her back. Two men soaked rags from a bottle and held them inside the huge mouth.

"I bet that's cocaine. The dentist used that once when I had a tooth pulled. I'm glad they aren't going to let her hurt any more than they have to," Lilly said sympathetically.

After waiting a while for the cocaine to take effect, Alberto himself used a large drill on the ailing tooth.

"Hey, Jerry!" Roxy yelled at a groom below. "What's Alberto doing now?"

"He's drilling a hole through the tooth so he can put an iron rod through it. Got to have something to hitch onto to pull it out."

"Whew!" Roxy shivered at the thought. She would never complain about the pain her dentist inflicted again.

With the iron rod inserted through the drilled hole, Alberto and Jim Oldknoe fastened a heavy rope around both ends protruding from the sides of the tooth, then attached the rope to the lead bar of a four-horse team.

On command, the team began to pull. The long-suffering Luly dug in and reared back in protest. The decayed tooth popped out and Luly fell back in a heap on her rump.

The watching circus population broke into a loud cheer as the elephant's chains were removed.

"Look at her!" Roxy cried. "The old girl actually looks as if she's smiling!"

Alice Granville approached her favorite elephant and shouted a command. Luly obediently stood on her hind legs and waved her released trunk triumphantly.

"That's the new stunt Alice has been teaching her, only Alice plans to stand on Luly's head at the same time. Now that the tooth is out they can go on rehearsing it," Lilly said.

In the crowd beyond the post office tent, Roxy saw Karl wave. She was about to return the gesture when she glanced at Mimi and realized to whom he was waving. Mimi nodded and smiled, then got to her feet and descended.

Roxy watched her go through the crowd toward the post office, then turned to Lilly. "Has Uncle Jules relented about those two?"

"Goodness no. I guess Mimi thinks what he doesn't know won't hurt him. She's getting awfully uppity these days. She'll be seventeen next week and thinks the world is her oyster."

Roxy walked slowly back to Frieda's tent. She must write Mama and Doug about Luly. Would Mama be glad she was learning some stunts on Jupiter? Would she want her in the ring if she ever got good enough?

And Doug? Well, she knew he'd be against it. Farm, farm, farm, that was all he ever thought of.

As for herself, all she ever thought of these days was circus, circus, circus!

Chapter 10

THE SPARK IN EUROPE

It was raining hard on June 27 as the train stopped with a jerk in Evansville, Indiana. Suddenly awake in her upper berth, Roxy could hear the rain beating a sharp tattoo right above her head. She parted the curtains and looked into the dimly lit aisle. Sticking out an arm, she glanced at her watch. Seven-fifteen! Grandma approached from the washroom.

Seeing Roxy, she said, "We're late this morning and from the looks of things I think we'll all wish we hadn't wakened at all. It's going to pour all day or I miss my guess."

Amy Travers stuck her feet out and sat on the edge of the upper berth next to Roxy's. "You said a mouthful, Gracie. The lot will be a loblolly of mud and everybody will be as cranky as all get out, including me."

Roxy pulled on her kimono and slippers, put her towel around her neck, and lowered herself until her feet touched Grandma's berth, then hopped down. "Oh, come on Amy. We've lived through rain before. Don't put on such a long face. And besides, think how good the rain is for the crops." Roxy tossed her braid over her shoulder as she looked up at Amy and laughed.

Amy made a wry face. "Gracie, tell this young thing to quit making fun on a morning like this. I can't bear it. You remind me, Roxy, of a book I read last winter about a girl who was glad about everything. Tripe it was and absolutely sickening. If you start pulling Pollyanna talk on us, we'll ditch you sure as shooting."

Roxy laughed again. "Oh, quit grumbling. I read *Pollyanna* too and this morning you sound like the old crosspatch in the story. Just a minute, I'll get the ladder for you."

Roxy had discovered these old ladies enjoyed teasing. She herself had learned to know and appreciate each one as a friend in spite of the variance in ages. She rather enjoyed being the only young one in Wardrobe now that she was out from under Grandma's jurisdiction during the day. Somehow it was easier to take from Frieda; she didn't know why. Perhaps it was because, waiting for Frieda in the connection at every show, she now felt more a part of the Big Top performance.

On the lot with raised umbrella in one hand, she held her skirts above her ankles with the other and waded through water and mud to breakfast. Her rubbers were brown with the oozy stuff. Heavens! It was after eight and the only tent up was the cookhouse. This was going to be one of those days!

The lot was a muddy lake dotted with roustabouts in long coats and dripping hats, trying to drive stakes and unroll wet canvas in the pounding rain.

Inside the cookhouse, Roxy lowered her umbrella and looked out. All across the space, wagons were stuck hub-deep in mud. An eight-horse team hitched to a heavy wagon pulled and strained to move the vehicle without success. Ed Nedosky shouted orders and another team of six was hitched to the rings on the side of the wagon. Mr. Hallock rode up on horseback and encouraged the teams as they pulled the wagon out of the slime. Poor Mr. Hallock, Roxy thought, imagine being responsible for this huge operation on a day like this!

She walked to the tables reserved for performers and

all personnel other than roustabouts. During her first days with the circus, she had wondered at the rule that roustabouts must eat together on one side of the cookhouse. It seemed snobbish. Soon, however, she learned the reason. The hundreds of workmen did not bathe and sitting near them destroyed the appetite. As Grandma said, "The boys stink to high heaven!"

Roxy got her plate and sat across from Mrs. Concello of the Marshall Midget Troupe and Jim Daggett, the ringmaster. A box on the bench raised Mrs. Concello high enough to eat comfortably from the table. She smiled at Roxy then turned to the ringmaster.

"Jim, don't you think there should be a law against anyone looking as pretty as Roxy does on a morning like this?"

Jim grinned wryly. "From the looks of things, you'll be the only pretty thing on the lot today, Roxy."

"How on earth can we parade, Mr. Daggett?" Roxy cut a bite of ham.

"Can't. We'll be lucky if we get set up for the afternoon performance. In a downpour like this, who would come out to see a parade anyhow?"

"Where is everybody this morning?" Roxy asked looking around at the empty tables.

"Sleeping I expect. Frank sent word to all cars that we aren't parading."

Her breakfast eaten, Roxy got her umbrella from under the table, walked to the front opening and looked out. The horse tent was up but Frieda's was not. The men were still struggling with the Big Top operation. The air was filled with shouts and orders interspersed with oaths at men, horses, and elephants as all three pulled, pushed, and tugged. If Papa could hear all this swearing, he would snatch her out of the circus so fast her head would swim, Roxy thought.

"Had your breakfast yet, Red?" Bo Bentley came up behind her.

"Yes. Have you?"

"Uh huh. Say, how about you and me walking over yonder to the end of the streetcar line, catching a car, and riding into town for a look around? Nothing we have to do this morning."

"Can't. I want to be on deck when Frieda gets here. This kind of weather is murder on her rheumatism. I help her with exercises to loosen her joints before she goes on. Then too, I want to check on her ringstock and be sure the boys haven't neglected anything."

"Say, the old girl's got under your skin, hasn't she? You sound as persnickety about her nags as she is."

"I sure am. A fine horse is only as good as his care. I aim to see that Frieda's stock gets the best."

"I don't think you need worry. Ed Nedosky is not about to let *any* horse be neglected. Why, we carry *four* veterinarians with the show and only *one* doctor. The animals get better care than the people."

"They should, especially horses. They can't tell what hurts them," Roxy replied.

Bo grinned. "Guess I should be a horse, then you might spend the morning with me. What have you got against clowns?"

"Not a thing. In fact I've always thought them the spice that flavors a circus. And Frieda says you're a good one and going to make a name for yourself."

"Oh, did she now? The old girl's getting soft. Well, run along to the horses, Roxy. I won't keep you."

Roxy put up her umbrella, held up her skirts, and stepped out into the rain, conscious of Bo's eyes upon her. Maybe she should have gone into town with him. It might have been fun. But there was Frieda and she would be sure to ask about the horses.

Next day was Sunday and the dry, sunlit lot in Louisville, Kentucky was a delight. Evansville mud was removed from rolling stock, from shoes, boots, elephants, and horses and outside every tent in the back yard, full clotheslines flapped in the breeze.

In the afternoon, Frieda and Roxy spent time in the practice ring. Abner had fixed a sidesaddle with a special handle for Roxy to hang onto during the stunt. With both legs on one side, however, she found she must adjust her balance. Now she felt she wasn't doing as well as when astride. But with Frieda snapping out instructions there was no letting up. Roxy wanted to ask how long it would be before she was ready for the Big Top but didn't. She knew the answer; when she and Jupiter reached perfection. Perfection was a long way off. And anyway the program was full. There was no place for a red-haired girl who could lean back on a rearing horse.

On Monday, Frieda dismissed her as soon as she got in from the parade. It was too soon to eat, so Roxy walked across the back yard to the parade wagons. She wondered why the "hushcloths" hadn't been put on yet. The wagons stood there uncovered in all their glistening splendor.

She walked closer and examined the carved flowers on number one band wagon. The care with which they were painted was amazing. Various shades of green were used on stems and leaves, and the flower petals blended from pastel at the center to a brilliant hue at the outer edge. She looked up at the gilded, life-size figures above.

"Well, Roxy, you beat me to it; already inspecting, I see." Mr. Hallock came up still wearing his parade clothes.

"Ever since I came I've wanted to examine the parade wagons at close range, but whenever I had the time they were always covered." Roxy pushed up the sleeves of her yellow-checked gingham dress.

"Looks like you came over at the right time today. I told the boys to leave them uncovered until I give them a once-over. After a day like last Saturday I like to inspect the rolling stock." He gestured with his hand toward the rows of wagons. "There's too much money tied up in these to neglect their upkeep."

"Do you mind if I tag along on your tour of inspection?" Roxy asked.

"Glad to have you. Each wagon is like a friend to me. Some are quite old; I could write a book about the other outfits they've traveled with and how I managed to get hold of them. Now take this one for instance." He pointed to band wagon number one. "This giant was built in eighteen ninety-four for Alf Connelly's Wild West Show. Alf went bankrupt in ninety-nine and I bought it for six hundred dollars."

Roxy gasped. "That much for a wagon?"

"That was a bargain. It had cost fifteen hundred dollars to build. Now this dragon and mirror wagon—" He walked on to a blue wagon covered with carved-silver dragons interspersed with mirrors. "This I designed myself ten years ago at a cost of a thousand." He pointed to the carved-silver spokes on a wheel. "Notice that the wheels have eighteen spokes instead of the usual fourteen. Would you believe it if I told you that each steel-rimmed wheel of this baby weighs three hundred pounds?"

Roxy laughed. "Sure, if you say so. No wonder every big wagon has to have at least a six-horse hitch." She followed Mr. Hallock as he walked around the wagon eying it up and down.

At the back he touched it caressingly. "This is the best hard maple we could buy, and the dragons were carved by a famous German wood carver I met in Bavaria. All right boys, cover her up." He signaled and a gang of roust-

131

abouts brought the "hushcloth" to cover the dragons and mirrors.

Hearing Frank Hallock talk about his rolling stock was fascinating. Every wagon had a name and a story. There were the Swan and Mermaid, the Red Riding Hood, the Asia, the France, the Sea Shell, the Great Britain, the America, the Mother Goose, the Columbus, the Ballet, the Ancient Greece. On each wagon, the carved, painted figures told stories in bright, gaudy beauty. And then there were the cage wagons, their iron bars framed in gilded designs with carved, life-sized figures at each corner.

"Well, we've looked them all over, Roxy. Nice to have an audience for my tales. Hope I haven't told you more than you wanted to know. Louise says I'm an old windbag when I talk circus. Say, you haven't met Louise, have you? Since the siding is so near, why don't you come over to our car and meet her?"

Roxy glanced at her watch. It was late and she might have to miss lunch in order to help Frieda dress for the matinee, but meeting Mrs. Hallock, and seeing inside their private car was worth it. "I'd love to, Mr. Hallock."

They walked across the lot to the railroad siding where the circus cars stood on the tracks in long, colorful lines. At the end of the third section on the far side, they arrived at the Hallocks' car. Roxy preceded Mr. Hallock up the steps. He opened the door for her and called out, "Company, Louise."

Roxy was awed by the elegant interior. It was like a handsome parlor, furnished with fine furniture and a thick carpet. The windows had velvet drapes and lace curtains. The white-haired woman who put down a newspaper and rose from a tapestry chair was even more beautiful than the room. She wore a pale-blue voile dress that Roxy knew had been made by an expert dressmaker;

it was so beautifully designed, with a stylish long tunic that reached below the knees of the slim skirt.

"Louise, this is Roxy Clark, Gracie's granddaughter." Mr. Hallock put his hat on a stand. "I've been giving her my wagon lecture."

"Roxy, how nice of you to listen to Frank's tales." She gently clasped Roxy's hand. "Sit here and let me have a look at you. You favor Gracie a little, but you don't look much like your mother or Marie."

"No, I guess I don't. I'm more like Papa they tell me."

"Ah, yes, your papa, the man who stole a fine rider from us." Mrs. Hallock laughed. "Well, after all these years I guess we must forgive him, especially now, since he has let you join us. I hear you're helping Frieda."

Roxy smiled. "Well, I try. I don't always do things to suit her. Occasionally we have words, although I'm getting better at holding my tongue."

Mr. Hallock sat down. "From what I hear, you're doing fine. You are the only rider Frieda has ever allowed to ride her stock."

Roxy gave an imperceptible start. So—he knew about the sessions in the practice ring! *And*—he had called her a rider!

Mrs. Hallock glanced at a watch pinned at her shoulder. "Frank, why don't you tell Henry to serve lunch in here now and to set a place for Roxy?"

Eating the lunch served by Henry at the mahogany table in one end of the car, and talking circus with Louise and Frank Hallock—Roxy knew this was a day to remember. There were white linen doilies at each place; the food was not the heavy fare put out in the cookhouse, and the thin china was a sharp contrast to the thick dishware on the lot.

Halfway through the meal, Mrs. Hallock rose and got the newspaper she had been reading when they came in.

"Frank, something has happened abroad that may be

the spark you've been predicting." She unfolded the paper and handed it to him, pointing to an article on the front page. She turned to Roxy. "Ever since we were in Europe last year Frank has been sure there would be some fighting over there before long. Every place we went we could almost hear the swords rattling."

Mr. Hallock took spectacles from his pocket, put them on, and scanned the paper. "You're right, Louise, this could be it."

"What's happened, Mr. Hallock?" Roxy asked.

"Yesterday the Austrian crown prince, Archduke Francis Ferdinand and his wife Sophie were shot at Sarajevo. That's the capital of the Austrian province of Bosnia. The killer is a Serb and Austria has been looking for an excuse to attack Serbia. This could just be the thing they've been waiting for. Austria would be delighted to extend its territory to the east."

Roxy had only a smattering knowledge of present-day Europe and Mr. Hallock's explanation meant little. Bosnia, Serbia, Austria were names of far-off lands that had nothing to do with her. As they finished the meal, the Hallocks talked about the assassination and its probable impact on various European nations. Roxy wished Mrs. Hallock hadn't interrupted the circus talk. She forgot the whole thing as she hurried across the lot to get Frieda ready for the afternoon performance.

As usual, Roxy waited in the connection way for Frieda to finish her last number. The sun was hot so she had brought a big umbrella to shade Frieda back to her tent.

"Here, I'll take that," Frieda said grabbing the umbrella handle. "You haven't had a chance to see Bo's new routine you were telling me about. Get along in there and catch it. I'll manage by myself today. For a change Martin is taking me into town for dinner. So you just see that you show up for tonight's performance. Enjoy yourself," she said as she walked away.

Roxy watched her for a moment. What had gotten into Frieda? Roxy had thought the word *enjoy* not a part of her vocabulary at all. She wished Mr. Jantry would take his wife out to dinner more often if it worked this kind of miracle.

Inside the entrance, grooms were bringing up the ponies that would perform next with "Mary Jane and Her Dog and Pony Show." Mary Jane herself stood outside holding six dogs on leashes. The performer was dressed like a little girl, a short white dress with a pink sash, long curls with a big pink hair ribbon, white sox, and black patent-leather slippers. Roxy knew, however, that Mary Jane was a long way from being a little girl. She was thirty-eight at least, and was the wife of Ted Adler, who walked a slant wire to the top of the tent without a net.

On the other side of the entrance, the many clowns were gathering for another one of their appearances. Roxy had learned that there were two kinds of clowns, "walk-around clowns" and "carpet clowns". The "walk-arounds" all entered the Big Top at one time and put on their zany routines as they walked the hippodrome track. This they did at high speed between the main acts; any clowning was taboo while stars were performing in the rings. The "carpet clowns" circulated through the audience, often before the show started. Pretending to be a part of the audience, the "carpet clown" could be very funny trying to find a seat and flirting with the ladies.

Roxy entered and squeezed in at the end next to the band. At this distance from the ring, Mary Jane did look like a little girl.

The band struck up a fast tune when the clowns took over. With so many parading around the track, each performing ridiculous business with some ludicrous prop, it was difficult to see them all. Anything for a laugh—gigantic shoes, three-foot cigars, a dog biting a clown's padded seat, a waddling duck led on a string, and on and on. And there was Bo!

Now how could that tiny pig pull the cart in which Bo was riding? It was only when he got right in front of her that Roxy saw that the cart was only a sham, and that underneath the covered sides Bo was walking. She laughed and clapped her hands. Bo lifted his tiny hat and bowed to her.

As each clown got once around the track, he disappeared into "clown alley" and left his prop, picked up another, and made the round again. Then when Jim Daggett whistled, the funnymen vanished immediately.

"Ladies and gentlemen," the ringmaster shouted. "In center ring I have the privilege of presenting to you the great Fritz Kassel and his incomparable liberty horses, fresh from a triumphal tour in which they performed for all the crowned heads of Europe!"

The liberty-horse act was a headliner and performed in center ring with nothing going on in either of the other rings. Roxy leaned forward. How distinguished the gray-haired Mr. Kassel appeared dressed in a white, long-tailed, formal suit.

On each of the twelve black horses' heads bobbed a tall purple and white plume, and another like it, fastened to the top of each white patent-leather bellyband, added style and snap. Numbered from one to twelve, each horse wore his own number. A long whip in his hand, Mr. Kassel stood in the center of the ring as the horses circled about him in numerical order. "The whip," he had told Roxy once in the horse tent, "is for effect only and for giving cues. I rarely touch a horse with it."

Roxy tried to see how he gave those cues to the moving blacks, but gave up, deciding that only the horses could read the position of that whip. How beautifully they drilled, in twos, threes, fours, and sixes. They formed two lines of six each; the lines approached each other and

136

crisscrossed in the middle. They lined up facing the re-served-seat section and stood on their hind legs in uni-son. The audience gave out with a roar of applause.

Then came the best, Roxy thought. A groom entered the ring and led out number eight. Number eight, Roxy knew, was Otto, one of the smartest in the troupe. The groom blindfolded the horse and led him down to the far end of the hippodrome track.

Now Mr. Kassel had the others move around the edge of center ring in single file, then he signaled the groom with a yell. The groom released the bridle and Otto, still blindfolded, galloped to center ring and entered the circling line. Getting between eleven and twelve, he took a few steps, then dropped out into the center of the ring and hesitated for only a moment.

Then, amid a thunder of applause, Otto entered the line in his proper place, between seven and nine.

Mr. Kassel took Otto by the bridle, signaled the other horses to one side, and led number eight to the center. The blindfold removed, Otto knelt on front legs and bowed his head to the applauding audience.

Roxy clapped until her hands burned as the black lib-erty horses galloped off, and Mr. Kassel clicked his heels together and bowed from the waist to every side of the Big Top.

How grand! Would she ever get to do anything in this canvas dome that would be exciting enough to make peo-ple applaud? Or would she always be helping people dress and mending costumes? She and Jupiter were get-ting better at the rearing routine. But what did it matter? There wasn't anyplace in the show for another act. But what about next year? Might not Mr. Hallock—?

Here came Mr. Donato and his elephants, with Alice working Luly and four others in ring three. Ring three being right in front of her, Roxy had a good view of the act. Alice had worked up a great routine and Luly responded beautifully for the spectacular ending. With the other four standing on round platforms, Luly stood on her hind legs in the center while Alice stood on Luly's head.

Roxy laughed at herself. Here she was a part of the circus and as thrilled as any spectator. How could Mama have left it all?

The end of the show was the exciting chariot race around the hippodrome track. Dressed in bright Roman togas, the drivers of the two chariots managed their teams so that the chariot that had been behind during the race won it with a sudden burst of speed at the end. The crowd loved it.

During the main show, as acts were changing, ticket sellers for the wild West show had moved through the audience and now, before the people rose to leave, they came again yelling the thrills in store for those who stayed for the added attraction.

"Only twenty-five cents, ladies and gentlemen! Stay and sit in the best seats for the wild West show. See the old West in action! Daredevil cowboys and Indians on the warpath!"

Roxy decided she would stay. These western riders were very good.

It was a noisy show with lots of gunfire and so much yelling, one could scarcely hear the band. There was some excellent rope spinning in the rings and lassoing on the track. An old-time stagecoach rattled in, was attacked by Indians and rescued by cowboys. There was Sam Dowd, an expert with a long bull whip, who, at a far distance, snapped bits of paper from his wife's hand.

It was after five when Roxy left the big tent. She would have supper first, then go to Frieda's tent and put away any costumes she might have left out. Frieda would probably be in a good mood tonight after a special dinner with her husband. Roxy had observed a deep understanding between these two. If they had been younger she would have called it love. But when people were that old, romantic love could be no part of their lives. And yet, there were Mama and Papa and they were well along in years. The look Roxy had often seen between them could *only* be love.

She wondered if real love would ever come into her life. She certainly thought it might have when she met Karl. If there had been no Mimi—? She brushed away the question. After squelching all those pangs with such difficulty, she must not get them going again.

Walking across the back yard, she paused outside the main dressing tent to tell Alice how great she and Luly were. Alice joined her and the two went on toward the cookhouse. Near the horse tent, Roxy put a hand on Alice's arm.

"Wait a minute. There's Mr. Kassel. I want to speak to him." Alice followed her to Fritz Kassel, who sat on a folding chair near the tent's opening. "Mr. Kassel, I caught your liberty act this afternoon. It's marvelous! Even better than when I saw it before in rehearsal."

Mr. Kassel stood up, folded the newspaper he had been reading, and bowed as formally as he had in the ring. "Thank you, Roxy. Good audience today."

Karl came out of the tent and greeted the girls. "Going to supper?" Roxy nodded. "I'll walk over with you," he said, then turned to his father. "Are you going to eat now, Father?"

"*Nein.* I finish reading this first." He turned to Roxy and Alice. "Reading English is not easy for an old German." He smiled briefly.

As they walked away, Roxy looked back and saw Mr. Kassel sit down again, open the paper, and frown at what he read.

"That's the fourth time Father has read the newspaper

today. He's worried about what is going to happen at home," Karl said.

"Do you mean that something will happen in Germany because that royal Austrian couple was murdered?" Roxy asked.

"It could very well be the thing we have all feared," Karl answered.

Chapter 11

"KEEP OUR SECRET"

On the Fourth of July, the circus showed in Columbus, Ohio. It was Saturday and the Midwest had turned into an inferno of summer heat. Roxy worried about Frieda parading on such a day and, finding Martin, suggested that it might be best for his wife to stay out of the sun.

"Don't even mention it to her, Roxy. She would just blow up and parade anyway. Frieda is a trouper of the old school. Hell or high water never stops her kind, and certainly not a hot sun." He smiled down at Roxy and gave her shoulder a pat. "You have been very good for her. And she has grown fond of you." He laughed. "The fact that your temper sometimes matches hers intrigues her, I think. You seem to understand her as few do. Frieda is a great lady. You and I know the pain she endures, yet she performs in the ring as though she were as young as the Kassel girls."

Roxy frowned. "But I do wish she wouldn't parade today."

"You just have a nice bath ready for her when she returns and see that she rests. She'll be all right." Martin took Roxy's hand in his and looked deeply into her eyes. "My dear, you are a good girl to take her welfare so seriously. She is very precious to me and I thank you."

Roxy smiled gently as she crossed the back yard. Looking into Martin's eyes, she had had a glimpse of something very rare and beautiful. Imagine—that kind of love after all those years!

It was still hot next afternoon in Dayton. As Bo had said to Roxy that morning, it was great it was Sunday so that the whole circus had time to sit back and pant. Roustabouts lay in the grass under wagons out of the sun. All across the back yard, in the shade of wagons or tents, performers sat on folding chairs or on the ground, some stretched out with eyes closed.

Too hot in Frieda's tent, Roxy brought two chairs outside and sat talking to her employer. Next door, outside Midgie's tent, lessons had been put aside and Midgie read aloud to the children. From the rapt expressions on their faces, Roxy thought it must be a fascinating book.

"We didn't show in Dayton last year," Frieda said. "First time we had missed coming here in ages."

"How come?" Roxy asked.

"Well, they had had a horrible flood in the spring and this city was no place for a circus last summer. Took them a long time to clean up and rebuild. They say the water was up to the top of the lampposts downtown."

"Oh, yes, I remember reading about that. I expect business will be good tomorrow," Roxy said. "Dayton people should be ready for some fun after all they went through last year."

Frieda took the pins from her hair and it dropped down below her shoulders. Roxy went inside the tent, returned with a hairbrush and began brushing the long, bleached hair.

Frieda turned her head toward Midgie and the children. "Look at those young ones, would you? They aren't moving a muscle. Run over there, Roxy, and see what on earth she's reading to them."

Hairbrush still in hand, Roxy complied. Midgie held

up the book and smiled. *"Toby Tyler or Ten Weeks with the Circus,* guaranteed to make us forget the heat."

Roxy laughed. "I should have known. Wish I could stay and listen too. Mr. Stubbs was always my very favorite monkey and of course Toby my favorite boy."

She returned and told Frieda. "That book has been around for thirty years or more, but I expect kids will always love that old-time circus Toby traveled with. Mama read it to all of us and I guess Grandma read it to her and Aunt Marie." Roxy continued with the hairbrushing.

Frieda closed her eyes. "Brush it a little more, then braid it tight, and pin it on top. As soon as it gets a little cooler, we'll go to the practice ring and let you and Jupiter have a go at it."

Sleep did not come easily in the hot car that night. All the windows were open and, disregarding modesty, curtains to the aisles were pushed back. Whenever she wakened from a doze, Roxy could hear the low conversation of circus folk walking along the tracks in robes and slippers, trying to cool off.

Before dawn a thunderstorm struck. There was a scurry to close windows in Wardrobe's car as the rain dashed in. By five, the rain had stopped and windows were opened again. A delightful coolness blew in. Roxy fell asleep at once and didn't waken until after seven.

It was a fresh, lovely morning she stepped into as she left the car to cross the tracks to the lot. Monday morning parades were usually good ones. Having rested on Sunday, people really felt like smiling at townsfolk on the streets. And with all this delicious, cool air, Daytonians would get Hallock's best, Roxy thought.

She ate breakfast with Jacques, Henri, and Lilly. Uncle Jules and Aunt Marie were at a table on the far side of the cookhouse. Roxy asked where Mimi was, and her cousins raised knowing eyebrows. Lilly replied that Mimi was taking a walk.

Henri laughed and winked at Roxy. "Yeah, taking a walk to see the scenery."

"Yeah, German scenery, if you ask me." Jacques grinned.

Karl was no place in sight. Roxy drew her own conclusions. Now that Mimi had passed her seventeenth birthday, she was getting bolder. What would happen when Uncle Jules found out?

Roxy saw Frieda and Martin come in and go to their table. Shortly thereafter Mr. Hallock and Mr. Kassel entered. This was unusual; Mr. Hallock ordinarily did not appear on the lot until closer to parade time. While listening to her cousins' chatter, Roxy watched the two men stop at the Jantrys' table while Mr. Hallock spoke to Frieda. Then Frieda looked across at Roxy then back at Mr. Hallock. What, Roxy wondered, was that all about? Was something the matter with one of Frieda's horses? No, if there were, Frieda would be off to the horse tent at once.

Roxy was not kept wondering for long. The two men came directly toward her and stopped on the other side of the table.

"Good morning, kids," Mr. Hallock greeted Roxy and her cousins. "A little problem, Roxy. Fritz tells me that Erma is ill. Had a bad night with a stomach upset. Doc Markley thinks if she stays in bed this morning she can perform this afternoon. Fritz wonders if you would ride Ludwig in the parade?"

For a brief time Roxy couldn't speak. Her spine prickled all the way to her neck. To ride one of the Kassels' beautiful parade horses even just on the lot would be— But in the *parade!!*

"Oh, Mr. Hallock! May I? Is it all right with Frieda?"

Roxy stood up and her napkin fell unheeded from her lap.

"Sure. I asked her if she thought you were up to managing Ludwig in the parade and she said you could manage any horse on the lot." Mr. Hallock laughed. "Coming from Frieda, that's about as big a compliment as you're ever likely to get." He turned to Mr. Kassel. "Now, Fritz, your problem is solved."

Mr. Kassel smiled and bowed to Roxy. "I thank you for my daughter. She will be relieved. Helga thought of you since you ride and also are about the right size to wear Erma's costume."

Roxy watched the men leave, then looked across at Frieda and Martin; both were smiling at her. Frieda nodded and waved. Why, those two old darlings; they were glad for her!

"Oh, shoot!" Lilly exclaimed. "You'll be behind us and I can't watch you. Hey, Rox! Where are you going? You haven't finished your breakfast."

"Who can eat when there's a parade to ride in?" Roxy stopped and glanced back at her cousins.

"I can for one," Henri answered, buttering a thick slice of bread.

"Well, I can't. I'm going over to Wardrobe and see if I can wear that costume." Roxy shrugged ecstatically and laughed. "See you at paradetime."

Grandma and Sadie Modosky were already in the main dressing tent when Roxy appeared. "Oh, Grandma, have you heard? Mr. Hallock says I'm to ride in the parade."

Grandma smiled and winked at Sadie. "We heard. That's why Sadie and I are here early to see if we have to make any adjustments on Erma's parade clothes for you. Get in there and take off your dress."

Roxy was sure she would waken from a dream at any moment as the two women helped her into the satin dress glittering with green sequins. It was a riding habit for sidesaddle and the skirt was voluminous.

With a pincushion tied around her left wrist, Sadie looked Roxy over critically. "Fits pretty well, don't you think, Gracie?"

"Uh huh. But I think we'll have to take the belt in a mite. Pin it a little tighter and let's see." Grandma stood off and watched as Sadie pinned the dress at the waistline. "Good. That does it. Take it off, honey. Here, try on Erma's hat."

Roxy removed the dress, then picked up the large green hat, its brim covered with green ostrich plumes. She sat down at the dressing table, put it on, and looked in the mirror. Even without the dress, the hat was gorgeously becoming.

The dress in her hands, Sadie watched. "You know, Gracie, they call that a 'picture hat.' Well, if I ever saw a stunning picture, it's your granddaughter wearing it. Green was just made for red hair."

"Thank you, Sadie. Isn't it a good thing I'm not riding with the Frontenays. Red is bad on me." Roxy pulled the hat on one side and smiled at the reflection.

"Take the thing off," Grandma ordered brusquely. "And since you don't have to report to Frieda this morning, you can give us a hand around here."

As performers began to arrive to dress for the parade, they greeted Roxy enthusiastically, pleased that she was riding with them. It gave her a warm feeling of belonging.

In one of the smaller dressing rooms, Gretchen helped her into the sequined dress and hooked it. Helga rouged Roxy's cheeks slightly and accented her mouth with red cream from a jar. Never before had Roxy worn lip rouge.

The hat pinned on, Roxy couldn't believe the mirror. If Doug could only see her now! Wouldn't his eyes bug out? Who would believe that this was an Indiana farm girl? And as if this outfit weren't enough, she was to ride Ludwig!

Out in the main dressing room, the ballet girls made a fuss over her appearance. Roxy had never felt so important in her life. Even Grandma patted her shoulder and said, "You look fine, honey. Enjoy yourself."

Enjoy was too mild a word for it, Roxy thought as she mounted the spirited Ludwig and lined up on the lot with the Kassels. Karl changed places with Erma's husband, Bernie, and rode beside Roxy. Two months ago, Roxy was sure she would have exploded. But now she knew that Karl only wanted to ride beside her because she was Mimi's cousin. But she didn't care! She was riding in the parade and looked as gorgeous and as glamorous as any woman in the show. Mama, Mama, how *could* you have left all this?

"There comes Mrs. Jantry," Karl said.

Roxy turned her head. Sure enough, Frieda had left her white coach and was walking toward the Kassel troupe.

"Had to come and inspect you," she told Roxy as she looked her over carefully.

"Will I do, Frieda?" Roxy pulled Ludwig out of line and the horse stepped around in a small circle.

Frieda nodded. "Yes. Don't forget to keep your head up and smile. Too bad you have to wear that hat."

"Oh, I like it. Don't you think it becoming?"

"It's becoming all right, but it covers too much of your hair. Your hair gives more flash and flare than sequins. Don't ever forget that."

Roxy got back into line beside Karl and the bands started playing. As the parade moved, she thought she was going to burst with the thrill of it.

When they reached the street Karl said, "You handle Ludwig very well."

Roxy patted the horse's neck. "He's a good mount. I'm

147

glad to get more practice with sidesaddle. I never used one until Frieda had me ride Jupiter."

"Yes, I've watched you in the practice ring. That's a fine showy number you've been rehearsing."

Now the clatter of their horses' hoofs on the paved street joined the rest of the circus symphony: rattling, rumbling wagons, swishing elephants, wild-animal noises, clanking harness, and brassy bands.

So great was Roxy's excitement, she scarcely knew what she said to Karl. One thing was sure, she would remember Dayton, Ohio forever. Its broad streets, its fine downtown stores, its magnificent courthouse, its tall monument in the middle of the street where the parade turned, and its crowds and crowds of cheering people packed from curb to buildings on both sides of beautiful Main Street.

Once when the parade stopped, Ludwig shied and stepped sideways out of line. Roxy reined him in and the horse reared on his hind legs. Alarmed, Karl rode to her. But, thanks to her experience on Jupiter, Roxy kept her seat, calmed Ludwig, and pulled him into line.

"Did you see that?" Roxy heard a man say in a loud voice. "That girl knows her stuff when it comes to horses!"

The parade moved on. Karl grinned across at her. "Are you sure you didn't do that on purpose?"

Roxy laughed. "I really didn't, but I might have if I had thought of it."

"Roxy, can you keep a secret?" Karl asked as the parade stopped again briefly.

Roxy smiled at the crowd on her side of the street. "Why, I think so."

"Mimi and I made plans yesterday. We want to get married some weekend soon. We wondered if you would help us."

It was a good thing Ludwig hadn't chosen that moment to rear or she might have fallen from the sidesaddle.

"Married! But how can— There's Uncle Jules—and—" For the moment she forgot to smile. "And how could *I* help?"

"We're not sure yet how we'll manage it. But we decided to tell you, so that when the chance comes, you would know and perhaps could help us tell your Uncle Jules."

"You'll need lots of help to do that if you really manage to get married. And if I know Uncle Jules, you yourself may need protection. He has quite a temper."

"So Mimi tells me. But the way things are going at home—I may—"

"Home? You mean Germany?"

"Yes. Most particularly Austria, right now."

The band just behind struck up "The Stars and Stripes Forever." Strange, thought Roxy, the way all that hullabaloo in Europe could affect Mimi and Karl.

Karl rode over a little closer. "You'll keep our secret, Roxy?"

"Sure."

"And help us?"

"If I can."

The band made it difficult to talk. For the rest of the parade, Roxy smiled at people but forgot to remember how gorgeous she must look in Erma's dress and on Erma's horse. She thought of her cousin up there riding near her father. How Uncle Jules would let fly if those two did pull off a wedding!

Back on the lot in the small dressing room, Roxy removed Erma's costume and took the stitches out of the belt so it would be right for Erma tomorrow.

In the main section of the dressing tent Mimi waited for her and the two walked outside.

"Did he tell you, Rox?" Mimi asked in a low voice.

"Yes. Oh, Mimi, have you thought this over carefully?

149

Shouldn't you wait until the season's over and we get back to Winter Quarters? By that time Uncle Jules will know Karl better and see what a fine person he is." Roxy tried to sound wise and reasonable. Being in on this secret put responsibility on her shoulders. To whom should she be loyal, Uncle Jules or Mimi? But she had to keep their secret; she had promised Karl.

"Roxy, Papa will never feel different about Karl, even if we waited until this time next year. And who knows what next year will bring, or for that matter, next month? On August first, a Saturday, we'll be rolling into Indianapolis. Last year Fran and Ed Murray got married in a little town just outside. They got their license in Indianapolis and went out to this place that specializes in quick weddings. We'll be in Indianapolis three days, Saturday, Sunday, and Monday. Karl and I thought we could get our license on Saturday right after the parade, then take the last interurban car out to Mount Green and get married after the night performance."

"But who would tell Uncle Jules on Sunday?"

"We hope you'll break it to him. We'll be back on Monday morning."

"Me! Oh, Mimi! Uncle Jules would eat me alive if I told him a thing like that! But anyway, your parents would miss you on Saturday night."

"No. I've thought of that. I'll tell them I'm spending the night with you in Wardrobe's car. They know there's an empty berth there since Florence got sick and had to go home."

"Mimi, I hope you're doing the right thing."

"I know I am. I'm not the first girl who has eloped, you know. Your mother and mine both had trouble marrying the men they loved. Strange how easily fathers forget the past when thinking of their daughters."

They parted at the horse tent where Mimi waited for Karl, and Roxy went on to Frieda's.

"Did you enjoy parading?" Frieda asked.

"Oh, yes. Ludwig is a fine horse, but of course I'm fonder of Jupiter," Roxy added quickly. Frieda was so sensitive about her horses.

"What about your horse, Kentucky? Isn't that his name? I haven't heard you speak of him lately."

Roxy felt a stab of conscience. She hadn't thought of Tucky for days and seldom about anyone else at home either. "Oh, I love Tucky, Frieda, and it won't be long until I see him, I hope, when we show in Westwood."

She arranged Frieda's pillows and turned away. With the elopement on her mind, she probably would think of little else from now until August. How she wished they hadn't told her!

Chapter 12

HOMETOWN

During July, the Hallock Circus rolled across Ohio, Pennsylvania, West Virginia, Virginia, North Carolina, Tennessee, up western Kentucky, and into southern Illinois. Roxy's excitement at the approaching July 28 date in her home town was overshadowed by apprehension of August 1. The responsibility of breaking news of the elopement to her aunt and uncle the next day was a heavy one. They might never speak to her again. And Grandma, what would she say? If those three were mad at her, they might see to it that she *never* got to ride in the Big Top no matter how good she and Jupiter became.

Every Sunday, and often at odd times on weekdays, Frieda instructed her at the practice ring. Roxy and Jupiter were beginning to understand one another. She felt that Frieda was pleased at her progress although she never said so, just nodded and told her to do it again.

One Sunday as they neared the practice ring they met Johnny Ames on his way to lessons. Frieda stopped him.

"Johnny, before you go to Midgie's run over to Wardrobe and tell Gracie Riley I want her at the practice ring."

Johnny smiled at Roxy, then nodded to Frieda. "Yes, ma'am," he said and dashed off across the back yard in the opposite direction.

Roxy glanced at Frieda questioningly but said nothing.

"You're doing well enough now for Gracie to see what

I've done for you," Frieda said, narrowing her eyes and pressing her lips into a thin line.

Roxy mounted Jupiter as Grandma arrived. Frieda told the groom who had brought the horse to put two chairs beside the ring.

Roxy wished she could hear what the two old troupers were saying to one another. At a call from Frieda, Roxy put Jupiter through the routine they had been rehearsing.

"Unbraid your hair and do it again," Frieda yelled.

Roxy did as she was told. Dismounting after doing the stunt, she held Jupiter's bridle, and led him to the two onlookers.

"Well, Grandma, what do you think of it?"

Gracie gave Frieda an icy glance. "Well, other than having your hair stringing down your back, I can't say it's enough different to be any great shakes. It'll be a cold day in June before Frank will have me figuring out a costume for you. So don't get any ideas."

Frieda looked at Roxy then at Gracie and gave a short derisive laugh. "Oh, don't be so opinionated, Gracie. It may interest you to know that Frank's already watched us and thinks Roxy shows promise."

Gracie rose and gave a scornful toss of her head. "Well, all I can say is that you're just spoiling a good wardrobe assistant, putting Big Top ideas in her head this way. Roxy is a fine seamstress and I have plans for her."

"And so have I!" Frieda stood up. "Plans that have nothing to do with a sewing machine."

"Oh, come on, you two," Roxy interrupted. "Don't quarrel about me. Maybe I have some plans of my own. Grandma, I'll always like to sew. And, Frieda, you know how I feel about horses. So maybe I'll just be a horseback-riding dressmaker." She laughed and rubbed Jupiter's nose. "Of course I'm not good enough for the show, Grandma, but Frieda has taught me so much and I'm grateful."

153

For once Frieda was silent. Grandma took a few steps and ran a hand over Jupiter's shoulder. "Good horse," she remarked. "Reminds me of Aldo that I rode in the season of ninety-six. Remember, Frieda?"

"I do indeed, Gracie. A good routine you had too. Roxy, take Jupiter back," Frieda said.

Leading Jupiter toward the horse tent, Roxy wondered if the two women were quarreling now or reminiscing. Did Grandma really think her riding mediocre or did she just want to depreciate Frieda's instruction? Well, no matter what Grandma said, Roxy knew she and Jupiter were good. *And*—Frieda had said Mr. Hallock had been watching them! Of this Roxy had been unaware. Engrossed in thought, she gave a start at a voice behind her.

"Good work, Roxy. You and Jupe have class. Real class." Bo smiled, gave her shoulder a pat, and hurried away before she could thank him.

On July 27, they showed in Vincennes, Indiana. As Roxy helped fasten the chiffon cape to the shoulders of Frieda's gold-brocaded parade dress, Frieda said, "While I'm gone I want you to look in the bottom of my trunk and get out a white riding habit you'll find there. Check it for loose sequins or any mending it may need."

"All right. Are you going to wear it this afternoon?"

Frieda turned around. "No. You're going to wear it in the parade tomorrow. There's nothing a town likes more than to see one of its own in the parade. We mustn't disappoint Westwood."

"Oh, Frieda!" Roxy clasped her hands exultantly, then hugged her own shoulders in glee. "Oh, won't Doug Gardner pop when he sees me!"

"Doug Gardner? Who's he?"

"A boy I grew up with. Lives on the next farm. He was always trying to boss me around. He didn't want me to join the circus. But, I'll show him!"

Frieda eyed the rosy-cheeked Roxy contemplatively. "You will indeed. You must ride a white, parade horse right in front of my coach. Tonight braid your hair tightly and then let it hang loose during the parade, and—no hat."

Moving toward Westwood that night, it was difficult to get to sleep. During the morning, she had tried on Frieda's sidesaddle riding habit. With designs outlined in silver sequins, the white satin dress was strikingly flashy. Imagine wearing it right down Main Street tomorrow, with all her school friends looking at her.

And what would Mama think? And Papa? He probably wouldn't approve of her being a part of the parade. He and Doug were so sure she should be back on the farm. Tomorrow, wearing the white dress and preceding Frieda's coach would be even better than riding with the Kassels in Dayton.

Roxy wakened as soon as the second section stopped. She looked at her watch. Five o'clock. It was noisy outside. She hopped down and ran out to the back platform. Even in the half-light of dawn the tracks and railroad yard appeared different from all the others she had seen during the summer. These were familiar!

George came out on the platform. "Well, you're sure up early this morning, Roxy."

"Sure am. This is my home town. Think the weather will be good today?"

"It'll be fine. Look yonder at that sun coming up. Going to see your folks?"

"Oh, yes!" Roxy descended the steps and looked up and down the tracks. Unloading was at its height. Parade wagons were being rolled off flatcars; men, horses, and elephants plied their skill and strength to the operation. Young townsboys ran here and there trying to see everything, scurrying to get out of the way whenever a circus boss yelled at them. Roxy knew that alarm clocks had been set the night before so these boys would waken in time to watch the circus unload. Later, on the lot, the boys would earn tickets to the afternoon performance by carrying water for the elephants.

She was about to return to the car to dress when two figures came running from behind a wagon.

"Roxy!"

"Allen! Janet! Where did you come from? I was looking for you." She hugged her sister and brother. "How did you know where my car would be?"

"Mama knew," Janet said. "She and Papa are coming back there, but we ran."

"Doug came too," Allen said. "Oh, there's Grandma."

There was a hearty family reunion outside Wardrobe's car. Roxy was hugged and kissed by Mama and Papa and Doug. It was wonderful. Her hair in two tight pigtails made her look like a kid, Doug said. He pulled the braids and asked her when she was going to grow up. She didn't tell him the reason for the tight braids. Her appearance in the parade was to be a surprise for all of them.

Mama asked what time the third section would be in, she was so eager to see Aunt Marie and her family. And did Grandma think they could all come out to the farm for supper tonight?

"Don't think so, Martha," Grandma answered. "Why don't all of you plan to eat with us at the cookhouse today. Roxy, you skidaddle in there and get dressed and we'll go over and have breakfast."

Roxy brushed out her long hair, wavy from the tight braiding, twisted and pinned the knot across the back, then put on her lavender dress. Frieda had said it was her best color. Mama came into the car and visited with the wardrobe ladies while Roxy dressed.

Walking across the tracks between Janet and Doug,

Roxy chattered excitedly, about the circus, its people, the animals, and the cities in which they had showed.

"Janet," Doug interrupted. "She's the same old Rox, isn't she? Doesn't give us farmers a chance to get a word in."

"Hey, Roxy," Allen called out ahead. "Come on this way."

"But that's not the way to the Lot."

"We have to go to the depot first." Doug took her arm and guided her toward the small red-brick station down the track. When they rounded the corner of the building, Roxy saw the reason for coming this way.

There tied to the hitching rack was Tucky!

Qualms of conscience burned inside her as she ran to him. She had been so full of circus, she hadn't even asked about him!

The horse neighed recognition as she clasped his neck, stroked his head, and murmured endearing words.

Papa laughed at the effusive reunion. "Well, there's no doubt that Tucky still remembers you. Allen got up before the rest of us this morning to ride him in to see you. Now that Roxy's seen him, son, I think you better take him over to the livery stable for the day."

Later in Frieda's tent, dressing for the parade, Roxy thought she would never forget this day. How Mama had enjoyed herself at breakfast, talking with so many old friends, and meeting the new acts. The Frontenays had joined them at the table and Aunt Marie and Mama had talked a streak. And after breakfast Roxy had escorted her family and Doug to the Kassels' table and introduced them, then Alice Granville and the Donatos came over, and Bo and Midgie, then Frieda and Martin. Doug had scored with Alberto and Alice when he asked them about the elephant with the toothache Roxy had written about. She had caught a fleeting glimpse of Bo's face as he left the group. His wistful half-smile touched her. Poor Bo, he had no family.

Holding up the full skirt, she came from behind the curtain and stood in front of Frieda, seated at the dressing table.

"Well, how do I look?"

"Turn around." Frieda rose, smoothed the white dress across the back, then stepped away. "You'll do. Now get your brush and sit here at the dressing table and take the pins out of your hair."

Frieda brushed the hair that rippled down below Roxy's waistline. Then taking a narrow, white satin ribbon, she slipped it under the hair in the back and tied it in a small bow on top of Roxy's head.

"There, that will keep it in place, yet let it hang free and bright on the white dress. You don't need any rouge this morning, your face is all peaches and cream. Just a little lip rouge and then we must be on our way. Ned is saddling Alexander for you. He's as white as Jupiter and very steady for parading."

Near Frieda's coach a groom held Alexander's bridle. Roxy put her left foot in another groom's hands and he gave her a boost to the sidesaddle. Frieda came nearer and arranged the full, sparkling skirt to her liking.

Long, white kid gloves reached to Roxy's elbow-length sleeves. She felt very elegant as Uncle Jules and Aunt Marie inspected her. Uncle Jules told her she was the prettiest girl in the circus. Roxy thanked him and winced, wondering what he would think of her this time next week.

As number three clown wagon rolled past to its place, Bo stood up, waved, wiggled his ears, and shouted, "You're all right, Red! Give 'em the works girl! Give 'em the works!"

The other clowns cheered as Roxy waved at them. Her cheeks burned with excitement. Bo liked her!

It was a striking figure that rode alone in front of Frieda's coach. With the exception of the long, bright, wavy hair, all was white, even Alexander's harness.

Holding the reins in one hand, Roxy's other hand was raised again and again to wave at friends calling to her from the sidewalks along Main Street. She could hear remarks.

"Say, isn't that Red Clark's girl?"—

"Hello, there, Roxy!"—

"Roxy, Roxy Clark! Yoo-hoo!"—

"Well, forevermore! That's the Clark girl!"

Her teachers, members of her church, school friends, Mose from the livery stable, county people she had known at Grange Hall, they all cheered and called to her as she rode by.

Up ahead she could see the courthouse where the parade was turning onto Washington Street. There on the corner near the curb stood the Clarks and the Gardners.

Janet saw her first, yelled, and shook her father's arm. "It's Roxy! Look, oh, look, Papa!"

Roxy waved and laughed at their astonishment. Doug's mouth dropped open, then spread into a grin as he waved his hat. He was saying something. Probably, "Well, I'll be darned!" How satisfying to surprise the old smarty for once!

Mama was nodding and smiling, probably remembering how it was to ride in a parade. Papa smiled at first, then frowned a little. Now what was going through that red pate of his? Roxy wondered as she rode on.

Back on the lot she found her family waiting in the back yard.

"I thought the parading you did in Dayton was a one-time thing. That's what you wrote," Papa said.

"Sure, it was. Today was just special. Frieda thought I should parade in my home town."

Janet stroked the parade dress. "Oh, Rox, it's so soft and beautiful. If you just had a crown, you'd look like a princess."

Roxy laughed. "Frieda said—nothing on the head—no hat—nothing."

Mama looked puzzled. "No hat?"

"Nope." Roxy reached over and rumpled Allen's hair. "It's the Clark hair, Mama. She likes it. Say, will you wait till I change, then we can go eat. Where's Doug?"

"Went home with his family to do some chores. They're coming back to see the evening performance," Papa said. "We have to go home too, to tend to things as soon as we eat with you. But we'll be back."

"Well, listen, let Allen and Janet stay with me. Frieda has given me the day off." Roxy turned to her brother and sister. "As soon as we eat, I'll take you kids to the side show."

She removed her parade finery, wrapped it in tissue paper, returned it to the trunk and sighed, feeling a little depressed. Her moment of grandeur was over. Had Doug liked the way she looked in the parade? Had he just gone out to the farm on purpose so he wouldn't see her and be tempted to give her a compliment? He was like that, the old prune! Now Bo had made no bones about it. He'd been pleased with her appearance and said so.

Janet and Allen watched their sister admiringly as she lifted a hand to the ticket taker at the side show saying, "Hi, Jake. These are my brother and sister."

"Hi, Roxy. Go on in."

Inside the large tent, she led them from platform to platform introducing them to side-show performers. These strange people were no longer freaks to Roxy, but friends with whom she ate and to whom she talked every day. She knew all about the tattooed lady's mother back in Iowa who had tuberculosis, about the trouble the giant had with his feet, about what they fed Gertrude to maintain her advertised weight, about the quarrels that went on among the Marshall midgets, about the fire-eater's love affair with one of the ballet girls, about the pride one of the oriental dancers took in the fact that her two sons were making good in the Big Top as tumblers, and that Mary Duncan, the snake charmer, dreamed of the day her five-year-old Susy would make the Big Top as a bareback rider.

Janet and Allen had very big eyes as these queer friends of Roxy's talked to them, asked them about school, what they were going to be when they grew up, how they were spending the summer—just like ordinary people.

Leaving the side show, Roxy took her brother and sister around to the back yard where preparations for the afternoon performance were in progress. She introduced them to her friends—performers, animal men, grooms, the postmaster, the cooks, elephant men, and on and on.

"Gosh, they all call you Roxy!" Janet exclaimed.

"Yep. Easy name to remember. But say, there's a fellow you met at breakfast. He calls me Red. Hey, Bo."

Bo Bentley, dressed and made up for his first entrance, approached with Herman in his arms.

"Hi there, you three Reds. Having fun?" Bo endeared himself to Janet and Allen by letting them pet Herman and lead him around by his harness. Bo showed them the mechanics by which he wiggled his huge ears, then took them into clown alley to see the wagon Herman appeared to pull around the track.

Allen was fascinated by Bo's make-up, the big nose, the extended red mouth, the black and red cheek designs on the white face, and the pointed eyebrows.

"Every clown with the Hallock Circus has a different face," Bo told him. "This one is my trademark. I invented it and I paint it the same everyday. We never copy another's face. It would be like stealing a guy's wallet."

Now the band started playing inside the Big Top. The performers began lining up for the grand entry; some walked, others rode in fancy vehicles, some were on horseback.

"Come on kids," Roxy said. "We'll watch in the connection."

They slipped around and between performers, and along the side of the connection way into the Big Top. Jim Daggett, just ready to make for center ring, saw them. He had met all the Clarks at breakfast.

"Having a good time?" he asked Allen and Janet. Speechless at being so near the tall-hatted ringmaster, they nodded. "Here, Roxy, why don't you take them right there to see the show. There's room at the end of the second row."

"Thanks, Jim." Roxy led the way to the empty place next to the connection.

Janet and Allen knew that Grandma had reserved seats for them for tonight's performance. But even those wouldn't be as good as here on the plain board seats so near to where the whole show entered, and practically every performer spoke to their sister. She told them about each one.

Bo tipped his tiny hat to them as he passed. And how Roxy especially loved Frieda that afternoon. Before each of her exits, she stopped right in front of them and her horse bowed. Janet was so thrilled the first time that she dropped her bag of peanuts on the ground under the bleachers.

The performance over, Roxy led the way to the cookhouse and found places for Janet and Allen, with three extra for Mama and Papa and—one for Doug in case he came back with them. She felt a certain satisfaction when

Doug, tall and sun-browned, arrived with her parents and climbed over the bench to sit beside her.

"Hello there, Roxane Clark, queen of the circus." He grinned at her. "You really thought you were some punkins this morning, didn't you? I hardly knew you diked up in all those spangles."

Across the table, Allen and Janet were telling their parents about the afternoon's adventures. Roxy settled back smugly. Now Doug was going to say how pretty she had looked on Alexander this morning, and how well she handled the horse.

"You should see the new calves out home," he said between bites. "And, Roxy, our wheat harvest is the best ever this year. Dad's bought the Goodman place there to the east of us. Going to put the fields into wheat and alfalfa next year."

"What's happened to the Goodmans?" She ate slowly. He obviously wasn't going to say a word about her appearance in the parade.

"They've moved to town. Lafe's getting too old to farm any more. Say, can you see the show with me tonight? I bought two reserved-seat tickets hoping you could."

"Now, Doug, that was crazy. I can see the show free any time."

"I know, but I want you to sit with me."

It seemed strange to Roxy to go through the front yard to see the show. The ticket taker at the main entrance raised his eyebrows at her as she and Doug passed through. "So, Roxy—they've kicked you out of the back yard, have they?"

"They sure have, Will." She laughed as she preceded Doug into the menagerie tent. "Come over here, Doug, and see Luly."

Seated in the reserved-seat section, she noticed that their seats were far away from the Gardners and Clarks.

Had Doug planned this? Maybe *now* he would say how lovely her hair had looked this morning.

"Aren't you getting a little fed up with all this circus whoop-la by now?" Doug asked as they watched Westwood people find seats.

"Heavens no! I love it. And I'm doing very well in the practice ring. Frieda is teaching me. She says Mr. Hallock has his eye on me. So—who knows, this time next year you just might be sitting here watching *me* perform."

"Rox, you're getting too old for such nonsense. It's time you came back where you belong. Doggone it, Roxy, I miss you. Why don't you quit the show right now and go home with your folks tonight."

"Doug, you're crazy. I won't come home until the season's over. I've got a job. Frieda Jantry needs me. I'm earning money and I love my work. If you just got me here to pester me, I'm leaving right now." Angered, she half rose.

"Oh, sit down and keep your shirt on! There's the band."

In spite of Doug's berating, she enjoyed explaining to him the backgrounds of her circus friends.

Watching Helga standing on a circling resinback with Karl on her shoulders, Roxy told Doug about Mimi's love affair. But concerning the prospective elopement, she kept silent.

Doug removed his coat, folded it, and put it across his lap. He took out the newspaper protruding from the side pocket and unfolded it.

"They got out an 'Extra' in town this afternoon," he said.

Roxy glanced over his shoulder and read the big headlines.

AUSTRIA-HUNGARY DECLARES WAR ON SERBIA

"Oh, so that murder in Sarajevo really did it! Mr. Hallock thought it might." She looked back at the ring

164

and saw Karl run from the center and leap astride the bareback horse.

"I didn't know circus people kept up with current events." Doug returned the paper to the pocket.

"We are really quite intelligent, Mr. Gardner." She watched the Hagens in ring three, then turned back to center. Did Karl know about this declaration of war? Was this the beginning of what he said he feared in Europe? Could all that was happening so far away touch this circus world of hers?

She turned and caught Doug looking down at her instead of at the performers. "You've got some real cute freckles all over your nose, Rox."

Roxy heaved an exasperated sigh. "Doug, you're a nut! Here I parade down Main Street looking like a queen and you don't even mention it, all you notice is freckles!"

"I'm not interested in queens. I just like a farm girl— Roxy Clark to be exact." He squeezed her hand and looked back at the Kassels.

Roxy watched Karl, and withdrew her hand. The way Doug downgraded the circus and performers made her tired! Stuffy—that's what he was! Him and his farm!

Chapter 13

THE ELOPEMENT

Again with Frieda next morning in Penfield, Roxy's mind wandered often to her exciting home-town day. Last night the Gardners and Clarks had escorted her to her car after the performance. Just as she had been about to board, Doug had led her away from the others into the shadows and placed a firm, no-nonsense kiss on her mouth.

"There, Roxy, my girl, that's to let you know how much I miss you. And if you don't come home pretty soon, I just might be coming to fetch you," he had said.

At the time she had laughed lightly and made a facetious remark. She had liked the kiss but she was going to forget it. Too confusing when she had more important things on her mind.

"I missed you yesterday," Frieda told her. "Guess I'm getting old. I like being pampered."

"Anyone who can ride as you do will never be old," Roxy said.

"It was good to see your mother again yesterday," Frieda said, sitting at the dressing table. "Farm life has agreed with her. She's as pretty as ever."

Roxy said nothing. She never thought of Mama as pretty. After all she was just Mama. But maybe she took both her parents too much for granted. Knowing they

166

would always be there when she needed them, other people seemed so much more interesting.

"That Gardner boy is a handsome lad," Frieda was saying. "He certainly has big eyes for you. Anything going on there in the romance department?"

"Goodness no! He's just the boy next door, so to speak. Known him all my life. I've told you how we've played and fought together for years. I expect some day Doug will be the best farmer in the county, maybe even in the state." Roxy put down the brush and coiled Frieda's hair into a soft knot.

"Well, my guess is that whatever he wants he'll go after." Frieda handed Roxy hairpins as she needed them.

"He sure will." It probably was a good thing Doug wasn't around the circus all the time, Roxy thought. His kisses probably could become distracting.

On Friday in Shelbyville, Mimi's secret weighed heavily upon Roxy. Mimi hadn't said another word about the elopement. Roxy hoped they had called it off. If they were going to be married, it would be so much better to wait until they got back to Kingston in October and could have a proper wedding. If she herself ever got married, she thought, she wanted to have it in their church at home with all the trimmings—walking down the aisle holding Papa's arm and wearing a veil a mile long, then have a big wedding supper for everybody out at the farm.

October would be a nice month to have a wedding. It was so beautiful at the farm in October. Every tree would be brilliant with color, and there would be that tangy scent in the air that you smelled only in autumn—the smell of the full corncrib, ripe apples, grapes, and there would be spicy catsup boiling on the kitchen stove.

She set the buckets in the tent behind the curtain. Well, Mimi and Karl probably weren't going to wait until October, so she'd better brace herself to face the music on Sunday. Perhaps Mr. Hallock himself might be displeased at the elopement, especially if Uncle Jules raised a howl. And when Mr. Hallock found out that she had known what was going on and hadn't told, she might even lose her present job to say nothing of any chance she might have in the Big Top.

In the cookhouse that evening, Roxy ate supper with Angie Heller. Angie brought her up to date on gossip among the ballet girls. Alice Granville joined them.

"Alice, you're looking a bit on the draggy side tonight. What's the matter?" Angie asked.

"You know, I think I've caught Luly's toothache. The whole side of my jaw is throbbing. I've got to hunt a dentist tomorrow in Indianapolis. I was wondering, Roxy, if you'd be willing to ride Luly for me in the parade in the morning." Elbow on the table, Alice held her aching jaw in her hand. "I spoke to Alberto. He agreed you'd be fine. You said you'd never ridden an elephant."

"Alice, I'd love to! That is, if Frieda says I may." Roxy hopped up. "Let's go ask her."

Frieda looked at Alice's swollen jaw sympathetically as she heard Roxy's request. "If you want to ride that rolling old mountain tomorrow, I suppose I can manage. Just be sure to tell Joe to have some one bring over my hot water."

"Oh, I'll arrange all that. Thanks, Frieda."

"I don't know what for. A ride on an elephant is pure torture. And don't forget we parade a long distance in Indianapolis. She'll find out, won't she, Martin?" Frieda turned to her husband.

"Roxy, with all this parading and the way Frieda tells me you and Jupiter are progressing, it looks as though you'll soon be leaving the ranks of us behind-the-scenes folks." He laughed and winked at Frieda.

"Well, not soon, Mr. Jantry," Roxy said. "This will just

be my third parade. And so far, Mr. Hallock hasn't been dangling any Big Top contract in front of my nose."

"I'll skin him if he does," Frieda said. "Now that I've trained you I'm damn sure not going to lose you."

Roxy looked down at Frieda. "Well, you haven't yet." Walking away she couldn't help wondering. If Frieda didn't want to lose her as a lady's maid, why all those hours teaching her in the practice ring?

Next morning in Indianapolis, Roxy took her diary from her suitcase and put it in her purse before leaving the car. She hadn't written anything in it since last Monday. With all that was going to happen today, she better write down the day in her home town before she forgot details.

She was early at the cookhouse and found a place back in a corner by herself. Eating with her left hand, she wrote about parading in white satin and sequins, and all the other events of the day, then—"Doug at Wardrobe's car!" There, that was enough. Anyone else reading this wouldn't know about the kiss. She added, "Doug disapproves of the circus, at least having me in it." That statement put the kiss in proper perspective.

As an afterthought she wrote, "Doug had a newspaper that said Austria had declared war today, July 28."

She put the marker at today's date, August 1, 1914. It was likely to be a big day in this big city.

It was fun being in the main dressing tent again. Alice had already left for the dentist, but had hung out the costume. Roxy put it on, long, royal-blue oriental trousers, a bright-red blouse, and a sleeveless jacket. A broad, gold sash went around the hips.

Grandma stepped in to see how she was getting on. "Hmmm. I don't like red on you," she said. "That veil over your head doesn't cover your hair."

"But Frieda said I should never cover any of it," Roxy remonstrated.

"Now don't start Frieda-ing me. In this department I'm the boss. Let's see what Alice has here." Grandma rummaged through the open trunk. "Here, this will do. Sit down there and pin your hair up higher."

Roxy complied and Grandma wound a piece of gold brocade around the red hair, completely covering it in a turban. Looking in the mirror, Roxy thought Grandma was right; it *is* an improvement.

Outside Alice's dressing room, Roxy saw Mimi dressed for the parade. "Oh, Roxy, today's the day! We're going to the courthouse right after the parade. Then tonight after the performance—" Mimi stopped and her eyelids lowered over her sparkling eyes as her mother approached.

"Well, don't you look cute, Roxy!" Aunt Marie said. "I hear you're riding Luly. Mimi, will you go back in there and help Lilly? She's grumbling about something of hers she says you lost."

Out on the lot, Roxy walked across to Luly who headed the long line of elephants. Luly was splendid wearing her red velveteen blanket and the gold-decorated howdah was perched on her back. Gus, the elephant man who rode on Luly's head, nodded and smiled at Roxy.

"Morning, Gus. I'm to be Luly's passenger this morning." She looked up at the howdah and gasped. How high it was up there!

On command Luly knelt, Gus gave Roxy a hand; she stepped on the trunk, grabbed Luly's harness, scrambled across her head, and climbed into the howdah. Seated, she watched Gus sit on the elephant's head.

Luly got up and now it was like being in a lookout tower. Roxy could see the procession forming ahead of her, the long string of elephants, camels, and calliope back of her. Alberto rode up on his black horse, waved, then took his place just in front of Luly.

Those ahead started to move out and Roxy was thrown against the side of the howdah as her mount lurched forward. She grabbed the sides and held on tightly. Side to side and up and down with a rolling motion, Luly rocked the howdah as a rough sea rocks a small ship. Roxy tensed every muscle to keep her seat.

How was she going to smile at people through miles of this? By the time they reached the city limits she was feeling nauseated. It was a good thing she had eaten an early breakfast, otherwise she might disgrace the Hallock parade.

Gus looked back at her. "How ya doing?"

"Not too well. Doesn't Luly ever move smoother?"

Gus laughed. "Nope. You'll do better if you sit loose and roll with her."

Roxy loosened her grip a little and relaxed, letting her body sway as it would. Why, that *was* better! Frieda said riding an elephant was pure torture, but maybe it didn't have to be if one got the knack of it.

She couldn't hear the bands ahead because of the calliope so close behind. Now, under the fingers of Hap Winters, that old steam piano back there was filling the streets with "Down by the Old Mill Stream," "There's a Long Long Trail," "Can't You Hear Me Callin', Caroline," and "Alexander's Ragtime Band." Hap played only popular music on the calliope, never the classical numbers Miles Wallace used in the band.

Indianapolis looked so different from this vantage point, Roxy thought, as they came to the business section. Alberto's outriders spurred ahead now, cautioning people with, "Hold your horses, the elephants are coming."

Several blocks ahead, as the parade turned into another street, Roxy caught the sparkle of red that was the Frontenays. Oh, dear! This time tomorrow!

Looking down into the admiring, upturned faces along the curbs, she wondered what those people would say if they knew that underneath powder and rouge and fancy costume, the exotic lady on the elephant was just a freckled-faced farm girl. She suppressed a giggle, waved, and smiled at her vast audience.

It *was* a long parade and Roxy was glad to see the lot come into view. Gus helped her down and said, "Well, how did you like it?"

"A good view from up there. But if I can have my rathers, I prefer parading on a horse."

Inside the dressing tent, Roxy stopped. Mimi, in street clothes, emerged from the dressing room she shared with her mother and Lilly.

"Say, how did you change so fast?" Roxy asked.

Mimi smiled. "Had to. It will hustle us to get back from the courthouse in time for the afternoon performance. If you can, keep out of Mama and Lilly's sight. I told them you and I were eating together."

"But Mimi, what shall I say if they do see me?"

"Oh, use your imagination. You'll think of something."

"I'm not a good liar. Mama could always tell when I was stretching the truth." Roxy untied her sash and folded it.

"Well, then go hide someplace." Mimi gave Roxy a quick excited kiss. "Wish me luck, Rox," she whispered and away she ran.

In Alice's dressing room, Roxy put away the costume and donned her own clothes. Now to avoid Aunt Marie.

What if she went over to the cookhouse to eat now and Aunt Marie saw her? She didn't dare run the risk of sitting at a table. If Aunt Marie questioned her about Mimi, she knew she'd give it away.

She walked behind the cookhouse tent and into the kitchen section where Ellen and Lem Ames managed the enormous cooking operation. Dishes clattered, kettles bubbled, and oven doors rattled as the kitchen crew took out huge pans of browned biscuits. Filling plates rapidly, deft hands set them out on a long table to be carried into the serving area. Roxy took a filled plate, grabbed a knife and fork, smiled at the cooks, and hurried out the backway to Frieda's tent.

A fine thing, having to hide away like this to eat, she thought as she set the plate on Frieda's trunk and pulled up a chair. Before she finished, Frieda returned.

"Well, did the ride on Luly do you in so that you couldn't make it to the cookhouse?"

"Oh, no. Just thought I'd eat here where it's quieter."

Frieda removed her dress, put on a kimono, and lay down on the cot. "Say, you didn't happen to see Karl Kassel anywhere did you?"

Roxy gave a start. "No, why?"

"Helga and Fritz were looking for him all over the place. Somebody brought word that Germany has just declared war on Russia. Fritz looked awfully worried. Helga said something about Karl's commitment to the Kaiser's army. I don't know what she meant. But I'd say all hell is breaking loose over there in Europe. I'd think the Kassels would thank their lucky stars they're in this country."

Roxy put down her fork. Suddenly she wasn't hungry and Europe didn't seem as far away as she had thought. Would this news alter Mimi and Karl's plans?

Everyone slept late next morning, even Grandma. Wakened by voices in the aisle, Roxy stuck her head out between the curtains. It was Grandma and Lilly.

"But, of course Mimi's here, Grandma," Lilly was saying. "Papa sent me over to tell her we are all going in town to church this morning for eleven o'clock service and she's to come with us."

"Mimi is *not* here I tell you. Whatever gave you the idea that she was?" Grandma frowned at Lilly.

"She told Mama she was spending the night with Roxy. I heard her."

Grandma looked up at the head protruding above. "Roxy, what do you know about this?"

"Me? Why, why—I don't know *where* Mimi is," Roxy replied truthfully.

"Lilly, you go back and tell your mother we haven't seen hide nor hair of her wandering child. Look in Alice's car, she could be there." Grandma reached back in her berth for a towel.

"But she said she'd be here," Lilly insisted.

"I don't care what she said. Now skidaddle. I've got to dress."

Lilly disappeared and Grandma looked up at Roxy. "Now, young lady, get down here and tell me what you know about Mimi."

Roxy descended slowly. Oh, dear, she'd have to tell. No one could lie to Grandma. She was as good at seeing through prevarication as Mama.

"I told you, Grandma, I don't know where she is." She looked into penetrating eyes.

"I know what you said. But you know something. I can tell by your voice. Now, out with it."

"Mimi—Mimi and Karl got a marriage license yesterday and went out to a little place called Mount Green to get married last night after the performance." There, it was out! Roxy sighed with relief.

"Married! Those two children? Oh, the little devils! Jules will hit the sky! And just how long have you been in on this, young lady?"

"Since Dayton."

Grandma scowled and shook her head. "That's almost a month ago. Why didn't you tell me?"

"I promised not to. And Grandma, they are *not* children. Karl is twenty and Mimi seventeen and both of them have good jobs. What's so awful about it? They're in love!" Roxy unbraided her hair.

"Jules doesn't approve of Karl, that's why."

"But Karl didn't want to marry Uncle Jules."

By this time the others in the car were in the aisle asking, "You mean Mimi and Karl are married?"

"It looks that way," Grandma answered. "Get dressed, Roxy. You and I have to go over and tell Marie and Jules."

Roxy knew she would never forget Sunday, August 2. She thought Uncle Jules was going to burst as his face turned to red and then to a near purple when Grandma told him. Sparks seemed to shoot out from the sharp points of his small, upturned mustache as he lashed out at Roxy for not telling him in time to prevent the "catastrophe," as he called it.

Aunt Marie took the news more calmly. Roxy wondered if she hadn't suspected all along that this might happen.

"I'll go over and tell Helga and Fritz," Aunt Marie said quietly. "Probably they have missed Karl by this time."

"You stay away from those Germans!" Uncle Jules shouted. For the first time Roxy heard him use oaths as he spoke of the Kassels.

"I don't care what they are, Jules. Their son is our son now. Nothing you can say will change it. Cool down. You forget I was just seventeen when I married you."

"But that was different."

"Oh, I don't know," Grandma said wryly. "You should have heard what Mike called you when he found out. You broke up a very good riding act. Remember?"

Uncle Jules looked startled. "Well, Mimi better not think of giving up trapeze for horses. I'll not stand for that."

Roxy caught Aunt Marie's eye and the two exchanged

quick smiles. How good it was that Aunt Marie hadn't forgotten how it was to be young!

The rest of the day was not as drowsy and lazy as most Sundays. It wasn't every day that canvas city had an elopement to talk about. When it was discovered that Roxy had been in on the secret, many came to Frieda's tent to get the details.

Ellen Ames arrived from the cookhouse to ask what time Roxy thought the newlyweds would return on Monday. She wanted to bake them a wedding cake. Jim Oldknoe went around with his big hat in hand taking up a collection for a wedding present.

Since they had already paraded in Indianapolis the day before, there was to be no parade on Monday. Roxy hoped Mimi and Karl would return by eleven or so; preparations were being made for a big celebration at the noon meal.

All Sunday afternoon Midgie had the children cutting out big letters and fastening them on a long string which said—YEARS OF HAPPINESS FOR MIMI AND KARL. This they hung across the middle of the cookhouse.

Early Monday morning, Jim Oldknoe and Jim Daggett went to town to buy the present.

The radiant couple reached the lot at ten minutes to twelve. Surrounded by well-wishers, Roxy couldn't get to them. Uncle Jules was not in sight.

Ellen's wedding cake was a work of art, Roxy thought. Mimi and Karl laughed and shook hands with everyone. Before the meal was over, Mr. Hallock himself presented the big box the two Jims had brought from town. It was a huge, silver tea service, deeply carved with fancy curlicues. The two Jims should have had a woman along on that buying trip, Roxy thought. What on earth would Mimi and Karl do with such a monstrosity?

Watching them, however, she could see they were

176

touched by the love that had come with the gift and gave no thought to its incongruity.

Later, eating ice cream amidst the hum of conversation, Roxy had a sense of ease and relaxation. It had all turned out very well. She had gotten over her crazy idea about Karl, she had kept their secret, they were married, and although Uncle Jules had blown up yesterday, he wasn't giving them any trouble today.

No sooner had the last thought crossed her mind than conversation began to fade. Roxy looked across to the entrance and hastily swallowed a spoonful of ice cream that froze her throat all the way down.

There stood Uncle Jules, his face white, his glance burning holes through them all as his eyes darted from table to table. Spotting Mimi and Karl, he waved a newspaper and almost ran toward them.

Slamming the newspaper down in front of Karl he shouted, "You damned dirty German! You took my daughter and now you fight my country!"

Karl looked at the headlines and turned pale. Aunt Marie, sitting next to Roxy, reached over and turned the paper around.

Roxy read the headlines.

GERMANY DECLARES WAR ON
FRANCE AND INVADES BELGIUM.

Chapter 14

NEW GROOM FOR JUPITER

The two Monday performances in Indianapolis went well. Standing in the connection watching the dainty Mimi fly to her father's hands as usual, Roxy again marveled at the perfection. Who would ever dream of the turmoil inside those two?

And Karl—his flawless performance, his dignified acknowledgment of applause—no one in the audience could guess his inner conflicts, Roxy thought. There must be joy at having lovely Mimi at last and anguish at being so disliked by Uncle Jules. But she imagined the European situation disturbed him even more than Uncle Jules's anger.

Next day, Tuesday, August 4, the circus showed in Marion, Indiana. As soon as Frieda was dressed after her last appearance in the afternoon, Roxy hurried to the cookhouse to eat an early supper. She must write to Mama while events of the last few days were vivid. Back at Frieda's she put a tablet on the trunk, sat down, and began to write about Mimi's elopement. Knowing how interested Mama would be, she included each detail of the scene in the cookhouse.

"And when he slammed that newspaper on the table, Karl turned white and so did Helga and Fritz. Must stop, Frieda just came in to dress for tonight's show. More later.

"Well, Frieda's off for the grand entry. Martin was here a few minutes ago to tell us the latest. England declared war on Germany today. He seemed awfully disturbed about it. Somehow I hadn't thought happenings way off there could affect us. But Martin says we have people in the show from almost all the countries involved in this thing and may have trouble on the lot. And of course none of it helps Uncle Jules feel more kindly toward Karl. Poor Mimi.

"I don't have time to write to Doug, so you let him read this letter. Tomorrow Toledo."

She signed it "With love," put it in the envelope, addressed and stamped it.

Standing outside waiting for Frieda, she looked up at the stars. What a fine summer night! She really did have time to write Doug, she admitted to herself, but somehow she didn't want to. She remembered his brown, lean face, his broad shoulders, his hard muscular arms that could push a plow for hours, wield an ax at the woodpile, carry a wobbly-legged colt into the barn as if it were a tiny baby, and that had held her so tightly there in the shadows by Wardrobe's car. If only he weren't so bull-headed.

Saturday, they set up in Cleveland for three days. On Sunday, Frieda and Roxy went to the practice ring at eleven. Roxy fed Jupiter the sugar and carrots she had brought, then mounted and rehearsed the routine again and again under Frieda's direction.

From the corner of her eye, she saw Mr. Hallock sit down beside Frieda just outside the ring. Roxy whispered to Jupiter, "Come on, boy! Do it right. The boss is watching!"

On the next round, however, she discovered that the boss was still speaking to Frieda and not watching the ring at all. Roxy gave out with a loud "Up, up, Jupiter!" to attract attention, but the two talked on without giving her a glance. Then Mr. Hallock got up, waved briefly to Roxy, and was gone.

Well, doggone him! She stopped Jupiter in front of Frieda.

"What did Mr. Hallock think of Jupiter and me?" she asked.

"He didn't say. Had other things on his mind. Get on with it, and get that horse up higher. This afternoon you are going to have a go on the hippodrome track."

Roxy clamped her right knee tighter around the saddle horn and pulled Jupiter to his hind feet. Clasping the handle firmly as she let loose of the reins, she lay back and caught a fast glimpse of blue sky. This afternoon she would be looking up at canvas in the Big Top!

Before the hour was up, Mimi and Karl came leading one of the Kassels' resinbacks. Both newlyweds wore practice tights. So—Roxy thought, already Karl was changing Mimi into a rider. Uncle Jules would be furious.

Frieda spoke to them, then called to Roxy. "That's enough for this morning. Be at the connection at two and we'll time your routine on the track. I'm meeting Martin. I'll stop at the horse tent and send a groom over for Jupiter, if you want to stay and watch Mimi's lesson."

"Thanks, Frieda." Roxy jumped down and led the white horse from the ring. "It's all yours," she said to Mimi and Karl. "Is Karl trying to get you off the trapeze, Mimi?"

Mimi laughed. "Oh, Rox, I've always wanted to learn to stand on a horse. I've tried but could never make it. Karl says it's easy and he'll teach me."

Karl nodded at Roxy. "Anyone who can fly as she does can certainly learn a few tricks on Bismarck's back." He turned to his wife and said softly, "Come on, *liebchen.*"

Jupiter's bridle over her arm, Roxy stood behind the chair Frieda had left and watched. With Mimi in front of Karl, the two sat astride the broad-backed Bismarck as he circled the ring. Karl got to his feet, bouncing on his toes with the up and down movement of the horse. He reached down.

"Now, give me your hands and get up," he told Mimi. "Bounce with the horse and always on your toes. Watch out for the heels."

As Mimi stood in front of her husband, Roxy gave a sigh of satisfaction. So handsome they were, with Mimi's black hair a perfect compliment to Karl's blondness. What a fine appearance they would make together in an act. Roxy began thinking of costumes she would like to design for them.

"May I take Jupiter, Miss?" a voice said behind her.

Roxy whirled around at the sound of it, her eyes opened wider, and she gasped incredulously.

"Doug!" The exclamation out, she was speechless.

"Well, well, at last I have flabbergasted the great Roxy Clark, even if I did have to come miles to do it. I arrived last night but I've been too busy on my new job to look you up. Your nice Frieda just came over and told me to come for your horse. Very understanding lady, Mrs. Jantry."

"Your job? But why—how—?" Roxy sputtered, trying to understand.

Doug took Jupiter's bridle from her and smiled down into her astonished face. "It's a long story which I'll tell you when I have time. Right now I've got to care for this horse according to Frieda's specifications. I understand from Ed Nedosky that she'll be around to check up on me in a little while. But I just wanted you to know that for the rest of the season there's a new groom in the horse tent. At your service, ma'am." He bowed facetiously, laughed at her still dumfounded expression and led Jupiter away.

Mimi slipped off Bismarck and ran to Roxy. "Hey, wasn't that Doug? And what's he doing here?"

Roxy, her eyes still on the new groom crossing the back yard leading Jupiter, shook her head in disbelief. "Search me. He says he has a job as a groom." She turned to Mimi. "But it doesn't make sense. He's a farmer, and at this time of year, there are a million things to do on a farm. I'm sure his father can't spare him. How did he get a job and why would he join the circus in midseason? I don't get it. But then Doug's unpredictable."

Mimi laughed. "You don't get it? Roxy, you're a dunce! Get along to Frieda's and look in her mirror, then you'll see his reason."

Roxy smiled then sobered. "Oh, you don't know Doug. He'd never neglect the farm just to see a girl. And besides he's always seen me every day. I'm old stuff to him."

Mimi looked Roxy over from head to foot. "You don't look old stuff to me. Riding breeches and boots become you and I bet Doug thinks so too."

"Mimi," Karl called. "Let's get on with the lesson."

Roxy walked slowly around the cookhouse tent to Frieda's. Had Doug really come because of her or had he just wanted some weeks of adventure? And how had he got the job anyway? Had he made some inquiries when the show had been in Westwood? But to desert the farm at this time of year—well, it was crazy, leaving his father in the soup like that. Absolutely crazy! And she'd tell him so the next time she saw him.

Frieda and Martin were sitting in front of the tent reading a Sunday paper. Martin looked up and smiled.

"Well, Roxy, I hear there's a new groom on the lot. How about that? I shouldn't wonder but what you'll be making more trips to feed sugar to Frieda's horses from now on. Right?"

Roxy looked closely at Frieda. There was a half-smile on her lips as she kept her eyes on the paper. "Maybe," Roxy answered. "Frieda, did you know Doug was on the lot?"

"Not until Frank told me this morning," Frieda said, dropping the paper to her lap.

So—that was what those two had been talking about! "Then *you* went over and told Doug to come for Jupiter?"

"Well, I told Ed that from now on I want Doug to care for my stock. He's sure to do a better job than any of those other lazy galoots over there."

"Did Mr. Hallock say how it happened that he took Doug on in midseason?"

Martin spoke. "We always need good grooms, Roxy. Roustabouts, animal men, and grooms fall by the wayside all the time."

"Yes, but why—?"

Martin looked down at his paper. "Things are sure getting in a mess over in Europe. The Germans are plowing right across poor little Belgium. Where is this all going to end?"

Frieda turned a page in her section of the newspaper. "I see they've made a play of that novel, *Daddy Long-Legs*, that was so popular two years ago. It's to open on Broadway in September. And Laurette Taylor may come back again later in the season in *Peg O' My Heart*. You know, Martin, I think we should go to New York in November and see some plays. Do us good to get some of the sawdust out of our hair."

"We'll do that, dear. Let's plan to go when they have the horse show at Madison Square Garden. You've always liked that." Martin picked up another section of the paper.

"Roxy, Martin and I have eaten. I'm going to take a nap now. But I'll be in the connection at two. You be there." Frieda got up and dropped the paper on her chair. "Doug has orders to bring the horses then."

Roxy strolled over to the main dressing tent and washed her hands at the washbench. She looked in the mirror above and wondered. Had Doug really come because of her? And did she want him on the lot? After all he was still the same opinionated fellow she had been arguing with ever since she could remember. She wished he *hadn't* come. The way things were going with Jupiter, she might stand a chance of being in the show next season as a performer. She still dreamed of a red-haired girl, in a lavender-sequined dress, performing on Jupiter with applause roaring through the Big Top. Doug might try to interfere with the realization of that dream.

After lunch she walked slowly toward the Big Top. A drowsy indolence had settled over the back yard. Clotheslines flapped with laundry, girls in kimonos, bath towels about their shoulders, dried their shampooed hair in the sun, men played cards in the shade of wagons, others slept on the grass; the animals seemed to be napping too, for there was only an occasional sound from the menagerie.

Roxy heaved a sigh of satisfaction. Four months with this circus and she felt she really belonged. Would she ever be satisfied on the farm again after this summer? Would Frieda want her for next season? Or Grandma? Or would Mr. Hallock hire her as a performer?

She kicked through the sawdust outside the connection. She had heard Grandma say that once a person got circus sawdust in his hair it was impossible to get it out. Her hair was getting awfully full of it, all right; circus sawdust, circus fever, whatever it was that made this whole way of life seem so excitingly attractive. Even rain, mud, humid heat, and sudden cold snaps were small inconveniences to suffer for thrills, sparkle, music, and applause. But would Papa let her travel with the show next year? Well, she would be eighteen in January, so—wouldn't she be her own boss then?

She looked at her watch. Twenty minutes before two. Inside the Big Top she climbed to the highest bleachers, sat down, and surveyed the empty expanse. How bleak without the flash of costumes, the perfection of extraordinary performances, the sound of the band, and an appreciative audience!

Doug would be here soon with the horses. If she got the chance, she'd find out *why* he had come. With him around, things weren't going to be quite the same. He was sure to check up on her comings and goings. But just let him try to stop her! She had managed very well all these months, had even learned to please the finicky Frieda. If only he had stayed on the farm!

She saw Frieda enter, then Doug, leading Jupiter and Sebastian. Roxy climbed down and walked to the entryway.

Doug winked and grinned at her as he handed over Jupiter's bridle. "Here you are, Miss Clark."

"Thank you, Mr. Gardner."

Frieda, dressed in smart black riding breeches and a white blouse, got astride Sebastian and rode out on the track. "All right, Roxy. Ride around the track counterclockwise so that when Jupe rears you'll be facing the audience on your lean-backs. Hold the handle with your right hand and lift the left in the air just as you rehearsed in the practice ring. I have a stop watch. I want to see how long it takes you to get around with Jupe up on every ten counts. Ride around a few times to give him a warm up."

Roxy mounted the sidesaddle and circled the hippodrome track, conscious that the eyes of the new groom followed her all the way.

After a few rounds, Frieda rode beside her. "Take the pins out of your hair." Roxy did so. "Here, I'll take them. I have a pocket." Frieda stopped Sebastian at the entryway. "Now, go to it, Roxy."

Roxy lightly touched Jupiter's flank with the heel in the slipper-stirrup and he sprang forward. She took a firm grip on the special handle and cried, "Up, Jupe, up!"

Left hand in the air she stretched back as the horse reared, then sat up as his forefeet came down. Again and again, between gallops, the horse rose on command and Roxy's flaming hair spread like a banner.

After once around the track, Frieda called out, "Smile at the audience on the stops, and this time, stop three times on each side and once at each end so everyone will get his money's worth."

Repeatedly, Roxy and Jupiter went through their act as Frieda timed and retimed with her stop watch. It wasn't until Frieda said "That's enough for today," that Roxy noticed she had more of an audience than just Doug. Alice, Rita, Bo, Martin, Jim Daggett, and Grandma sat on the bleachers near the connection.

As she rode by, Bo yelled after her, "You're great, Red, simply great!"

Outside the connection she hopped down and patted Jupiter's neck. "We *were* good, old boy. I know we were, you beautiful, beautiful creature!"

Frieda came out on foot; Doug followed with Sebastian. "We'll work out again on the track next Sunday," Frieda said. "You're doing all right. Even Gracie said so." Frieda narrowed her eyes. "We'll have her making that lavender costume for you yet; just mark my word." She laughed as she walked away.

Doug looked after her. "Now tell me what that's all about. And who was that fresh guy who called you Red?" His tone had the familiar, disapproving rumble Roxy knew so well.

"You want to know too much. Bo isn't fresh. He always calls me Red and I like it. He's been with the circus all his life. He's a clown." Leading Jupiter, she walked beside him toward the horse tent. "And speaking of wanting to know—how could you leave the farm just now and how did you get a job here?"

Doug grinned. "I thought you'd wonder about that.

Well, after you were in Westwood, your father and I got together and decided it would be a good idea if I joined the circus and the sooner the better."

"Papa? But why?"

"Roxy Clark! That's why! Your father got quite a jolt seeing you in the parade just as though you belonged to the circus."

"Well, I do. I belong more every day."

"I'm here to see about that. Your father sent Mr. Hallock a telegram and he wired back that he could use a good groom for the rest of the season. So here I am."

"But the farm—"

"Your father took care of that too. He and your hired man are giving my dad a hand with harvest. So you see, when men put their heads together they can manage anything, even a headstrong girl who has left home."

"Doug Gardner, you are an interfering old snoop! You'll never manage me! Never, never, never!" She threw him Jupiter's bridle, stomped a booted foot, turned and ran across the back yard, around the cookhouse, and toward the tracks.

By the time she reached Wardrobe's car her face was flushed and tears of anger stung her eyes. Papa and Doug were conniving to keep her from becoming a circus performer and Mr. Hallock was helping them. Well, she'd show them!

Inside the car, she removed her riding clothes and took a sponge bath in the washroom. She brushed her hair, then remembered that Frieda still had her hairpins. Braiding her hair, she put on a yellow voile dress. She opened her trunk and got out a new pair of black pumps with silver buckles that she had bought in Canton.

The afternoon workout had made her hungry. She'd eat an early supper. No, she wouldn't! The grooms usually ate early. Well, she would anyway. She wasn't going to let Doug bother her. She'd ignore him completely.

She stepped off the car and crossed the tracks. That Papa! She could almost hear him telling Doug how he, as a young farmer, had joined the circus in midseason because of a girl rider. And Papa had brought *that* girl back to the farm!

Chapter 15

SOFT TALK

Monday afternoon as usual, Roxy stood in the connection while Frieda and Sebastian did their dressage routine. Beside her, Doug waited for Sebastian.

"Your Frieda is quite a girl on that horse," he said close to Roxy's ear to be heard above the band.

Roxy moved away a step. Sometimes Doug's presence confused her and the girl in lavender on a white horse grew dim. Last evening he had sat at one of the grooms' tables facing her across the cookhouse. The half-smile, the cocky tilt of his head as he looked at her from time to time, had made her furious.

He moved nearer and repeated, "I said your Frieda and Sebastian are very good."

"Yes." Another step and now she was next to the bleachers and could move no farther.

"That was a nice yellow dress you had on last night, just the color of ripe corn. Glad you remember how much I like yellow." Again his head was close to hers as he spoke in her ear.

"I just happened to wear it," she said snappishly.

The band changed tempo and, much to Roxy's relief, Sebastian galloped into the connection and Frieda dismounted. Doug took charge of the horse and Roxy helped Frieda remove her red coat.

"Good to get out of that. It's unusually hot in there,"

Frieda said taking off her hat and running her hand through her damp hair. "Here, I'll take the coat. You run along and get some hot water."

Hurrying across the back yard for Frieda's buckets, Roxy could see Doug leading Sebastian toward the horse tent. How often she had seen him leading a horse. He was already right at home here on the lot, it seemed, and if she knew Doug, he would soon know the workings of the whole circus business. He was like that, interested in everything, full of questions, and always remembered the answers. Admirable qualities in a man, but—

"I like the way your Doug grooms my horses. He's a very nice fellow. Must like you a lot," Frieda said when Roxy returned.

"Oh, Frieda, he's not *my* Doug at all."

"No? Well, he must think you are *his* Roxy. Why else would he be willing to sleep night after night in one of those crowded, stinking cars in the first section if not just to be near you during the day?"

"I suppose he just wants a change from farm work."

Frieda turned her head and looked back over her shoulder at Roxy and smiled. "I may be an old lady, Roxy, but romance I can spot a mile off. That boy is in love with you. Reminds me of when Red Clark came along years ago to be near your mother. And you know how that turned out. I had thought you and Jupiter might be in the show next season, but now I'm not so sure."

"Oh, Frieda, Doug Gardner doesn't mean a thing to me—romantically that is. Do you think I *could* be good enough with Jupiter for next season?"

"Yes. Frank has had an eye on you for some time. But of course you can't have it both ways. If Doug persuades you to be Mrs. Gardner, you'll be a farm wife, not a circus performer."

"What an idea, Frieda! Doug hasn't proposed to me and I tell you he won't. I won't let him!"

"Then you think you want to continue perfecting the routine with Jupiter?"

"Oh, yes, yes!"

Later, eating supper with Sadie Modosky, Lilly, and Henri, Roxy sat with her back toward the grooms' tables. If Doug was there, she wouldn't have to look at him. Frieda's words had put her on guard. She was *not* going to give him one crumb of encouragement and maybe he would leave the circus. She wasn't going to let him spoil her chances in the ring.

"I saw a map in the paper this morning," Sadie said. "Those Germans are just making mincemeat of that little Belgian army. Belgium's King Albert said he refused to let his country be used as a road to France. If France and England don't get over there quick, it looks as if the Germans will be in Paris before you can say Jack Robinson."

"The French will stop them, never fear," Henri said confidently. "The Germans will never get into France. I predict inside of a month they'll be pushed back into Germany and the war will be over. As Grandma Gracie would say, the Kaiser has just gotten too big for his britches."

"Speaking of Gracie," Sadie said, rising, "she and I have a fitting job to do. We're making a new red coat for Jim Daggett. He's put on a little weight and his old one is too tight."

For the most part, during the following days, Roxy was able to avoid Doug. Instead of standing in the connection to wait for Frieda, she managed at each performance to find a seat in the unreserved bleachers near by, where grooms were not permitted. But she could feel his eyes upon her as he waited for Sebastian.

They showed in Pittsburgh, Buffalo, Rochester, Syracuse, and on Saturday, August 15, in Utica. That Saturday night they rolled on to Albany to show there on Monday.

Roxy was eager for her Sunday-practice session in the Big Top, but hoped another groom would bring the horse. At two o'clock sharp, however, Doug led Jupiter through the connection.

Frieda and Martin were sitting on the first row with Roxy. "Go mount up," Frieda told her, "and gallop Jupe around a few times."

Roxy wished she didn't have to speak to Doug with no one else near. His cocksure manner made her boil.

"How's the show girl this afternoon?" he grinned at her. "Been avoiding me like the plague, haven't you? I was just telling Jupiter here to put in a good word for me while you two are out there cavorting around the track."

Roxy took Jupiter's bridle. "You're crazy, Doug, just crazy. How come this sudden interest in me? Back home you and I were always just friendly enemies. Remember?" She stepped in his cradled hands and he boosted her to the saddle.

"Sure I do. But after you left, I knew we had to have you back on the farm. And I'm just the guy who's going to take you back in a few weeks." He grinned at her again, nodded emphatically, and winked.

As she grasped the reins, a bolt of anger shot through her. "Like hell you are!" she said tensely and dug her heel into Jupiter harder than ever before. The surprised horse galloped furiously onto the track.

Halfway around Roxy caught her breath and the flush of anger gave way to a pallor of shock. Why, she had let out with that word for all the world like Frieda! What would Doug think of her? And Papa? She slowed Jupiter.

Reaching the connection again, she slipped off the horse and stood in front of Doug. "Sorry I said that. It just slipped out. But you made me so mad!"

"Hmmm. All I can say is I got on the lot just in time. Pretty soon you'd be swearing like a roustabout."

Roxy stuck her tongue out at him and remounted without his help.

As the routine progressed, she felt she and Jupiter were outdoing themselves. It must be that spurt of anger that had given her added zip and vigor. She was delighted when she passed Frieda and Martin and noted that Mr. Hallock had joined them. Good, now *he* would see her at her best.

"Hi—yi, Jupie!" she yelled. "Let's show them!"

But on the next round Mr. Hallock was not looking at her; Karl was speaking to him, and on the next time around she discovered that the two had left. Now why did Karl have to interrupt? What could be more important to the boss than her act?

When Frieda called out, "That's enough for today," Roxy dismounted in front of the Jantrys.

"Very good, Roxy," Martin said as he stood, then gave a hand to Frieda. "You two have worked out a nice routine there. Frieda, it looks like you are going to be minus a dresser next season."

Frieda nodded. "Could be, Martin, could be." She gave Roxy a brief smile.

Roxy laughed happily.

"Well, Douglas," Frieda said as Doug came forward and took Jupiter's bridle, "what do you think of our girl's riding today?"

"*Our girl*, Mrs. Jantry, has always been a fine rider. You should see her jump the fences back home on her horse, Kentucky—a great sight and just as showy as the stunts on Jupiter." Doug looked down into Roxy's eyes. There was no smile of approval as he led Jupiter away.

Removing her riding clothes in Frieda's tent, Roxy's elation over her performance vanished. Doug made her feel guilty, as though, loving the circus so much, she was being disloyal to her family and the farm.

After supper, she went back to Frieda's tent to see if

she was needed, but Frieda wasn't there. Nearby, Midgie Dexter strummed on a mandolin and sang with tiny Mrs. Concello and Mary Duncan.

Roxy strolled over and sat on the ground by Midgie. "Got your snakes tucked in for the night?" she asked Mary.

"Sure, and my Susy too. She's so tired. Ted put her through a tough rehearsal at the practice ring. How'd your rehearsal go today?" Mary asked.

"Good. Frieda thinks I may have an act next season." Roxy idly fingered the loose end of a guy rope knotted around a tent stake.

"Well, if Frieda thinks so, you are as good as on next season's bill," Mrs. Concello said, pulling up her child-sized feet and hugging her knees.

Midgie ran her finger over the strings and hummed a little. "Do you girls know the words of 'Let Me Call You Sweetheart'?"

"Sure, most of them."

Midgie plucked the strings and they sang.

> *Let me call you sweetheart,*
> *I'm in love with you.*
> *Let me hear you whisper*
> *That you love me too.*

Roxy looked up at the first stars glimmering through the dusky sky and sang an alto accompaniment to the others' soprano. Beautiful romantic words! They reminded her of a love scene in a Mary Pickford moving picture she had seen last winter.

Mrs. Concello clapped when they finished. "Say, we're all right. Roxy, you harmonize beautifully. Play some more, Midgie."

They sang "The Rosary," "Down by the Old Mill Stream," "It's a Long Way to Tipperary," "Bill Bailey

Won't You Please Come Home," "On the Banks of the Wabash," and "The End of a Perfect Day."

As it grew darker, the singing attracted others who joined in. Roxy noted that Frieda and Martin were seated next door, listening, and that Bo Bentley sat on the ground nearby.

A man came around Rita's tent and stopped to speak to the Jantrys. What was Doug doing over here? Grooms should stay with the horses. Frieda pointed at her and he came across and dropped down on the ground beside her. She saw Bo rise and walk away.

The others went on singing. "What do you want?" Roxy asked.

"Could we get away from here? I just heard something that you should know. Come on."

"No. I want to stay here."

"It's about Karl and Mimi. I think your cousin may need you soon. She's sure going to need somebody."

Her curiosity pricked, Roxy got up and followed Doug. Side by side they walked slowly across the back yard, around the side-show tent to the deserted front.

"All right, what about Karl and Mimi?"

"A little while ago Mr. Kassel and his two sons-in-law were in the horse tent giving Bismarck a once-over. He's been ailing. I've been caring for the horse so I was with them. Well, I couldn't help hearing their talk about changes they're going to make in their different acts. It seems Karl won't be with us after tomorrow night's performance. He's taking a train down to New York City and shipping out Tuesday on the *Bremerhaven* to Hamburg to join the German army."

Roxy stopped and swallowed hard. "But he can't leave Mimi! They were just married! And his numbers in the show! No one can fill in for him!"

"Evidently the Kaiser and the Fatherland come first with Karl. Mr. Kassel thinks it's the right thing for him to do, although his brothers-in-law seem to think him a little touched in the head."

"Oh, Doug, poor Mimi! And this will make Uncle Jules dislike Karl all the more, because now he really *is* going to be fighting France. I should go over to third section and see if I can do anything for Mimi."

"I'd wait. She's going to need you more after he leaves. Let's cross the tracks and walk to the edge of town."

"All right."

"I wonder," he said, "how come we don't show in New York City since we're so close?"

"Frieda says it's because the Ringling Brothers' Circus has things sewed up there at Madison Square Garden. Martin says routing a circus is the most important job of all. Hitting a town just after another circus has been there murders business. He says anyone can run a circus but it's the wise showman who knows where to take it. We go to Philadelphia, Tuesday."

"Yes, I know."

Doug took her arm to help her as they crossed the tracks and walked along the edge of the road. Ahead, where the sidewalks began, a streetlight hung above, casting a yellow light on the area.

Roxy's mind was jumbled confusion. Why was Karl doing this to Mimi? They had been married two weeks, and they were so in love. Why would a man leave a beautiful wife to go off across the sea to fight a war? What kind of a hold did the Kaiser have on his people? If Karl had responded to that terrible crush of hers, she might be the wife he was leaving.

Without thinking, she put her hand on Doug's arm. He reached over and pulled her hand through and gave it a pat. Quickly she withdrew it.

"Nice night," he said. "I bet the folks back home are sitting out in the front yard right now. Maybe your folks are over at our place and the kids are chasing lightning bugs."

"Janet and Allen are too old for that."

"Maybe so. Remember how we used to fill glass jars with them at night, running all the way down the lane to catch them, and then when we had a lot, we'd let them all go? Didn't they make a fine show, though, with so many lighting up and flying away at once?"

"They sure did. Remember the time—" Roxy stopped short. He was reminding her of home on purpose!

"Yes? Remember what?"

"Oh, nothing. I wonder how Helga and Fritz will manage their bareback number in center ring without Karl. The three of them are so great. Why do you suppose he's leaving her, Doug?"

Now they were walking on a brick sidewalk and the streetlight shone on their faces. "Somewhere somebody said 'I could not love thee half as much loved I not honor more.' Maybe that's the way Karl feels."

"Honor? It doesn't seem very honorable to me for an army to go roughshod across Belgium killing people and blowing up their towns the way the Germans are."

"If you were a German you'd probably be able to justify it. I read in the news that yesterday the Germans took the great Belgian fortress of Liège. It looks as though the way they're going, they'll occupy Brussels in a few days."

"Poor, poor Mimi with Karl going into the midst of all that! And Uncle Jules—! And I thought that once you got married you lived happily ever after."

"It all depends on the fellow you marry. Maybe Karl wasn't the one for Mimi. Now take me, for instance. I'm going to marry a girl from my own neighborhood, one I know all about—her bad temper, her get-up and-go, a girl who is so beautiful tonight in a lavender dress that she's set me on my ear."

Before Roxy could catch her breath at such an unexpected pronouncement, he drew her into the shadow of a tree, kissed her, and held her close.

"Oh, Doug!" she gasped. For a moment she rested her head just under his shoulder.

He leaned down and kissed her again. "Roxy," he said with a sigh, "I wonder why didn't I tell you this before you left home? Then we could have all been spared this circus spree of yours."

Something clicked inside Roxy and she pushed him away. What was she doing, letting him soft talk her like this? "Let's go back to the lot."

"What's the hurry? I like it here." He put his arms about her again. "Frieda doesn't need you now. We've got the whole evening. You are the reason I joined the circus. You knew from the beginning, didn't you?"

"I guess so."

"Listen, Roxy, if Karl can leave the show tomorrow, why can't we? We could be back in Westwood by Tuesday if we caught a train in the morning. What do you say?" His voice was low and compelling.

With all her might she shoved him away, turned, and started walking at a fast clip toward the lot.

"Hey! Where are you off to?" he called, stepping fast to catch up.

"To the circus where I belong," she said firmly. "And I'm not going home, Doug Gardner, until the season's over. So just put *that* in your pipe and smoke it!"

"But Rox, I asked you to marry me. Didn't you understand?"

"Sure I understood. But I didn't say yes, did I? And I'm not going to. Why don't you just catch that train tomorrow and get along home to your farming? You don't belong with a circus!"

The moon was up now and ahead, across the fields, she could see the myriad of tents making up the traveling city of which she had become so fond.

She wasn't going to leave it, she just wasn't!

Chapter 16

DISASTER AND TRAGEDY

Sunday nights when Wardrobe's car was not in motion, Roxy usually found it difficult to get to sleep. Tonight it seemed that sleep would never come.

They had all gotten to bed late; the old ladies exclaiming as she told them the news about Karl. Grandma had been very disturbed, thinking of the unhappiness in store for Mimi.

But it wasn't only Mimi's trouble that kept Roxy awake. Every time she closed her eyes, and even when they were open, she thought of Doug and his proposal. Could a girl be in love with a man just because she liked being kissed by him? Enough in love to marry him?

Here she was right at the door of success, so to speak; she had only to open it, and perhaps next season she could be the lady in lavender on a white horse, with applause on all sides. She couldn't give up that chance. She must be so firm with Doug that he would go back to Indiana right away.

Thinking of the door to success reminded her of an English course she had taken on the short story. One story that they had discussed at length had to do with doors. It was about a king who, instead of giving an accused man a trial to decide whether or not he was guilty, put him into a huge arena surrounded by spectators. At the side of the arena were two doors. The accused must choose which to open, his choice to prove his guilt or innocence.

Behind one door was a beautiful lady; if by chance he chose this one he was deemed innocent, married her at once, and lived happily ever after. Behind the other was a tiger; if he chose this one he was presumed guilty, and the tiger made a quick end of him.

At the end of the story, the hero was about to open one of the doors. Was it the lady or the tiger? And that was the end of the story. The author, Frank Stockton, had written it so cleverly that everyone in the class had a different opinion about the ending.

Well, she knew exactly what was behind her doors and which was which. Behind one there was a red-haired girl in lavender sequins on Jupiter, and the whole circus family she had grown to love. Behind the other door was Doug. And with Doug would come all the responsibilities of farm life. Could she cope with them as Mama had? And did she want to?

Which door should she open? Well, she didn't have to choose tonight. She must get to sleep. Poor Mimi! Tomorrow morning she would ride in the parade in front of Karl for the last time. How would that girl be able to perform tomorrow, knowing that Karl was watching from the connection and that next day in Philadelphia he would be gone?

At parade time next day, Roxy walked with Frieda across the lot to the white coach.

"There she is, Frieda. Oh, my, doesn't she look terrible?" Roxy pointed to the already mounted Frontenays.

"The poor child. She won't be any paler when she's in her coffin, that's for sure. But she's young, she'll bounce back. Youth is like that. It's us old birds who can't take it. Why, if Martin ever— Well, that's something I never permit myself to think about." Frieda lifted her skirts and stepped up into the open coach and sat on the white leather seat.

Roxy reached in and arranged the gold-brocade skirt and purple cape to show to best advantage. Unconsciously, she gave Frieda's gloved hand a little pat.

"Thank you, Roxy. You're a comfort to an old woman. Don't know how I ever got along without you." Frieda smiled then turned grim. "But I shouldn't brag on you. Praise so often spoils a workman."

"Oh, I don't know," Roxy said as she laughed. "Grandma often says, 'Brag on a fool's work and he'll kill himself doing more.'"

"But you're nobody's fool."

I wonder, Roxy thought, as Frieda's coachman drove the conveyance into line. Hadn't she been all kinds of a fool to *let* Doug kiss her? If she had stopped him, she might have avoided the proposal.

At the afternoon and evening performances, the connection way was crowded with performers to see Karl's last appearances with the Kassel troupe. Mimi stood silent beside Roxy, but her tight clasp of Roxy's hand spoke volumes. Roxy felt her own heart break as she observed her cousin's sad little face—dark eyes on center ring, a constant stream of tears rolling down white cheeks. On the other side of her, Aunt Marie had an arm about the drooping shoulders. Uncle Jules was no place in sight.

Next morning, in Philadelphia, brave Mimi, head held erect, rode off in the parade as usual. That empty place back in the Kassel troupe must be killing Mimi, Roxy thought. What a magnificent trouper she was!

The Hallock circus rolled on, performing to enthusiastic audiences just as though nothing had happened. Harrisburg, Baltimore, Washington, Richmond, Norfolk, Raleigh, all seemed the same to Roxy as the circus went south. She wished they had struck Washington on a Sunday so she could have had a glimpse of the country's capital. But they showed there on a Friday. She would have liked to have seen the White House where President Wilson lived and where, according to the newspapers, he sat writing note after note to Europe saying the United States was neutral and that his government was "impartial in thought as well as action."

Maybe that was the way President Wilson felt, but he should be in the circus back yard some Sunday afternoon and hear the fights that went on as the Europeans discussed the war. Roxy heard Martin say he wondered how long Mr. Wilson could stay out of it, especially since the City Bank of New York had loaned France ten million dollars.

Roxy noticed that many on the lot shunned and avoided speaking to the Kassels. She wondered how it was with Helga and her daughters in the dressing tent. Surely Mimi and Aunt Marie would still be friendly toward them. After all Mimi was a Kassel now.

Doug had changed his tactics and was now ignoring Roxy. After a while she quit looking for a seat as she waited for Frieda, there was no need. Doug waited outside, coming in just as Frieda and Sebastian made their exit. When Roxy caught his eye he put on a sad, hurt look, and turned away.

Oh, that devil! She knew him so well! He was pulling that long face on purpose to make her sorry for what she had said to him. She wasn't sorry and she wasn't leaving the show. She was going to forget that proposal.

Each Sunday afternoon at her practice session in the Big Top, he brought Jupiter and helped her mount as impersonally as though he had never known her. She wanted to kick him in the seat of the pants as she often had when they were children.

Almost every Sunday, Bo was in the stands watching her rehearsals. His evident admiration of her riding skill was so encouraging. When he wasn't there she was disappointed.

Crisscrossing the states, they stopped in cities and towns in South Carolina, Georgia, Tennessee, Arkansas, Missouri, Oklahoma, Texas, and Louisiana.

Saturday, September 12, the circus showed to good audiences in New Orleans, Louisiana. Many of the performers were in extremely good spirits and Roxy knew why. The newspapers were full of the details about the battle of the Marne. Marshal Joffre had stopped the Germans at the river.

It was only about one hundred forty miles from New Orleans up to Mobile, Alabama, and tomorrow was Sunday. Into her berth at eleven, Roxy thought she would get up early in the morning even if it was Sunday. It had been so hot and sticky during the past week; she had quite a washing to do for Frieda and herself. And she wanted to write a long letter home. It would be more than a month before she returned and Mama and Papa seemed to enjoy her letters so much.

The wheels clicked rhythmically and the car swayed, and, like a gently rocked, tired child, Roxy fell into a sleep invaded by the usual incongruous mixture of joys, fears, and frustrations that make up dreams.

Mounted on Tucky, as he stood on a small platform high in the Big Top, she was about to dive down with him into a small tank of water. This would make them applaud louder than they ever did for any one else, she thought exultantly. "All right, Tucky, let's go!" she yelled and he sprang from the platform.

Wham! The train stopped with a terrific jolt and her head hit the end of the berth with a thump. She sat up to rub the hurt.

Oh, my goodness—Grandma! She pushed aside the curtains and stuck her head below.

"Grandma, are you all right?"

"Banged a bit but I'll live," came the familiar voice.

"What do you suppose is the matter?"

"No idea, but I intend to find out. I told Frank yesterday we were about due for something. Things have been running too smoothly around here."

Kimono and slippers on, Roxy descended into the aisle and went from berth to berth to see if the wardrobe ladies had suffered any broken bones. With the force of the stop, they very well could have. Grandma joined her. They examined a cut on Jenny Thompson's forehead. Grandma got peroxide and bandages, Roxy soap and water.

"Now it's all right, Gracie, just a scratch. Hand me my kimono and let's get out and see what's the matter," Jenny said when the cut was bandaged.

Roxy and the others went to the back platform and looked down. George stood in the dark at the bottom of the steps.

"What's the trouble, George?" Grandma asked.

"Mrs. Gracie, I think there's something wrong with the first section up there ahead."

Roxy put her hand to her throat. The first section! Doug was there! She followed Sadie down the steps. Now some men were lighting red flares along the track and others were running ahead.

Roxy walked out a way from the car and tried to see up the track where a few flares were beginning to flicker.

Alberto Donato came from the car behind Wardrobe. "Know anything, Gracie?"

"I just sent George up to see. We should know soon, if he doesn't get so interested that he forgets to come back."

"Well, I think I'll wait here. If there's bad trouble, they may want the elephants. I've got my boys ready to mount up if they're needed."

Now Jim Daggett and Mr. Hallock ran by. The third section must have caught up with them, Roxy thought.

Shortly after that, Martin followed, stopping to speak to Grandma.

"What's the matter, Gracie?" he asked.

"We don't know, Martin. Some kind of trouble with the first section."

"Oh, my! I better get up there and check on Frieda's horses. If anything happened to them—" He noticed Roxy in the red glow of the flares. "We know what they mean to her, don't we, Roxy?"

"We sure do, Martin."

She watched him hurry away in the eerie light. Always so faultlessly dressed, it was queer to see him with his blue nightshirt stuffed into his trousers.

Now more people ran past from the third section. Among them Roxy recognized Fritz Kassel, Uncle Jules, and Conrad Hagen.

"Grandma, can't I go up there too?" she asked.

"No. If there's bad trouble they only need people who can help. We'd only be in the way."

"Oh, Gracie, let her go and find out something, anyway," Sadie cried impatiently.

"There comes George."

Puffing from the run, George stopped and panted. "Three cars jumped the track," he said in gasps.

"Anybody hurt?"

"Don't think so. But one was a horsecar and some of the poor critters are doing a lot of awful screaming. I think they're hurt bad. Listen. Can't you hear them?"

Roxy *could* hear them and she stuffed her fingers in her ears to shut out the sound. Those beautiful, wonderful circus horses! It was horrible! What if Jupiter, or Caesar, or Sebastian were one of them? Or Bismarck, or Otto, or even any of the heavy draft horses.

"Grandma! What will they do? Why don't they help them?"

"There's only one thing to do, unfortunately," Grandma

said grimly. "Shoot them and put them out of their misery."

Even as she spoke, the air was pierced by gunshots. Roxy shuddered and felt as though she were shriveling inside. Tears flowed and her chest hurt so she thought her heart would stop beating. And what if someplace up there in all that confusion, Doug had been hurt.

Jim Daggett ran up. "Alberto! Frank says to bring up six elephants to help clear the stuff."

Roxy wiped her eyes on her sleeve. Grandma and the others were crying too. Helga Kassel walked to them. "I heard shots, Gracie. The horses?" she asked in a sad, knowing voice.

"I'm afraid so, Helga."

Helga leaned against Wardrobe's car as though all strength had ebbed away. "First our Karl, and now this," she murmured.

"Your horses might not be the ones," Grandma said.

"Perhaps. But all horseflesh is precious to me. Thank God they are not suffering now."

"Look, Gracie, isn't that Frank coming there?" Amy Travers asked.

"Why so it is and going so slow too. I wonder—" Grandma walked a few steps toward the circus owner, Roxy and the others close behind. "Frank, what is it? Is it a bad wreck?"

Frank Hallock paused near a red flare and Roxy could see tears glistening on his cheeks and his shoulders shaking with sobs.

"Oh, Gracie! Right this minute I wish I'd never been born! We had to shoot Sebastian. Martin himself told us to do it. Dear old Martin! He started back to tell Frieda, walked around a car in a kind of daze, I suppose, and walked right in the path of a moving freight on the other track! Killed him instantly! Dear God, dear God, how am I going to tell Frieda?"

Roxy thought she was going to faint. She walked to the car and grabbed the handle by the steps.

"I'll go with you, Frank," Grandma said in a husky voice. "You come too, Helga."

Roxy watched the three move back toward the third section, their bodies throwing out strange shadows in the red flicker of the flares.

Not a word was spoken there beside Wardrobe's car. Some things were just too horrible for words.

At dawn Roxy dressed and went up to look at the wreck. She was numb and scarcely saw the overturned cars and wreckage along one side of the track. She looked for Doug, but among the gang of hundreds at work on clearing the track, she could not find him. She drew reassurance from what Frank had said—that no men had been hurt. None but Martin! That dear, dear man, so kind, so loving and thoughtful of his Frieda. And what would happen to Frieda? She was a strong, wiry woman, but could she withstand such a blow? Roxy knew how the old tartar loved and depended on her gentle husband.

She felt a hand on her arm. It was Bo.

"Are you all right?" he asked.

"As right as I can be." She looked up into his dark eyes and her own filled with tears again. "Oh, Bo, what can we do for Frieda? She loved him so."

He patted her shoulder. "There, there, Red. Don't cry. Circus folks have to learn to take hard knocks. Buck up. You'll find a way to help her soon enough. Old Frieda's been rough on me plenty of times when I wanted to sock her, but heaven knows I never wished the likes of this on her."

"Was your little Herman hurt?" Roxy asked.

"Nope. Queer though, isn't it? A fine man like Martin killed and a valuable animal like Sebastian destroyed,

207

when the circus could lose Herman and me much easier. A clown and a pig wouldn't be missed."

"Don't say that, Bo! I'd miss you."

"Would you, Red? Honest?"

"Honest, Bo."

As he walked away toward the wreck, she wondered.
Tough and full of bravado on the lot and a crazy, zany
clown in the ring, Bo Bentley was quite different inside.
The real man was sensitive and hungering for affection;
he had had so little of it.

Slowly she returned to Wardrobe's car.

All day, crowds of townspeople flocked out to see the
train wreck. Watching men, horses, and elephants at
work on the havoc was almost as exciting a show as one
in the Big Top. Fortunately, the cars carrying cages were
spared and the wild animals were safe. The loss, however,
of twenty-seven valuable horses was severe.

It was noon on Sunday before Roxy saw Grandma
again. She and Louise Hallock were leaving with Frieda
on a train from Mobile. They would take Martin's body
back to his home town in Illinois to be buried, Grandma
told the others as she packed a suitcase.

Sticking a long hatpin through the crown of her hat,
Grandma looked down at Roxy, seated forlornly on a
berth. "Frank wants to see you, honey," she said in a
strangely soft voice. "He wants to talk about you filling
in for Frieda tomorrow. Now you remember there's a lot
of Riley in you. Don't you let your old grandma down.
Make them glad that Roxy Clark's in the ring."

Roxy jumped up and threw her arms about her grandmother. "Oh, Grandma," she sobbed, laying her head on
the strong shoulder. "I couldn't! I'd remember Frieda and
how grieved she is and I'd think of Martin and cry."

Grandma pushed her away and held her at arms
length. "You'll do no such thing! You'll get out there, do
your best, and smile! Hear me! Smile! You haven't seen

Mimi sniveling in the ring have you? She's got plenty to weep about. All my granddaughters are troupers, including you, and don't you forget it!"

With that she grabbed her suitcase and hurried out of the car.

Roxy climbed to her berth, lay on her stomach, and cried into the pillow. This was her chance to help Frieda, the chance that Bo had said would come.

All along she had prayed for an opportunity to show what she could do in the Big Top.

But, O God, not this way, not this way!

Chapter 17

GIRL ON A WHITE HORSE

By one o'clock the cookhouse staff had set up a long table near the tracks and everyone was fed, but few felt like eating. Roxy got a sandwich, crossed the ditch beside the tracks and sat on the ground with her back against a fence post. She took a small bite. It was like paper in her dry mouth. Her throat burned and ached from sobbing; her eyes felt as though they had been seared by the fire-eater's torch.

All along the railroad, circus performers crowded about, some picking up food at the makeshift cookhouse, others talking in small groups, others, like Roxy, sought solitude by the tracks.

Each one, Roxy surmised, was filled with thoughts of Martin, and no doubt, like herself, was wondering how Frieda would manage without him. But Roxy had something else to wonder about too. If Mr. Hallock did ask her to fill Frieda's spots, could she? There were five, the parade, the grand entry, the spec, the two-wheeled cart act with Jupiter, and of course the dressage spot with Sebastian. This last even Frieda could not fill, now that the beautiful black horse was dead.

Roxy swallowed hard and the food seemed to scrape her throat. She gave up and dropped the sandwich in her lap on a paper napkin. Closing her eyes, she leaned her head against the post. Minutes passed and she wished she had not already cried herself out. More tears might ease the pain in her chest.

"How're you doing, Red?"

"Fair, Bo." She looked up at him. Unshaven, his shirt was torn and his hands grimy. "Been helping clear the wreck?"

"Yep." He dropped down beside her. "I shouldn't sit down. I'll never want to get up, I'm that tired. I just came down and ate and then I saw you over here." He glanced down at the scarcely touched sandwich. "You should eat that. We don't expect to roll until this evening. It will be late before the cookhouse is set up in Mobile. Come on, now, eat."

"It's so hard to swallow."

"I know. Mimi told me that it's noised around that you're to fill Frieda's spots tomorrow. If that's true, then you'll need your strength."

"Mr. Hallock hasn't talked to me."

"He will. Right now he's concerned only with getting us to Mobile."

"I don't think I can do it, Bo."

"Sure you can. You'll do it for Frieda and Martin. You can't just sit around here and cry about what's happened. Sebastian's gone, to be sure, but Jupiter and Caesar are just rarin' to go. You can't do them out of their spots, Red. They thrive on applause. You want to become a performer don't you?"

"Oh, yes, Bo, but I didn't want it to happen because of a wreck and, and—" her eyes filled with tears as she turned away, "and—all the rest."

"A performer can't be choosy. When his chance comes, why he gets in and does his best. Now come on, eat that sandwich like a good girl." Bo smiled at her encouragingly.

All afternoon, railyard workers, roustabouts, animal

men, and male performers labored to clear the track. It was half past seven before the first section moved and covered the five miles into Mobile. By the time Roxy stepped off Wardrobe's car at the edge of the city, it was dark. The lot was across the tracks and beyond a road. She could hear the stake drivers at work.

Amy Travers came up behind her and said, "Let's go over and have a look. Cookhouse should be in business soon and I'm starved. Aren't you?"

"No. I don't suppose I'll ever want to eat again." Roxy walked beside Amy.

"Oh yes you will. Circus people have to get used to death, honey. Old Mr. Icy Fingers is always hanging around just waiting to snatch one of us. Maybe a flyer who takes too big a chance, a wire walker who loses his balance, a rider who falls from his horse, a trainer who trusts a cat too much, or a roustabout trampled because he went to sleep too near the elephants. It's the price we pay for being with the show. Has Frank talked to you yet about tomorrow?"

"No. I haven't seen him."

"Well, he will. If this thing had to happen, it's good it happened on Sunday and so close to our stop. Otherwise we might have lost a day's showing," Amy said as they crossed the road.

By the time Roxy had finished her meal and stepped outside the cookhouse, the lighting plant had the entire lot illuminated; the horse tent, dressing and side-show tents were up, and the Big Top was beginning to rise. Roxy wondered that the men didn't drop from fatigue. Where else would you find such faithful workers? If Mr. Hallock did want her to fill in for Frieda tomorrow, she must try.

Sadie Modosky joined her. "Roxy, I just saw Frank in there eating. Poor man, I think he's sitting down for the first time today. He looks awful. He says I'm to have

Frieda's costume trunk put in the main dressing tent, and that you're to try on her outfits tonight so I can make any necessary adjustments before morning. Come on. He'll be over when he finishes his meal."

In the dressing tent with Sadie, Roxy opened Frieda's trunk hesitantly. Only last night she had packed it in New Orleans. And now—! Tears came as she placed the red coat on a hanger and put it on a rod, then hung the other four costumes beside it.

Sadie looked at Roxy studiously. "Looks like you and Frieda are about the same size."

"We are. You won't have to do much to them, if anything. What should I try on first?"

"Well, let's start at the beginning with her parade duds."

One by one Roxy tried on the costumes, feeling as though each were a cloak of mourning. Though she knew it foolish, she felt responsible for the whole awful tragedy; that somehow, in her desire to show off, to perform, she had wished too hard for the opportunity. Now that her chance was here, it tasted bitter, very bitter.

Mr. Hallock came in just as she stepped from behind a curtain wearing the big hat and full-skirted dress with the roses.

"Hello, Roxy," he said. "I see Sadie has filled you in. You look pretty in that. Do the others fit?"

"Yes. But I didn't try on the red coat with white breeches. She wore that for Sebastian's dressage number." Roxy's voice choked as she spoke the horse's name.

"I know. The routine you and Jupiter have been working on will just fit into the time slot of that dressage number. I timed it when I watched you last Sunday. Sadie, do you have a becoming sidesaddle riding dress she can wear for it?"

"I'll find something, Frank."

"Good. Now, Roxy, I'm sure you can do the parade,

the grand entry, the spec, and the part you've been re-hearsing on Jupe. But do you think you can manage Jupe with the two-wheeled cart?"

"I don't know. I've watched Frieda do it often enough."

"Well, you be over at the Big Top at seven in the morning and have a go at it. Wear that dress; you'll need to learn how to manage the wide skirt in the cart. If you can't do it, Helga can, although it wouldn't give her much time to change for her next spot."

"Mr. Hallock, do you think Frieda will be back soon?" Roxy asked.

"That's hard to say. Under any other circumstances I would say yes, she is such a staunch trouper. But, losing Martin—!" He shrugged his shoulders. "As you know Frieda has rheumatism, and emotional stress has always made the disease worse. Martin knew this and kept all worries and strains from her. With the blow she has received today, however, anything could happen to her."

"The poor darling," Roxy murmured, looking up into Mr. Hallock's eyes. "I've grown to love her very much."

He patted her shoulder. "Good girl. Glad you got through her tough hide. Few of us have escaped her temper, but we love her in spite of it. See you in the morning. I'll speak to Ed about having Jupiter hitched to the cart early." The circus owner left.

"You know Wardrobe, Roxy; can you think of some-thing you could wear for that last spot?" Sadie asked.

"I wonder if Erma would mind if I wore her parade dress. Remember, I wore it when I filled in for her in the parade at Dayton."

"Yes. As I remember, though, we had to take it in for you. You couldn't both be using it. But I've got a case of extra things I'll go through. There's a green one there I think we can make fit you."

"How about a lavender one?"

"Don't think so. How come lavender?"

"Oh Frieda always said I should wear lavender sequins for that number. Green will do. But I won't need a hat. Frieda says I should always work without a hat."

"When it comes to pleasing an audience, Frieda knows her stuff. No hat it is."

Climbing into her berth, Roxy was sure she couldn't sleep, but would toss, cry, and worry about tomorrow. Exhausted, she closed her eyes, then there was Sadie calling her to get up. It was six o'clock.

The two of them ate breakfast and hurried to the dressing tent where Roxy put on the snug-bodiced dress with the wide, full skirt. It was white satin, sprigged here and there with sequined roses.

"Let down your hair," Sadie said. "Frank will want to see you exactly as you'll appear at a performance. Sit there at the dressing table."

"Say, it's hard to sit with all this skirt!"

Sadie brushed Roxy's hair back of her ears, slipped a narrow white ribbon under the back, and tied it in a small bow on top. "Your hair looks nice rippling down your back. Curls a little at the ends too. Frieda's right. Well, get along with you. When you come back, I'll help you with the parade dress."

Seeing Roxy cross the back yard in costume so early, others followed to the Big Top to see what was going on. In the connection, Roxy found Mr. Hallock and Helga. Jupiter, hitched to Frieda's dainty, rose-entwined cart, stood on the track with Doug at his head.

Roxy nodded to Mr. Hallock and Helga. "I'm ready."

"You look lovely, dear," Helga said.

"Very nice, Roxy." Mr. Hallock smiled briefly. Roxy thought his eyes looked like two large black patches. He was shaved and had on clean clothes, but the lines in his face were even deeper than last night. "Now, Helga," he said, "let's review this routine with Roxy."

Roxy paid close attention as the two instructed her in the cart number, a number she had watched Frieda do again and again.

"Fortunately, Jupiter is used to you and your voice. Before you begin, you might go over there and talk to him a little so he'll know he's in friendly hands," Mr. Hallock said.

Lifting her skirt off the grass, Roxy crossed to the horse's head. She looked up at Doug and murmured, "Good morning, Doug."

"Morning." He pulled Jupiter's head down, patted the nose, and said softly, "Did you ever see such a beautiful girl, Jupe?"

"No compliments now, please, Doug. This is very serious business. I feel as though the whole show were on my shoulders." She put her hand on Jupiter's head. "Jupie, honey, you and I must come through for Frieda and Martin. Understand, baby?" She pulled him closer and laid her cheek briefly against his white head. The horse neighed and nuzzled the hand that had often fed him sugar.

"If only you had stayed at home where you belonged," Doug grumbled beside her.

Roxy frowned at him, then glanced at her audience of interested performers. By this time several more sat in the bleachers, Bo among them. The bandmaster, Miles Wallace, stood alone in the bandstand with his cornet, ready to play Jupiter's music.

The cart had special, extra-long shafts that curved up and were attached to the harness at Jupiter's shoulders, thus leaving the horse's hind legs free and far enough away from the cart for the rearing stunts and unusual gaits he performed in the act.

Roxy went back to the cart. Mr. Hallock held the horse's head, while Doug helped her up onto the small seat that perched above the two high wheels, then

216

handed her the long, white leather lines. Helga came over and arranged the full skirt.

"Once around the track, first," Helga directed.

Again and again the red-haired girl and the white horse went through Frieda's cart routine. Roxy knew that the melody from Miles's cornet would be playing in her ears till doomsday. Mistakes got fewer, but Roxy felt success was due more to Jupiter's talent than to her own handling of him. Still—she was getting the feel of it. And how satisfying when there were no mistakes and fellow performers broke into applause.

"That's enough, Roxy," Mr. Hallock called out. "I think you'll do."

Down from the cart, Roxy ran to the connection where Aunt Marie, Uncle Jules, and Jacques gave her all kinds of praise. Bo smiled and nodded approval as she caught his eye.

Mr. Hallock came up, a yellow piece of paper in his hand. "Listen to this, folks, a telegram just came. It says, 'Heard of wreck—What do you need?—Acts—canvas—animals—horses. Am in Tallahassee—can send right away.' It's signed, John Ringling." He slipped the paper in his pocket. "Good old John! A tough competitor, but what a heart!"

Back at the dressing tent Roxy found the wardrobe ladies opening parade-costume cases.

"How'd it go, honey?" Sadie asked.

"Well enough. But it's easier to work on Jupe's back. Did you find a riding dress for the last number?"

"Yes. Here it is." Sadie held up a Kelly-green satin riding dress; the short-sleeved bodice was covered entirely in green sequins; fleur-de-lis sequined designs spread over the skirt in sparkling splendor.

"Oh, that's lovely."

"And it will be lovelier on you, honey," Sadie said. "Come on, get out of that and try it on."

So much had happened in the past thirty hours that, riding along the streets of Mobile in Frieda's white parade coach, Roxy was sure it was not she sitting here dressed in gold brocade and purple chiffon, but some stranger with whom she wasn't even familiar. Red curls hung about her shoulders and Frieda's narrow gold crown rested on her head. She should feel like a princess.

This exceeded any dreams she had dreamed last April. But reality was so different. What an effort to keep on smiling and raising her hand in greeting to the crowd along the curbs on either side.

The band music, the click of horses' hoofs on the pavement, the yells from the clowns as they made the crowds laugh, all sounded a dirge in her ears, sad and depressing. Dressed in regal grandeur, Roxy smiled and waved, and winced each time she was cheered and applauded. This afternoon might be easier, she would have to concentrate on performance and wouldn't have time to think.

Her first two appearances would be easy. All she had to do was ride Caesar in the grand entry and then in the spec, with a change of costume between. But the last two would be real challenges to her horsemanship. Well, Jupiter was a smart horse and she herself knew the routine; she shouldn't worry.

Back from the parade, in the dressing room, Jenny Thompson helped her out of the gold brocade. "I had one of the boys bring some hot water." Jenny pointed in the corner of the curtained area. "Thought you'd want to freshen up before you eat."

"Oh, Jenny, I could have gotten it. That's one of my jobs, you know."

"No. You're filling a star's shoes today, honey, so you get a star's treatment."

In the cookhouse as Roxy ate her lunch, many friends came to wish her performance well.

Uncle Jules put his hand on her shoulder. Roxy looked up at him. Since the elopement he had seemed to avoid her. Now he gently touched her hair and smiled. "I shall be watching you *ma petite* Roxane. As Cyrano said to *his* Roxane, 'Your hair is such a shining light that, just as after looking too long at the sun, one sees crimson circles everywhere, so when I turn from your overwhelming blaze, my dazzled eyes meet only golden clouds.'"

"Oh, Uncle Jules! I'm afraid you're flattering me. But it's nice to be compared to Cyrano's Roxane."

Mimi came up and stood beside her father. "Mama says you did fine with the cart this morning."

How thin Mimi appeared, Roxy thought. Beside Uncle Jules, she looked like a child instead of a married woman. Uncles Jules looked down at her wistful, sad face. Roxy watched his eyes soften as his arm encircled Mimi's shoulders. Roxy looked back at her plate, and a warm wave of thankfulness eased recent sorrows. Uncle Jules had forgiven his daughter.

A memorable day, September 14, 1914—the day she performed for the large audience in Mobile, Alabama!

Mounted on Caesar and wearing a yellow riding habit, she lined up in the back yard for the grand entry. High on Luly, Alice yelled at her. "You look gorgeous, Roxy!" Roxy waved and smiled.

Back from the first appearance, Sadie helped her into the white spec costume. Roxy gave a sad little laugh as Sadie fastened it under the arm.

"What's funny?"

"I was remembering the first time I met Frieda and she bawled Grandma out about this dress. She was not about to have a high neck and long sleeves."

"That's right. And we had the devil's own time making it over to suit her too, the fussy old darling." Sadie sighed and hung the yellow dress on a hanger.

It was amazing the way the show clicked off as usual, Roxy thought later, as she stood in the connection dressed for the cart number. If the wreck had not occurred yesterday so near Mobile, she was sure the audience could not have guessed their trouble from this afternoon's performance. At least everything had been right until now. In a few minutes, however, Hallock Circus perfection would be in her hands.

Doug led Jupiter inside and helped her into the cart. Roxy firmly grasped the white lines in her gloved hands and took a deep breath.

Now came the musical cue from the band, and the white, rose-entwined cart rolled onto the track; pulled by a handsome, white horse, driven by a beautiful girl with flaming hair, it was a pleasing sight.

The girl tossed her head and smiled at the audience as she tightened the lines and brought the horse to his hind legs, then loosened them as he stepped down and began a gait to the beat of the music. At the turn, up again, and down, with a change to another faster sort of dance step.

Roxy tingled and thrilled. Jupiter, oh Jupiter, you darling! You wonderful, talented horse! Frieda would be so proud of you!

By the time the equipage reached the reserved-seat section, the Big Top was a steady roar of applause.

The once around took less than three minutes, then there was Roxy in the connection and Doug lifting her down. Mr. Hallock stepped up and hugged her.

"Good girl, Roxy! You *are* your mother's daughter."

In the dressing tent, flushed with excitement, Roxy scarcely knew when she stepped out of the white-satin-with-roses and when the green-sequined-fleur-de-lis was slipped over her head by the deft Sadie.

"Sit, so I can fix your hair and touch up your make-up," Sadie ordered.

Running across the back yard, holding up the green skirt, Roxy glanced up at the blue sky piled with cotton-candy clouds and gave a brief prayer. "Thank You for the cart number. Now please let this one come off well. Not for me, but for Frieda."

The Eldonas ran out of the connection as Roxy entered. Little Gina Eldona stopped and pulled her mother's hand. "Oh, I want to stay and watch Roxy, Mama, can I?"

"Sure. I will too."

The elephants were finishing their turn in the three rings. Roxy watched Alice put Luly through her stunts. The old girl got better every day.

Leading Jupiter, Doug came up beside Roxy. "Say, that dress is a real knockout. I never saw Frieda wear it."

"No. It was an extra in Wardrobe." Roxy caressed Jupiter, then ran her hand over the buckle on the saddle girth.

"*Some* extra. Saddle all right?"

"All right. I'll mount now."

Doug put his hands together, Roxy stepped in them and sat on the saddle. He put her left toe in the slipper-stirrup then spread her skirt.

Roxy smoothed the long green gloves above her elbows and took the reins. The music changed and all twenty-seven elephants lumbered around the track behind Luly and Alice, and made their exit on the other side to the menagerie tent.

Now the band struck up Roxy's music. With a "Hike, you, Jupie!" the horse got onto the track and galloped around the entire hippodrome, his white tail streaking out behind him even as red hair streaked behind his rider.

On the next round came the rear-ups and the lean-backs. Jupiter outdid himself, almost standing straight up again and again as Roxy leaned back to smile and wave at the applauding audience.

In the connection, Doug caught her as she jumped down. Mimi crowded close and hugged her. "Oh, Roxy, you're great! You've got such a sense of showmanship. I wish Grandma could have seen you. She would be so proud."

"You did all right, Red! You sure did all right!" Bo Bentley called out as he stood nearby with Herman in his arms.

Roxy nodded, smiled at the clown, and gave Jupiter a pat as Doug led him away. For a short time she had been able to forget Martin.

Knowing now that she *could* do it, Roxy approached the evening performance like a seasoned trouper. Well, perhaps not quite like one; she wasn't sure that she would ever ride out onto the track without a thrilling tingle of excitement. But then, maybe even the old-timers felt the same in the Big Top.

That night, her last number over, Roxy removed the green dress, put on her yellow gingham, and packed Frieda's trunk as she had all summer. Then she gave "the girls" a hand at putting other costumes in place.

When she left the dressing tent, she walked around to the front yard to take a short cut to the railroad yard. The menagerie tent was already down and many of the cages gone. Elephants pushed and pulled loaded wagons. The last gunshot of the wild West show had banged out, and the audience streamed out from the Big Top.

Roxy paused to let a family go by. The mother held a small girl's hand, the father that of a somewhat older boy.

"Well, what did you like best?" the father asked.

"Oh, the cowboy who chased the Indians away from the stagecoach," the boy replied.

"Not me!" the other child exclaimed. "I liked the girl on the white horse. Her green dress was beautiful and her red hair so pretty. Didn't you think so, Mama?"

"Yes I did. She was a fine rider too."

Roxy wished she could thank that little girl and her mother.

Chapter 18

THE LADY OR THE TIGER?

On to Montgomery, Birmingham, and Nashville, the circus moved without mishap, the new rider filling in at every performance.

After her last number on Friday afternoon in Cairo, Illinois, Roxy went back to the dressing tent and found that Grandma had returned.

Clasping Roxy in a hug, Gracie then held her off at arm's length. "You look nice in that shade of green. We must have had you in mind when we made it. Frank telephoned yesterday and said Frieda wasn't to worry about the show. You were doing a good job filling her spots."

"How is she, Grandma?"

"Not well at all. Louise Hallock and I are very worried. Louise decided to stay with her a while longer. She's at the home of Martin's youngest sister. The day after the funeral Frieda went to bed and hasn't been up since. It's terrible trying to get her to eat."

"Oh, I'm so sorry! Don't they have any horses? She should get out and ride. I bet anything that would help her." Roxy stepped into a dressing space and unfastened the top hook at the back of her dress.

Grandma followed. "Here, let me unhook you. No, they don't have any horses. They live in town and just have one of those crazy, sputtering, Henry Ford contraptions. That man should be put away, getting those noisy things all over the streets to scare the living daylights out of horses!"

That evening, Sadie and Amy insisted that Grandma sit in the grandstand to watch Frieda's understudy. Later, after her last number, Roxy started to help with the packing in the dressing tent. Grandma came in and took a costume from her granddaughter's hands.

"This is not your responsibility now. Frieda was right. You don't belong in Wardrobe."

"Then—you think I did all right?" Roxy looked into Gracie's face.

"Now, don't start fishing for compliments. You wouldn't be doing Frieda's spots if you weren't up to snuff. Frank would cut the program rather than have a poor fill-in. Run along and get your sleep. Performers must look fresh as daisies."

On Sunday in Decatur, the circus caught its breath. Only a week since the wreck, Roxy thought, and already she was beginning to forget. What kind of an inconsiderate girl was she? Her mind filled with shining costumes and applause, the occasional thoughts of Frieda's sorrow were causing less pain.

Last Tuesday, Ed Nedosky had gone off to Kansas to buy horses. After lunch Roxy joined Lilly and the two went over to see if he had returned with the new stock.

"Where's Mimi?" Roxy asked her cousin.

"Writing to Karl. What else? Since he left, she's written him enough to fill two thick books. And if he's with the German army by now, I don't suppose he'll ever get what she writes."

"Has she heard from him?"

"Only twice."

"Oh, my! And he's been gone more than a month!"

The new horses were in a roped-off corral near the horse tent. Roxy looked them over critically. Most of them would do as draft horses, but not one could replace the valuable Sebastian. He was as irreplaceable as his mistress, she thought sadly.

"Here comes your friend, Doug," Lilly announced.

"Well, what do you think of them?" Doug said as he came near.

"Not bad, but certainly not ring stock," Roxy answered.

Lilly laughed. "Say, doesn't she sound like the old expert, though? You'd think she'd traveled with the circus for years."

"She catches on fast," Doug said, a disparaging note in his voice as he looked at Roxy.

Roxy looked away. Concentrating on her performances as she had, she scarcely ever thought of Doug *or* his proposal. But sooner or later she was going to have to, she supposed. Doug wasn't the kind to give up easily.

"Well, I'll leave you two and go find Rita. She's teaching me to crochet. You should see the lace edge I'm putting on a handkerchief." Lilly turned to leave.

Roxy frowned. "I'll come with you and watch."

"Now why did you leave him?" Lilly wanted to know as she and Roxy arrived on the other side of the horse tent. "If ever such a good-looking man gave me the eye he's been giving you, believe me, I wouldn't run away."

"Lilly, you run off at the mouth too much. When I want to talk to him, I will. Doug will be around."

"Don't be so sure. Boy, oh boy! If I were three years older, would I ever give you a run for your money with that farmer."

Roxy examined Lilly's face closely. "You could. You get prettier every day."

"Thanks, Rox. Now that Mimi's married, maybe I'll have a better chance with the boys around here."

Sunday morning in Bloomington, Illinois, when Roxy got off the car at seven-thirty, she found Mr. Hallock talking to George at the bottom of the steps.

"Good morning, Roxy. I've come to take you to have

breakfast with Louise and me. She returned late yesterday. Your grandmother has gone on over to our car so Louise can give her the latest on Frieda."

"How is she, Mr. Hallock?"

"Not well at all. Her sister, who lives in Ohio, came and took her home with her yesterday morning. There are some things I want to talk over with you and Gracie. So I thought we could do it over breakfast."

In the Hallocks' private car, Henry again served the meal. Halfway through, Mr. Hallock said, "Louise, why don't you give Roxy her note from Frieda?"

Surprised, Roxy took the pale-blue envelope from Mrs. Hallock. The others were silent as she read the shaky handwriting on the dainty note paper.

My dear girl Roxy,

Just a few words of thanks to you for doing my turns. Frank telephoned and told me the audiences like you. Being Gracie's granddaughter I knew you had it in you. If you keep at it, you may even be a *great* rider someday.

My joints are acting up like the very devil. Even if I had the will to return, I know I could not. My riding days are over. My only desire now is to join Martin as soon as possible.

This letter is mainly to tell you that I am giving you Jupiter and Caesar for your own. On condition, however, that *you yourself* ride them in the show. Louise is bringing the necessary legal papers to transfer ownership to you.

Tell Gracie I said you were to have lavender sequins next season. Green is good, but lavender is your color.

Now don't let that farm boy talk you out of the Big Top. It's where you belong.

Thinking of you with affection,
Frieda

Tears filled Roxy's eyes as she handed the paper to Grandma. Turning to Mrs. Hallock, Roxy asked, "Is it true that she won't be back?"

"I'm afraid so. She's in a very bad way."

"Imagine, giving those beautiful horses to me! You would think she'd want some relative to have them." Roxy dried her eyes.

Grandma put the letter on the table. "Well, Miss Clark, you now have two of the finest horses in the show, provided of course you come back next season. Frieda gave them to you because she wants them and you to stay with this outfit. Right, Frank?"

"Yes. And that's what I want to talk to you about, Roxy —next season. I think in time you could become a head-liner. How about it?"

Roxy didn't answer, but turned questioningly to Grandma.

"Don't look at me," Grandma said brusquely. "You were good help in Wardrobe but who am I to keep a rider out of the ring. What do you think your folks will say to such a thing?"

"I don't know."

"*Of course* you'll want to talk it over with Martha and Red," Mr. Hallock said. "The contract need not be signed until January first. So there's plenty of time. How do you feel about it?"

Roxy twisted the linen napkin on her lap. "I would like to do it, but—"

"Now don't push her, Frank," Mrs. Hallock interposed. "A girl has to consult her parents. Henry, please bring us some more coffee."

In the back yard the next afternoon, as Doug held Caesar for Roxy to mount for the grand entry, he said, "I hear Frieda gave you her horses provided you stay with the show."

"Yes."

"Why doesn't she get back here and ride these nags herself? Doesn't she know that I already have to buck more than my share with all the supercolossal whoop-la around here?" He stroked Caesar's neck.

"I don't think she'll ever ride again. It was Martin, you know, who kept her at it in spite of her ailment. Now it's just no go."

"Well, she should have given the horses to someone else on the lot. Darn Frieda anyway!"

"Don't say that! I love them and now they're mine." She touched Caesar's dark mane.

As Roxy rode into line, Doug gave the horse's rump a gentle slap, half-affection, half-exasperation.

During the following days, riding horses, contemplating the contract Mr. Hallock wanted her to sign, knowing that Doug watched her disapprovingly through every performance, Roxy felt uneasy. But with all this success how could she be undecided about next season?

Each time she hopped off Jupiter and ran toward the dressing tent to remove the green costume, she would exult in the thought—next year she might be here wearing lavender for that number! Then, remembering Doug's penetrating eyes as he had reached for Jupe's bridle, she wondered.

Feeding sugar to Caesar and Jupiter in the horse tent, she tried to guess to whom Frieda would give them if she decided *not* to sign the contract. If she did sign it, perhaps Mr. Hallock would let her bring Tucky along next season. With all the experts on the lot to advise her, she was sure she could teach him a routine for the ring.

On Sunday, October 4, in Galesburg, Mr. Hallock asked Roxy to pose for some photographs. "I want to be prepared if you do decide to come with us. With that bright hair you are a natural for Bert Jackson, the artist who does our posters. So we'll try to get some photographs for him."

That afternoon, in the back yard, Roxy posed for the photographer as a crowd of performers looked on. She noted that Bo, always in the connection during her numbers, was now near the front of the group. His obvious admiration was exhilarating. Was it her skill with Jupie that drew him or—?

Doug brought Jupiter and stood aside after Roxy mounted. Dressed in the green costume, her hair down her back, she pulled the horse to his hind legs, leaned back, waved, and smiled at the camera. Several times she went through the stunt as the photographer exposed enough plates to assure a good one.

Perhaps next year, she thought, all across the land, posters would appear showing a red-haired girl on a rearing white horse, with the words—ROXY CLARK, EQUESTRIENNE OF EXTRAORDINARY ELEGANCE—or perhaps—ROXY CLARK, RADIANT RIDER OF THE RING. There she would be, in store windows, on fences, barns, and billboards to entice people to the circus grounds to buy tickets to see her.

"There!" said the photographer as he put the last plate in the box. "You said something about another costume, Mr. Hallock."

"Yes. Roxy, get into the white-satin-and-roses. And Doug, hitch Jupiter to the white cart."

Roxy held up her skirt and started toward the dressing tent. Leading Jupiter, Doug caught up with her. "So— you *are* coming back next season," he said.

"I won't decide until I talk with Mama and Papa. You know that."

"Mr. Hallock must be pretty sure of you or he wouldn't be having these pictures made."

"He said it was just in case."

"Yeah, I just bet," Doug growled. "With a circus and two fine horses dangling before a girl's eyes, what chance does a guy like me have? I've got about as much chance as a snowball in hell."

"Watch it, Doug. Don't start talking like the roustabouts, or like Frieda," she added.

"I'd cuss a blue streak if I thought it would help," he said as she disappeared into the dressing tent.

October days were cool and crisp as the Hallock circus wound its way through Illinois and Indiana toward Winter Quarters. Roxy had been performing for more than a month. Each time as applause filled the Big Top, she tingled with the thrill of it. The clapping was for her! Could she, she wondered, ever be happy again without it?

On Sunday morning, October 25, she opened her eyes, then closed them again. This was a day she wished had never dawned. The wheels had stopped and she knew that when she went outside she would see the familiar Kingston railyards. The season was over; they were back at Winter Quarters.

Packing suitcases, looking everywhere to be sure no belongings were left, the wardrobe ladies hugged Roxy as they said good-by.

"You'll be back, honey, but you probably won't be traveling with us anymore," Amy said sadly. "But we'll see you. And we're going to make you the prettiest dresses ever. Just wait and see!"

Grandma was giving George instructions about her trunk. "Send mine to the house as usual, but send Roxy's to the station. She's taking the eight-thirty in the morning to Indianapolis on her way home." Grandma turned to Roxy. "Are you ready? My carriage will be here in a minute. My neighbor always gets in some groceries for me. So we can get breakfast at home."

"Would you mind, Grandma, if I come into town later on the interurban trolley? I want to see Jupiter and Cae-

231

sar before I leave, and could you take my suitcase in your carriage?"

"Sure, honey. I know how you feel about Frieda's horses."

"What will happen to them if I don't come back, Grandma?"

"Oh, I suppose Frieda will give them to Frank, and he'll find someone else to ride them in the show."

Thoughtfully Roxy crossed the tracks to where the first section was still unloading. Beyond stretched the Quarters, red and yellow buildings waiting to receive and shelter the caged animals, the elephants, camels, and horses, through the cold winter months.

Was it only last April she had arrived here? It seemed so much longer. The places she had been! The people she had grown to know and love! The things that had happened to her!

Walking along a cinder path toward the barns, she imagined she appeared about the same as she had last April. She was wearing the same navy-blue suit, the same felt hat, the same button shoes. But inside, what a difference. She was a circus rider! She had had a proposal of marriage! Two very opposing facts.

Wagons of equipment rolled along the roads, equipment that would be overhauled and carefully stored for next season. At the barns, Roxy asked about the ringstock and went on as directed.

Inside barn eight, she walked down the center and looked at the horses on either side. Finding the two she sought, she bent and went under the rear chain at Jupiter's stall.

"Hello, baby," she murmured, stroking his head. "Got to say good-by now, sweet Jupe. But I'll be back. I'll be back to see you even if I don't sign Mr. Hallock's contract. If someone else rides you, do a good job, boy. Do a good job."

At this point Caesar stuck his head over the partition and neighed. Roxy smiled faintly. "Oh, I love you too, you old scalawag." She went into the other stall and rubbed Caesar's nose.

Outside she looked about for Doug. He had mentioned that they would ride to Westwood together tomorrow. Well, she supposed she'd see him at the station in the morning. She walked across the grounds to the gate and waited for the interurban.

"Hey, Red! Wait!"

Roxy paused as Bo ran from between two barns. "How come you aren't on your way home, Bo?"

"This *is* my home. I stay here all winter. Just wanted to tell you I'll keep an eye on Caesar and Jupiter for you till you get back next spring."

"Well, thanks. But I still don't know whether or not I'll be back." She looked up and thought the depth of his eyes belied his usual, offhand, brusque manner. There was so much about Bo that she didn't know. She should have made more opportunities to talk with him. But Doug had come along and—

"Oh, you'll be showing up here, come spring. Once the circus gets hold of you, Red, there's no letting go." He took off his cap and ran his fingers through his hair. The wind blew wavy strands across his forehead. He reached into a pocket and drew out a sealed envelope. "Got something for you. You're not to read it until you leave Kingston. Promise?"

Roxy turned the envelope over in her hand, noting that the Roxane Clark was written in fine, delicate script. Who would have guessed that this could be Bo's handwriting? "Sure I promise. I'll like reading a letter from you."

He put his cap back on and stuck his hands in his pants pockets. "If you should feel like answering it, write me here at Winter Quarters. And I could write you from time to time about your horses if you want me to."

"I'd like that, Bo."

Down the track the black interurban rounded the curve. Roxy hurried outside the gate, Bo beside her. The car stopped and she climbed aboard. On the platform she looked down and waved. "Good-by, Bo."

"Good-by, Red. I'll be seeing you."

Seated inside, she dropped the letter into her pocketbook. Now what on earth could Bo have written her? she wondered. Why hadn't he said it just now? He was a strange one, that was for sure. Leaving him at this moment, she felt that she hadn't half appreciated him.

By the time she reached the brown house on Wheeler Avenue, the Frontenays had arrived and the place was filled with confusion. Half-unpacked trunks, boxes, and suitcases were strewn over the living and dining rooms.

Grandma sat in her rocker reading a letter and sipping coffee. "Find your horses?"

"Yes. Where are—"

"Oh, they're all upstairs. I'm just waiting till they clear up this mess before I unpack. This is a letter from your mother. She'll meet your train tomorrow. I take it you didn't write her about next season."

"No."

"Hmmm. Well, I'm not saying a word, one way or the other. Oh, yes, Doug Gardner telephoned. He can't make that morning train from here. But he's going to take a later interurban and will meet you in Indianapolis and ride down to Westwood with you."

Roxy took her suitcase from near the door and mounted the stairs to unpack the things she would need for overnight.

Next morning the Indianapolis train was crowded with circus people. Roxy sat with Alice Granville, returning to her home in Cincinnati. They talked on and on, recalling the season, the good days, the bad, the successes, the tragedies.

234

In Indianapolis Alice had to run to catch the Cincinnati train. Roxy sat in the waiting room and wondered if Doug would make it. She had packed enough lunch for two. She kept her eyes on the door to the street.

There he came! He stood beside her and pulled out his watch. "Made it, and with fifteen minutes to spare. Any place here to get something to eat? I'm starved."

Roxy touched the shoe box beside her. "I made us some lunch."

"Good. Guess we better wait and eat it on the train."

"Yes. There wouldn't be time here."

Seated beside him on the Westwood train, Roxy opened the box and they ate. By the time they finished, rain was pelting the window. Doug put his apple core in the box and took it to the end of the car to discard it.

Roxy looked outside and shuddered a little. The trees were bare, the land looked cold and desolate. Bleak November was practically on the threshold, ready to force them all inside to shiver near stove and fireplace. After her summer of color and glitter, winter was going to be an awful letdown. But Mama, Papa, Allen, and Janet—and Tucky—were waiting for her.

Doug came back and sat down. "Well, now that we've eaten, how about some serious talk? I know all about that contract Mr. Hallock wants you to sign. But I want you to marry me." He squeezed her hand tightly and looked down into her eyes. "You know why I joined the circus. Your father was sure I would bring you back to stay. And if it hadn't been for that train wreck and all that followed, you wouldn't be so hesitating, would you?"

She turned away and watched the raindrops chase each other down the window. "I don't know, Doug. At this moment, I'm confused."

"You sure are. As you'll remember, the house on the Goodman place is in fine condition. I aim to wire it for

235

electricity right away. We could be married around Christmas, move in, and have the place in good shape by spring-planting time."

Roxy closed her eyes and saw herself in the kitchen at the Goodman house. A blue-checked apron tied about her waist, she stood by the table and jounced the dasher of a churn up and down—she peeled potatoes—she cleaned a chicken—she made jelly—then outside, she fed chickens—she milked a cow—she hoed an onion bed!

The pictures faded, and there was a girl in sequins on a white horse!

"You love me, don't you Rox?" he asked softly.

"Well, I liked it when you kissed me, but that's not enough for marriage. I'm sure of that." She pulled her hand away, clasped her other one and held them together tightly in her lap. "Doug, did you ever read a story called, 'The Lady or the Tiger'?"

"Oh, come on now, let's not change the subject."

"I'm not. Did you ever read it?"

"Oh, I guess so, way back in high school."

"Well, you remember how at the end the hero had to choose one of those doors, and the reader doesn't know which he chose, the lady or the tiger?"

"Yes. But what does that have to do with—?"

"Well, I feel sort of like that man. Only I know what's behind each door and the choice is mine."

Doug laughed briefly. "So—I'm the tiger, am I?"

"Yes, at times. But if Rita can manage Rajah, I probably could learn to get along with you."

"I'd sure like to have you try, Roxy." He took her hand again. "And what about the other door?"

"You know what's back of that—Roxy Clark in lavender sequins, Jupiter and Caesar—and applause." Again she removed her hand from his. "Maybe you could join up again for next season and I'd have more time to make up my mind about you."

236

"No! It's out of the question. I'm a farmer. There's a war in Europe that's getting bigger every day. The Germans have taken Antwerp now and no telling what it's going to take to stop them. The people over there are going to be busy defending their homelands with no time to raise crops. My job is in the fields to help feed them. And besides if we don't take the Goodman house now, my father is going to put a hired man on the place. That farm needs both of us, Rox. A farmer has to have a woman to make a go of things. You know that."

Yes, she did know. She turned her face again toward the rain-spattered window.

Which door was she going to choose, she wondered, the lady or the tiger? How she would welcome some sort of positive nudge in the right direction.

Her pocketbook slipped from her lap and Doug retrieved it. Holding it again, she remembered Bo's letter and took it from the purse. Slitting the envelope she looked up at Doug. "Forgot I hadn't read this letter," she explained.

"If you aren't the limit! Here I'm talking about our future and you read a letter!" Doug crossed his knees, stuck a foot into the aisle, and looked angrily out the window on the other side.

Roxy moved away from him. "Oh, quit beefing!" She scowled. "I'll make up my mind when I'm good and ready and read letters whenever I please."

Doug didn't answer.

Roxy settled nearer her window and relaxed. Back on the old antagonistic footing with Doug was a relief. She opened Bo's letter.

Dear Red,

I've been writing this letter to you in my mind all season. Many's the time I've wished I'd paid more attention back there in Kingston High School English classes so I could come up with some high-sounding words. Mrs. Hallock made me go to school, but I sure didn't hit the books very hard.

Ever since the day I saw you sitting on the fence I haven't been able to quit thinking about you. And when I watched you riding Jupiter in the practice ring, I thought you were just the prettiest thing I had ever seen. You weren't like the other riders; you were kind of wild and fiery with that red hair blazing all around you.

About the time I got up nerve enough to try to get acquainted, why along came that fellow from your home town. *I don't like that guy!* He's too cocky, always hanging around you like he owned you. And he never understood what riding and the circus means to you. Then after the wreck you were a headliner and I was still just a small bit clown and I lost my nerve.

Summers when I was a kid, Mrs. Hallock made me have lessons with her so I wouldn't be behind my class when the season was over. Me being an orphan, she felt responsible, I suppose. Well, during my high school days, she gave me a big dose of poetry. Some of it—! I'd sooner have taken castor oil.

But now I'm glad she did, because I still have the book in my trunk. For the last three weeks I've been reading in it, looking for some right verses to put in this letter, some verses with the highfalutin' words I feel but don't know. I figure John Keats said it about right.

> I met a lady in the meads,
> Full beautiful—a faery's child;
> Her hair was long, her foot was light,
> And her eyes were wild.

I set her on my pacing steed
And nothing else saw all day long;
For sideways would she lean, and sing
A faery's song.

And there she lulled me asleep,
And there I dreamed—ah! woe betide!—
The latest dream I ever dreamed
On the cold hill's side.

Now, there, Red! You show up on the lot next season! I don't like dreaming dreams "on the cold hill's
side." Hallock's Circus would be a mighty chilly place
without you.

> Your great admirer,
> Bo Bentley

Roxy rested her head on the back of the seat, closed her
eyes and her mouth formed a gentle smile. Why, that
sweet Bo! Whoever would have thought—? She opened
her eyes and watched raindrops slide down the window-
pane. Was Bo's letter the positive nudge she had wished
for?

Imagine! A clown who quoted Keats!

ABOUT THE AUTHOR

Elisabeth Hamilton Friermood has written many lively romances for teen-age girls, "a long list of good stories with fresh, interesting backgrounds." (*The Horn Book.*) Most of her books have period settings and the Midwest as locale.

Mrs. Friermood, a native of Marion, Indiana, studied at Northwestern University and the University of Wisconsin, and was children's librarian in Marion, Indiana, and Dayton, Ohio, before moving to Pelham, New York, in 1944. Until his recent retirement, her husband, Dr. Harold T. Friermood, was the National Director for Health, Physical Education, and Sports of the Y.M.C.A. The Friermoods have a married daughter, Libby, Mrs. Herbert Franck.

J34